A TICKET TO ZULULAND

AuthorHouse™
1663 Liberty Drive
Bloomington, IN 47403
www.authorhouse.com
Phone: 1-800-839-8640

© *2013 Anya Ashe. All rights reserved.*

No part of this book may be reproduced, stored in a retrieval system, or transmitted by any means without the written permission of the author.

Published by AuthorHouse   12/29/2012

ISBN: 978-1-4817-8000-1 (sc)
ISBN: 978-1-4817-8003-2 (e)

This book is printed on acid-free paper.

Because of the dynamic nature of the Internet, any web addresses or links contained in this book may have changed since publication and may no longer be valid. The views expressed in this work are solely those of the author and do not necessarily reflect the views of the publisher, and the publisher hereby disclaims any responsibility for them.

A TICKET TO ZULULAND

'The Place of the People of Heaven'

ANYA ASHE

A Ticket to Zululand

'The Place of the People of Heaven'

is dedicated to
my grand-daughter,
Isabelle

ACKNOWLEDGEMENTS

My biggest vote of thanks as always goes to husband who once again carried out a great deal of research to help ensure the facts I have quoted are correct.

I would also like to thank the tour guides and all those who travelled with us around South Africa. In this instance, I am not going to mention any names, but there might be some hints in the book as to who they were. Further thanks go to the people of South Africa who made us so welcome during our visit.

Finally, I would like to thank all those who have purchased this book. I do hope you enjoy reading it.

AUTHOR'S NOTE

This novel is a work of fiction, which is definitely the case with regard to the criminal acts that have been included. At the time of the author's visit, South Africa was not a dangerous place for tourists who took sensible precautions. In many parts of the world, tourists are targeted because they are easy prey for pickpockets, etc. This is especially true of those people who flash their money around, leave wallets, purses and other valuables exposed to view, and/or visit places where they are recommended not to go.

All names and characters in this book are the product of the author's imagination and any resemblance to actual persons, living or dead, is entirely coincidental. However, the locations described and some of the establishments mentioned actually exist and some, although not all, of the situations reported were actually witnessed by the author. Where historical facts have been quoted, the author has tried her best to establish that these are correct at the time of writing this book in 2011. She has also tried her best not to add any personal bias. However, it should be noted that all opinions expressed are personally those of the author.

As a self-published author, Anya Ashe has to publicise her own work. She regularly carries out book signings and tries to support local charities. She can be contacted by email (anyaashe@gmail.com) and also via Facebook.

For further information about Anya Ashe, try reading her blog: www.anyaashe.blogspot.com

PROLOGUE

Amy looked down at her husband lying peacefully in bed. Then she turned away and went quickly into the guest bedroom where the suitcase she had been packing for sometime was just awaiting a final check before she closed it firmly, tightened the straps and wheeled it out of the room.

For what seemed like a long time now she had been slowly filling this suitcase whilst at the same time she had been withdrawing money from their various bank accounts. Now all the savings accounts and even the joint current account were empty. All the money had been changed into South African Rand (ZAR) and was securely concealed about her person and in the assorted hand luggage she was intending to carry.

As she closed the front door behind her, she said to herself "You are a Bad Woman". Then she sighed. She had looked after her husband twenty-four hours a day for thirty-five years and now it was time to live her own life.

Therefore, with a rueful smile, a knapsack on her back, another bag on her shoulder, and dragging her suitcase along the uneven paving stones, she walked to the nearby Underground Station.

* * * * *

On the same day, in Beijing, two Chinese businessmen were having last minute discussions in their office before leaving for the airport. They were also intending to board a flight to Johannesburg.

"I don't understand why we have to do this," the smaller and older of the two complained.

Having heard this particular rant many times before, his companion replied in a resigned voice,

"I've already explained that we need to expand the business, or it will not survive. We have plenty of silk, but we need to be different from other manufacturers. Also, we need to be one of the first in this country to obtain a long-arm quilting machine. Then not only will we be able to manufacture exquisite quilts filled with silk, but we will also produce king-size quilt covers beautifully quilted. They will be top of the range and in great demand throughout the world. Once we have one machine, we will be able to copy it and manufacture others. We can program them to run twenty-four hours a day, have staff working day and night, and our production rate will be fantastic. We will not only be the largest manufacturers of silk quilts, but also suppliers of cheaper versions of these machines throughout China. We will dominate the market. Our future will be assured, but we need to act now. The long-arm quilting machine is very expensive and the bank will not give us any more financial assistance so we are going to obtain money by other means."

"But why do we both have to travel to South Africa," moaned the other man. "Can't you go on your own?"

"It's a very risky business, and it's only fair that we share the danger. After all, you're going to benefit as well so we are both going. I have made all the contacts. Everything is arranged, and now we must leave for the airport."

A taxi was waiting for them outside the factory gate, and so it was that two more people started on a journey during which they would experience a different world.

* * * * *

Two days previously two other people had also been discussing their trip to South Africa; they had been in the luggage section of a large department store in the centre of London where they had been overheard saying,

"I think we've left it a bit late to be buying new suitcases when we fly out to Johannesburg this coming Saturday night. Why couldn't we use the ones we've already got?" one of them complained.

"Because everything has to be new," the other replied. "It's a new start."

The shop assistant who had been listening to their conversation, could not believe his luck, or was it fate? He had a very specific suitcase that needed to go to Johannesburg and the person who was supposed to collect it, was not now available. The shop assistant wanted to get rid of the suitcase as soon as possible; he definitely did not want to have to explain why it was not being displayed for sale, or even worse, find out that one of his colleagues had discovered it in its hiding place under the counter and sold it. He had already sneaked that suitcase out of the store for modifications to be made, and then smuggled it back in again so that it could be sold in a bona fide way. Now here was his opportunity to get rid of it and ensure that it travelled in the right direction.

"Can I help you?" he enquired politely as he approached the two potential customers.

"Yes, we would like to purchase two good quality suitcases," one of them replied, while the other added, "and they must be exactly the same."

"Then I suggest Samsonite," the assistant stated as he lifted out a case from under the counter. "I can do an extremely good price if you purchase two of these. In fact, I can sell you this particular case at half price. They come in many different colours. You could have this one, and one in another colour so that you know whose is which."

"No, we want them both in exactly the same colour," came the adamant reply.

"Do we really?" her companion asked.

"Yes, we do."

Seeing that there was not going to be any question of the lady changing her mind, the shop assistant set himself the task of finding another suitcase of exactly the same make, size and colour.

"The special price is for this particular suitcase, but I'll try to find another one," he said as he sorted through the piles of suitcases on display while the customers inspected the one he had been hiding under the counter.

"It's a very good quality case, and for half price it's a real bargain. I think we should definitely have it," one of them stated while the other individual stressed, "only if there's another one like it."

"I've found one," the shop assistant stated breathlessly as he extracted a suitcase from the bottom of a pile that teetered precariously as he did so. Luckily, he was skilful enough to remove it without the whole stack of suitcases falling over and thereby ruining the display.

He carried the suitcase over to the counter, where he was pleased to learn that the customers had definitely decided to purchase both suitcases.

"Did I hear you say you were travelling to Johannesburg on Saturday night? Will you be travelling British Airways?" he asked.

"No, Virgin Atlantic," came the reply.

"Oh, that's great," the shop assistant continued. "I travelled to South Africa with Virgin Atlantic last year and had a fantastic time. By the way, do you have a store card?"

"No, is that necessary?" one of the customers asked.

"Well, if you join now, I can give you another 10% discount. You just have to fill in a form," the shop assistant explained as he passed one over to them.

"Might as well then," the customers agreed, and they filled in the form while the shop assistant removed the security tag from one of the cases and tied plastic bags around the handles of both to indicate that they had been purchased.

After returning their completed form and paying for the suitcases with a credit card, the customers happily left the store wheeling a suitcase each whilst at the same time agreeing with each other that they had managed to obtain a bargain.

The shop assistant was also happy. He now had details of which flight they were booked on, credit card details, a full name, and even an address, home and mobile telephone numbers.

* * * * *

CHAPTER 1
'O R Tambo'

As the road traffic announcer completed his broadcast with the words,

"Traffic at a Standstill on Motorway"

Jerry said miserably,

"I think I am destined to have those exact words included in my obituary," before continuing,

"A frustrated driver who died whilst in traffic at a standstill on motorway."

Dawn didn't bother to answer as she was quietly praying,

"Please, Oh please, not again. Don't let us miss our flight. We did allow five hours for this two-hour journey. It can't be a repetition of when we nearly missed our flight to Malta; then we were stuck for five hours on the M25 because of an accident. On that occasion we were going to Gatwick. Now we want to get to Heathrow. Why don't the police direct the vehicles off when they close the road?"

The traffic had hardly moved at all for the last two hours. Jerry and Dawn found it so annoying as they sat glumly looking out of their car windows at the stationary vehicles all around them. All they could think about was that they might not be joining the 17-night **Grand Tour of South Africa**, which they had booked to celebrate their 40th Wedding Anniversary.

Then the cars that had moved across onto the hard shoulder, started to edge forward. Perhaps it was not 'total gridlock' after all.

Jerry tuned in the radio to the traffic news again and reported,

"There should be a slip road ahead. The accident is on the other side of that. Just check on the map and find out if we can pick up the North Circular Road from there."

Dawn dutifully checked the map and found that from the next exit they could get onto the A10 and that would take them to the North Circular.

1

"It's going to be a nightmare driving into London suburbs on a Saturday afternoon, but we can't sit here doing nothing any longer," Jerry said as he indicated and waited for someone travelling slowly along on the hard shoulder to let him pull across.

Eventually, he managed it, but then even this line of traffic was almost stationary. However, gradually they crawled along and half an hour later reached the exit.

Dawn just pointed out the road signs and helped Jerry with directions to make sure they did not stray from their chosen route, but she didn't say anything else as she tried to ensure that Jerry concentrated on his driving. There were road works and more traffic jams, but Jerry did the best he could, working his way across lanes on roads which were choked with traffic, until eventually they saw signs for Heathrow Airport. It was only then that he breathed a sigh of relief.

"We should be okay now," he said. "Just got to park the car and get the bus to the terminal."

"Never again," commented Dawn. "If we do another trip like this one, we stay overnight in a hotel at the airport. It doesn't matter what time the flight is."

When they got to the check-in desk, it was obvious that they were among the last to arrive, but luckily Jerry had reserved seats on-line so they were able to sit together.

Knowing that they were having a meal on the plane, they just grabbed a drink in the Departure Lounge and then made their way to the Gate for the overnight flight from London Heathrow to Johannesburg.

Once on board Flight No BA55, Dawn settled herself in the window seat, and put a copy of the itinerary and the bulky travel guide, 'Lonely Planet', in the back pocket of the seat in front so that she could study them both during the twelve-hour flight.

Jerry had 'drawn the short straw' and was occupying the middle seat when a young lady arrived to claim the seat adjacent to the aisle. She introduced herself to Jerry and Dawn before sitting down. Then she explained that she was from Mexico and was travelling to South Africa via London with her mother who had a seat in First Class.

Eventually, the plane took off an hour late, and by the time the refreshments arrived both Dawn and Jerry were ravenous. However, as always seems to happen in these circumstances, the aircraft hit turbulence just as the drinks were being served, and they had to drink quickly to avoid accidents; Dawn particularly did not want to spill her cranberry juice, thinking quite correctly that it would make a terrible mess.

The meal comprised of salad as a starter, chicken, leeks and potatoes for the main course, with the alternative being pasta with mushrooms, and then there was a very nice dessert, although no one was certain exactly what it was.

One of the films available for viewing was "The Young Victoria", but although Jerry tried to watch it, the Mexican lady spoke to him during the majority of the flight time – apart from when he pretended to be asleep, that is. Dawn on the other hand, settled down to sleep after the meal and, even though it was quite cramped and she moved about restlessly all night, she did not fully wake up again until the lights went on and breakfast was served approximately an hour before the aircraft reached its destination. It was at this point that the pilot announced that time had been made up during the flight and they would be landing on schedule.

Dawn did not completely escape joining in the conversations with the talkative Mexican, however, as she was obliged to do so towards the end of the flight. The Mexican appeared to be keen to gather as much knowledge as possible about a wide range of subjects. Her English was remarkably good, but very distracting; so distracting, in fact, that it was not until they were walking through immigration control that Dawn realised she had left both the itinerary and the travel guide on the plane. She hadn't had a chance to delve into either of them!

When Jerry and Dawn came out into the Arrivals Hall, they immediately saw their travel guide holding up a large sign and went over to meet him. The guide introduced himself and explained that as they were the first to arrive, they could leave their suitcases with him and explore the many shops in the vicinity.

This Jerry and Dawn were pleased to do, and they started to wander around, discovering that O R Tambo terminal buildings were of a very modern construction with glass and gleaming stainless steel everywhere.

There was also an excellent range of shops and numerous restaurants in the Arrivals Hall. One discovery they made was that Marks & Spencers in South Africa went by the name of Woolworths, and they just had to go in to have a look round; however, the only item they purchased was a bottle of water. Later their guide explained that many local people, especially those living in the farming areas around Johannesburg, now travelled to the airport on a high-speed train to shop and treat themselves to a meal out.

Another discovery was that the price of books in South Africa was extremely high. As a result Jerry and Dawn decided against buying a replacement travel guide; they were thankful that Jerry had had the foresight to input all the information about the places they were to visit, together with the itinerary, into the small laptop that he had brought with him.

* * * * *

Dawn and Jerry had not noticed Amy on the aeroplane, nor did they see her while they went in and out of bookshops. However, she was wandering around the Arrivals Hall at the same time as they were, but she had no idea of where to go and was looking absolutely lost.

Whereas Dawn and Jerry had been among the first off the plane, had joined the front of the queue going through Immigration Control, and had immediately spotted their tour guide and his sign as they walked out into the Arrivals Hall, Amy had not been so lucky.

She was also feeling ill. Her flight had not been a good one. She had been hemmed in by large people seated on either side of her in the middle row at the back of the plane, and despite the fact that she had treated herself to two gin and tonics, as well as drinking the two small bottles of wine that she had managed to persuade the stewardess to supply as part of the inclusive meal, the alcohol had not induced sleep.

Her sorry state might also have been due to the fact that she had eaten little of the breakfast or the evening meal on the flight. In fact, she had had virtually nothing to eat since she had left home. She had also been squinting at the small screen on the back of the seat in front of her, trying to follow the film and listen to it on the headphones until she ended up with a headache.

As a result of all this and the time it had taken to gather all her belongings together, get her hand luggage and coats down from the rack, she was one of the last to get off the plane. A further problem was experienced just when she joined the queue heading towards the Immigration desks; a crowd of Chinese people joined her as their flight had landed only minutes after the Heathrow flight. They talked loudly and incessantly to each other. Also, they already had their cameras out and were taking photographs of each other until they received a warning from staff that unless they put their cameras away they would be confiscated.

Eventually, she had reached the baggage hall and found the right carousel where only her suitcase remained, still going round and round on the conveyor belt.

In the Arrivals Hall, she was watching other people being met at the airport and wondering what to do next when she remembered that she had been given a telephone number that she could use to contact the tour guide on arrival.

She dumped all her bags (she now had several more than when she had left home) and coats (two of them) in a pile on the floor while she turned out her handbag, looking for this information. Finally, she found what she wanted on a screwed up piece of paper at the bottom of her bag. She dialled the number and joy, oh joy, someone answered who directed her back to the area to the right of the door from which she had exited previously. She could not understand why she had not seen the guide before; his sign was big enough, and he was not hidden behind a pillar or anything else.

Dawn and Jerry, returning from their explorations, soon joined her and the tour guide introduced himself again saying that his name was Brian. He explained that he would now take them to the area where they could wait for the coach. After that, he had to come back to meet their fellow travellers: two more couples who were travelling on a Virgin Atlantic flight expected to arrive shortly.

As they walked along together, Jerry asked Brian,

"Why is it named O R Tambo Airport?"

Brian replied, *"It was named after Oliver Reginald Tambo who was a founder member of the ANC Youth League with*

Nelson Mandela and Walter Sisulu. The ANC sent him to England to mobilise support and, possibly interestingly for you, he lived in exile in Muswell Hill, London, after he fled South Africa. Nelson Mandela was best man when he married Albertina. His mother was a domestic worker and his father worked on the railways. The renaming of the Airport was in recognition of the work Oliver did for the cause. This Airport is just one of the many things that were renamed after the demise of apartheid. I'll be explaining more about this during our travels around this part of South Africa."

Jerry had not expected quite such a long explanation, but he thanked Brian as they went into a waiting room where a row of seats faced windows overlooking a coach park.

Little did Jerry realise that this was just the start of the wealth of information that Brian would supply during the trip.

* * * * *

In amongst the Chinese tourists, who had joined Amy in the Immigration queue, were two Chinese businessmen. They were looking at their fellow travellers with dismay, ashamed of how they were behaving abroad.

"What a terrible noise they're making, chatting incessantly while they take photographs," one said to his fellow traveller whose reply was of a more serious nature.

"I just hope they don't draw attention to us," he whispered to his colleague.

Having arrived after a long flight - they had flown on Dragonair Flight 993 leaving Beijing at 1830 hours on the Saturday which arrived in Hong Kong at 2205 hours from where they had changed onto a South African Airways Flight 287 leaving Hong Kong at 2355 hours and arriving at O R Tambo Airport, Johannesburg at 0710 hours on the same Sunday morning as the British tourists – they were exhausted.

Luckily, they were easily recognised as they walked into the Arrivals Hall (being the only Chinese people in business suits) and were quickly whisked away by two shabbily dressed black men who grabbed their suitcases and escorted them to a rather dusty vehicle waiting in the street outside.

"We will take you to a hotel downtown," one of the men uttered as they quickly exited the airport building. "There you will be able to recover from your flight before you continue your journey. We just have to wait for a friend who should be here shortly."

The businessmen noticed that the men they were with were looking around nervously, and realised that possibly this was because there were a lot of obvious 'No Parking' signs, indicating that the car should not have been parked in its current location.

* * * * *

Brian had been back, standing in his special location just outside the doors through which passengers came into the Arrivals Hall from air side, for only a short time when he identified the two couples he was expecting to arrive on the Virgin Atlantic flight; it was obvious from the tags on their luggage labels.

He waved and beckoned them over, but just as they were moving across to join him, a young man cannoned into two of them, knocking them both to the ground whereupon their suitcases flew out of their hands. A crowd gathered round, the two people were helped to their feet and the suitcases were returned to their owners. However, when they looked round to see if the young man was all right, he had completely disappeared.

"Oh, look," the woman wailed. "One of our new suitcases has an enormous scratch in the shape of a 'V' all across one side."

* * * * *

When a young man ran out of the terminal building and jumped into the car containing the two Chinese businessmen, it was driven off at speed. The young man was obviously not in a good mood and was muttering angrily, which prompted the driver to ask, "What went wrong?"

It was fortunate (or possibly unfortunate) that the Chinese could not understand the reply provided in the Zulu language, because they might have been concerned if they had learnt that they were actually travelling with a person who had just attempted to steal a suitcase.

* * * * *

While waiting in the coach station for their fellow passengers to join them, Dawn and Jerry discussed their flight experiences with Amy who was eager to tell them all about herself.

Dawn also watched the many vehicles of different shapes and sizes, entering and leaving the coach station just outside the room in which they had been told to wait. She was particularly intrigued by the Magic Buses, which she noticed took a maximum of seven passengers plus a driver. Some of these had a trailer attached to the back into which the driver put the luggage before the tourists climbed aboard.

However, it was not a Magic Bus, but a Mega Bus that was summoned by their tour guide after he had escorted the four additional members of their party into the waiting area. As it drew up outside the automatic sliding doors, Dawn noticed that this type of bus could carry a maximum of sixteen passengers so they would have plenty of room to spread out as their group only consisted of seven tourists, a guide and a driver. It also had a trailer, and as they all trouped outside with their luggage, they were greeted by the smiling driver who manhandled the luggage into the trailer, locked it and opened the doors for the passengers to get onto the bus.

On the walk to the bus, Jerry had mentioned to Dawn,

"You can't help feeling sorry for Amy. She's obviously an intelligent woman – she said she went to Oxford University. Then when she finished University, she got married and has been looking after a disabled husband full-time every since. It was lucky that she was able to find a carer to look after him while she made this trip."

Before they set off, Brian introduced the passengers to each other and to Dan, the driver. He then explained that the drive to Pretoria would take approximately one hour, and that they would be stopping at various places of interest along the way before arriving at their hotel, the Court Classique, where a welcome dinner would be served that evening.

It was a lovely, warm day with not a cloud in the sky, and the guide explained that it was the start of the South African Spring when it rained occasionally during the day, but mainly at night. Small shrubs and plants were flowering prolifically in the airport grounds; in particular, the petunias provided a blaze of different colours at the base of the many Jacaranda trees that were not yet in bloom.

As the bus travelled along wide motorways that they were informed had been built for the World Cup that had taken place the previous year, the passengers chatted to each other.

Amy, Jerry and Dawn, had been joined by Meryl and Peter, and Anne and Catherine (who said she preferred to be called Cathy). Anne explained that she was Cathy's mother, and that while she and her husband had been living in South Africa, Cathy and her elder brother had been born. Now she was bringing Cathy back to see the country she had only known as a very young child, but which Anne had grown really fond of twenty years earlier.

Meryl and Peter said that they were on their honeymoon, and that it was a second marriage for both of them. They told of how they had first met and fallen in love when Meryl was still at school, but due to pressure from their parents, they had eventually gone their separate ways. Each of them had married and had families, but when their children were teenagers, both had split up with their partners. Then, just like a fairytale come true, they had met again and their love had blossomed once more.

After that Jerry and Dawn's story of their straightforward life of marriage, children, grandchildren and now retirement, appeared to be really boring. But then Amy retold her story, which managed to silence everyone, and Jerry and Dawn felt that their life had not been so bad after all.

Later, Jerry remarked to Dawn,

"It's funny. When Amy was speaking to us she said that she had looked after her invalid husband since leaving University. To the group she said that although her husband is disabled, he is a Head Teacher at a private boys' school."

"That doesn't mean she hasn't looked after him all their married life," Dawn replied.

"No, but the story is changing," Jerry continued.

When they reached the main road, Brian picked up the microphone and started his commentary; one of many such commentaries that would bring the sights they were about to see to life and make the tour even more interesting.

"The total population of South Africa is currently (in September 2011) made up of approximately 36 million people from 9 different African tribes, 6 million former Europeans, 2 million Indians/Asians and Cape Coloureds which is an ethnic group resulting from young Dutch or German men marrying Asian girls, plus there could be as many as 5 million illegal immigrants. There are eleven official languages. The most widely spoken home language is Zulu, although English is the second most popular language spoken by over 40 million people. Six million people speak Afrikaans (similar to Flemish or Dutch)."

"South Africa produces more than 70% of the world's gemstone diamonds, and a huge diamond was found just two years ago. There are nine diamond mines in South Africa, and recently diamonds have been found in the recycling dumps in Kimberley. Today, the Phoenicia Mine is producing the most diamonds. There are ten different types of diamonds which are assessed by carat (weight), colour (white is the most valuable), clarity (the least flaws the more valuable), and cut (58 facets is the most beautiful cut, but an amazing 66 facets has now been developed)."

"Sugar cane and maize are our biggest crops. We produce at least 7 million tons of maize a year, but sometimes this can be as much as 10 million tons. Eighty per cent of the crop is white maize rather than sweet corn, as this has a ten-year storage capacity. The staple diet of the African people is maize eaten daily as a corn porridge (mielie)."

"In January and February the countryside looks beautiful with maize growing to between ten and fifteen feet high."

"Ethanol is also obtained from maize and sugar cane. All our aircraft use synthetic fuel and two hundred aircraft a week fly into Johannesburg; two million people travelling from overseas and seven million individuals from within South Africa on airlines using Johannesburg Airport each year. With regard to foreign tourists, the British come to South Africa in the highest number with half a million visitors from the United Kingdom annually, second are the

visitors from the United States and Canada who like it here. Despite the fact that they have a long journey, the North Americans have now overtaken the Germans who come third and the Dutch are now in fourth place."

"Our biggest trading partner is Germany. Next comes the United States, third is Japan, fourth is the UK and fifth is China. We also import oil from Saudi Arabia."

After providing so many facts, their guide then let them enjoy the magnificent open countryside in silence, and it was not until they were nearing their destination that he imparted more information.

* * * * *

CHAPTER 2
'Pretoria'

"Pretoria, the capital city of South Africa was named after Governor Pretorius, and is the political and diplomatic hub of this country."

"Although Pretoria is the largest city in South Africa in terms of area, it is only the fourth largest in terms of population. Johannesburg has the largest population, Durban is next and Cape Town comes third. Durban is a popular city for South African tourists. 700,000 motor cars are built in South Africa each year and the biggest factory is in Durban: VW and Toyota have factories there."

"Pretoria is a multicultural city, and although there is a strong Afrikaner influence, English is widely spoken. You can also hear other languages on the streets so it has an international flavour."

"Our first stop will be at the Voortrekker Monument. After this, we will pass the University of South Africa (UNISA), visit the historic Church Square (originally called Market Square) where there are many imposing buildings of architectural interest, and then we will go up to the Union Buildings from where there are fine views across the whole city."

As they travelled along a good road, all the passengers continued to look out of the coach windows at the beautiful countryside laid out before them until a sign announced the Voortrekker Monument on the right. They drove up a hill towards an imposing building on top, and parked in a car park below steps that led up into a walled area around the monument, which housed a museum and a cenotaph in its basement.

Then standing in the courtyard garden they spotted a magnificent coral tree with dark red blossom, where the white and purple flowers in the bed underneath resembled a velvet picnic blanket circling the base of the tree. Brian pointed out that these were Protea, the national flower of South Africa and that 300 species of these plants grew in this country, before he explained the history of the building that stood before them.

"The Voortrekker Monument was built over an eleven-year period, between 1938 and 1949, and is made of granite. It *is forty metres high and forty metres wide, ie it's a cube, and in total there are 220 steps inside the Monument. The wildebeest are the symbols of the four regiments of the Boer Army and on each corner of the building there is a different figurehead. Around the inside of the walls circling this courtyard there are six wagons representing a laager (a circle of wagons), which is the arrangement that the Voortrekkers used when they set up camps on their long journey to their new homes so that they could defend themselves against attacks from local tribesmen."*

Before going inside the monument itself, the tourists took photographs of the monument sign, the coral tree, the outside of the monument, the statue of a Voortrekker woman in traditional dress with two children at her feet that stood below the steps leading up to the entrance, the wagons depicted in the walls, and a view of the city of Pretoria with the Magaliesburg Mountains in the background; apparently this was where the Cullinan diamond (the world's largest rough gem quality diamond that Edward VII had cut into seven pieces) was discovered in 1905.

Once they were inside, Brian took them over to the walls where there were scenes depicting the journey of the Voortrekkers and the dangers, trials and tribulations they encountered before they settled in what later became the Natal region of South Africa. He told the story of the Battle of Blood River, which was the result of the Zulus reneging on their agreement to allow the Voortrekkers to settle on their lands. After losing this battle, the refugee Zulus (later known as the Matabele) left to go to an area of Bulawayo that became Matabeleland.

"Unfortunately," he added, "despite the efforts of the Boers to get away from the British influence in the Cape Town region, the British annexed Natal in 1842 as the area was rich in minerals. In fact, in the mid 1880s gold was discovered in the nearby Transvaal and this ultimately led to the Boer War in 1899."

Then he pointed out the hole in the ceiling through which the sun shone down directly onto the cenotaph at a specific time of the year, saying that celebrations took place in the monument on 16th December.

The tourists then wandered around inside the building, looking at the carvings at ground floor level, the tapestries in the basement museum and, after climbing up the stairs to the viewing platform, down into the cenotaph itself and at the views of the surrounding countryside where springbok grazed in the fields.

Their second stop took place after driving into the centre of Pretoria, along streets full of shops with bars on their windows, but where only a few were open as it was a Sunday. Despite this, people mingled on the pavements and traffic was quite heavy. Their guide explained that most people now lived in the suburbs where there were big shopping malls and the city centre was becoming a depressed area.

"Imagine what it must be like during the week," mused Jerry. "There are a lot of office blocks so I presume it would be even busier than now."

After getting off the bus in an ornate square, they gathered round Brian as he pointed out the buildings surrounding the gardens in the middle of which stood a statue of former President, Paul Kruger; the same Paul Kruger who in 1897 decreed that land be set aside for what would eventually become the Kruger National Park.

The buildings (or national monuments) included a station designed by the British, Pretoria City Hall, the Transvaal Museum, the Palace of Justice, the General Post Office, the First Mint, and the earliest coffee shop (Café Riche).

In one corner, a group of black women, all wearing identical green outfits, were gathered. Brian explained that they belonged to the Women's ANC movement and were campaigning for Women's Rights. He then added,

"In the South African Parliament we have the largest number of women members (compared to other countries) with 47% currently holding office. With regard to jobs in South Africa, women get priority and then black people. Since the abolition of apartheid, we have positive discrimination in South Africa. In August, there is a Ladies' Day, or National Women's Day, which is a public holiday. There is also a Secretaries' Day."

"So are you saying that those qualified to do jobs, possibly will not be employed, or promoted, because they are not women or black?" asked Jerry. "You could then end up with people in charge being less able than those working under them."

When Brian just shrugged, Jerry added,

"Well, that could lead to problems in future."

The tourists then strolled around the Square taking photographs whilst the locals gazed at them. Picnics were taking place on the grass, people sat chatting on park benches, children ran about, and there was a lot of activity around areas where car washing was being carried out for a fee.

Their third stop was at the Union Buildings on top of another hill overlooking Pretoria, where Brian explained,

"The Union Buildings are the administrative headquarters of South Africa. They are built of sandstone and limestone, and were designed by the British architect, Herbert Baker, ie the same person who was responsible for the Naval Hospital in Greenwich. You will notice that the domes on top of the towers are an exact replica of those you might have seen in Greenwich. The President's office is in the West Wing of this building, but the South African Parliament is in Cape Town."

"How long does the President remain in office?" asked Jerry.

"Five years, but it is possible to stand for a second term of five years. Unfortunately, Nelson Mandela did not do so," Brian replied. *"The President makes his inaugural speech in the amphi-theatre in the centre of this building."*

Brian then pointed to a tree in the gardens adding:

"That is the yellowwood which is South Africa's national tree. You will also notice animals of South Africa on the front of the Rand notes, and on the back pictures of industries that depict the infra-structure, such as mining etc."

Flags of South Africa were flapping in the breeze in front of the enormous, but magnificent building before them. Then on the other side of the road, ornamental gardens stretched down the hillside. There were views of the skyscrapers of Pretoria with the Central Bank of South Africa (the equivalent of Fort Knox in the USA) in the centre and the Voortrekker Monument in the background.

"Now, if you have taken sufficient photographs," Brian said, "we will take you to your hotel. You have had a long flight and you might like to rest this afternoon. Tomorrow we have a lengthy drive. It will take approximately six hours to reach our next stop. With breaks and sightseeing on the way, it might take a little longer, but by late afternoon we will be near the Kruger National Park."

Everybody climbed back aboard the bus which travelled around the outskirts of Pretoria, past parks and gardens, along wide one-way streets with four lanes of traffic all travelling in the same direction, before drawing up in front of the Court Classique Hotel, an elegant building in colonial style, beautifully restored to its former glory with the relief in wood and metal painted red, blue and green.

The driver had to park the bus on the wide pavement outside because the main gates to the hotel were locked, but the passengers could get out and walk through a small side gate that led into the front gardens. From there they were able to continue to the reception area where Jerry managed to get the guide's attention and asked another question.

"Why are there such wide roads in Pretoria?"

Brian replied, *"The roads were originally designed so that a bullock cart drawn by eight animals could turn round in the road. You will also find that most towns in South Africa are approximately 35 miles apart (56 kilometres) because this is the distance that oxen can travel in a day,"*

Thereby, Brian provided yet another example of an interesting fact, and by the end of the trip, the tourists would be marvelling at the breadth of his knowledge. There didn't seem to be a question he could not answer, and he encouraged them to ask, explaining that this was what made his job even more rewarding.

After welcome drinks had been handed round in the garden and room keys distributed, Dan drew up with the bus. The cases were unloaded and marked with room numbers before the guests made their way to their rooms.

* * * * *

The two Chinese businessmen had arrived at their hotel sometime earlier, but it was definitely not as nice as the one Dawn, Jerry and their fellow travellers would be staying in. It was, in fact, a very shabby hotel in one of the seedier districts of downtown Johannesburg, and the man on the Reception Desk eyed them suspiciously before stating,

"Payment required in advance. I no want no bilking."

The Chinese looked round at the South Africans who had accompanied them into the hotel, and asked,

"What is bilking?"

"That's leaving a hotel without paying," one of them replied. "It's better if you pay for at least four nights' accommodation now."

The Chinese did as suggested, but when they were left alone in their room, the smaller of the two remarked in Chinese,

"What a dump this hotel is. I didn't like the look of those two who met us. Can we trust them? Also, that young man who travelled in the car from the airport, he was very angry - he could easily become violent."

"They came highly recommended," his partner replied. "What do you expect the people we're dealing with to be like? We're about to do something highly illegal. This hotel is just right. We don't want to be seen in a high-class establishment."

"Well, I don't see how we can leave the hotel to go sightseeing without running the risk of being mugged."

"We're not going to be doing any sightseeing. We'll get some sleep now so that we are ready for the job we are going to do later."

"You mean we've come all this way, and we're not going to see anything of South Africa apart from the view from this room and from the windows of any vehicles we travel around in?"

"That's right. We don't want to draw attention to ourselves. Now get some sleep. Our contacts will be calling round later to discuss the plans for getting what we want."

* * * * *

Dawn and Jerry were so impressed with their hotel that they took photographs not only of the outside, but also inside their room, which was furnished in a traditional style, with mahogany panelling and dark wooden doors dividing the lounge from the bedroom. The walls were as white as the linen, which was crisp and luxurious, and there was even a small kitchen area with refrigerator and microwave.

After freshening up, they decided to have a light lunch before taking a siesta. It was an interesting experience walking out of the hotel as they had to negotiate an automatic gate system, before they went in search of the highly recommended pancake house that they had passed on the approach road.

They crossed wide roads when traffic lights allowed them to do so, noticing that all the buildings, whether they were houses or blocks of flats, had high fences around them, and signs showing that alarms had been fitted with some even mentioning 'Armed Response'. Even the apartments on the ground and first floors had bars at the windows. But they had been told that it was not dangerous for tourists to walk around the city, and they took a short cut across a park where groups of people were enjoying lively discussions whilst seated on the grass and where others dozed in the shade of trees.

Eventually, they reached Harries' Pancake House situated in a small complex of shops bordering a car park on the corner of an intersection of busy roads.

The restaurant was very clean, with chrome tables and chairs, and Dawn and Jerry chose one close to the windows overlooking the street. The menu was also very varied, and listed fillings for pancakes which they had never experienced before. Dawn chose a pork and peach one whereas Jerry selected a Thai curry filling, which arrived with a hot and spicy sauce that brought tears to his eyes.

After enjoying their meal, they took the same route they had used earlier and returned to the hotel for the promised siesta knowing that in the evening they were expected to join their fellow passengers for a welcome dinner.

The dinner actually turned out to be a wine tasting event that took place in a basement restaurant in the hotel. Dawn and Jerry arrived promptly at 6.30 pm, but nobody else was there apart from the gentleman who was providing information about the wines. It appeared that there had been communication problems, but after telephone calls were made, the remainder of the party and the guide joined them. They were served a different wine with each course and their host explained the origins of the wines in a very interesting way. The food was also excellent: beef tartar or soup with pasta and pawns, followed by beef cooked over two days or sardines, and for dessert, chocolate brownie with a cherry sorbet or sweet cous cous with fruit compote and coconut ice cream.

After consuming the wonderful meal, drinking several glasses of wine, port and amarula, Dawn and Jerry were in bed by 9.00 pm. Knowing that they had to be up by 6.30 am, they quickly went to sleep.

* * * * *

Once again in contrast, the two Chinese businessmen had not had such a good first day in South Africa.

When they woke from their slumbers, they were hungry and telephoned Reception to try and find out if there was a restaurant in the hotel, or if room service was available, only to be told that a sandwich could be brought up to their room.

As there was no alternative, they had agreed to this, but when someone knocked on their door, they were surprised to find that the sandwiches were actually just thick slices of bread across which had been laid what appeared to be a sausage.

"What is this?" asked the larger Chinese businessman.

"Biltong," came the reply from a man holding out a tray, which the businessman took from him.

The biltong was not actually to their taste, much too salty, but they ate it anyway. Then they sat around in their room restlessly waiting for their associates to turn up as promised. However, they did not do so until late evening.

It quite dark outside when they heard the next knock on their door, and the larger of the two men checked by looking through the peephole before he opened it.

"Hardly worth the effort of checking who is there," thought his colleague, "Even the people we are expecting, could be a threat to our existence."

Nevertheless, he followed his associate who went down the hotel stairs with the two men who had met them at the airport, and they all got into a car that was waiting with the engine running. It was explained that they were being taken to a bar to meet others involved in the plot in order to finalise the plans.

From the outside the bar looked no more than a tin hut, but when they walked inside they found it was quite spacious with many tables and chairs, an enormous flat screen TV on one wall silently screening a football match, and a bar counter along the length of another wall. Although most of the room was dark as there were no windows and the atmosphere was full of smoke, the bar itself was well lit. It was fitted with lights that illuminated the optics, and rows and rows of bottles of alcohol on the back wall; the lights were also reflected in the mirrors positioned behind them and they twinkled on the glasses hanging above the counter. It looked very smart and acceptable in the eyes of the Chinese businessmen who knew of many similar bars in China.

Some of the occupants of the building looked up as they entered, but quickly looked away again and continued with what they were doing: drinking, laughing and talking together.

Among them they recognised the young man who had joined them in the car from the airport. He was sitting at a table talking angrily with two other men, one of whom signalled to the men the Chinese were with and pointed to the back of the building. The other man was a very smartly suited gentleman who appeared to be as out of place in the bar as did the Chinese.

As the group walked past, it was only those who understood the Zulu language who realised what the angry young man was saying,

"It wasn't my fault. Nobody warned me that they would have two suitcases the same colour. I couldn't snatch both. I went for the one I saw first, got confused when I saw the other one and that delayed me. All I could do was mark one of them so that it will be easier to recognise in future."

"A lot of good that will do if there are two matching suitcases," replied the smartly dressed gentleman, who had been recognised by some of those who had just entered. "We still don't know which is the right one."

The group then went through many smaller, but still noisy areas leading off the main room.

In one such area, they noticed that there was a full-size snooker table in a bad state of repair. In fact, the places where pockets of netting would normally have been found, were currently in the process of being reinstated by a man who was forcing a sharp piece of angle iron into the correct shape, but there was no sign of any netting to go around it.

Just as they walked past, a man shouted out and they turned to see him near one of the repaired pockets, holding up a hand that was dripping with blood. Although they could not understand what was being said, they immediately realised that the person carrying out the repair was scolding the man with the bleeding hand.

What he actually said in Zulu was,

"I told you not to touch it. It is sharp. I am going to install the covers on the pockets next week."

The Chinese businessmen were not allowed to linger anywhere, however, but were quickly led into a room at the back of the building where the man who had gesticulated earlier soon joined them and introduced himself as Rocky. Other men also joined them, and eventually, there were seven people in the room. They all sat round a large table, beers were ordered, and the Chinese asked if there was any chance of getting a meal.

The others thought this was a great idea, and slapped the Chinese on the back before Rocky, who was obviously in charge said, "Bobotie all round" to the person who was serving the drinks.

Surprisingly, the Chinese found the 'Bobotie' to their liking. It was a lamb curry with sultanas and nuts, served with boiled rice and mango chutney, which suited the Chinese admirably.

Everyone around the table tucked into their meal and beer was swilled down, with the glasses being refilled regularly. Initially, there were angry exchanges in Zulu that the Chinese listened to, but obviously could not understand. However, eventually agreement appeared to have been reached, and the Africans then spoke animatedly in accented English that the Chinese could just understand. It appeared that they were making an effort to put their guests at ease, which the Chinese appreciated.

After the meal had been cleared away, everybody was in a better mood and they got down to discussing business with their Chinese associates.

Joseph, one of those who had joined them earlier, but had not spoken, was introduced as being "the man on the inside". The Chinese were given to understand that he had once been a Park Ranger trained in the art of tracking animals; it was going to be his job to find a large herd of rhinos in the Kruger National Park and direct a helicopter to land nearby.

The Chinese, realising that they were expected to pay, questioned why a helicopter was needed whereupon it was explained that because of the size of the Kruger National Park and the fact that the animals were allowed to roam freely, wherever they wanted, it would be difficult if they used any other means to get to the herd quickly and out again before they were spotted.

Although a helicopter had not been part of the original deal, the Chinese agreed to this, and were then told that they would be taken to meet the helicopter pilot the next day when he would expect payment.

The price was discussed, together with the amount those present expected to receive for their contributions to the arrangements, and as there was no option, the Chinese had to agree. After all, they had come this far and there was no going back on the deal now; they could also see from the attitude of those present that even if they had wanted to renege on the deal, trouble would result.

However, they had to explain that they didn't carry large amounts of money with them, but they had arranged for a bank transfer to be made to the Johannesburg branch of the HSBC where the driver of the car agreed to take them the next day.

It was after midnight when they were driven back to their hotel after having paid for all the food and drink consumed by the whole group and arrangements had been made for them to be collected at ten o'clock the next morning. On reaching their hotel room, the Chinese thankfully fell onto their beds and slept.

* * * * *

But what of Amy? How had she occupied her time after arriving at the hotel in Pretoria?

Quite sensibly, she had decided not to leave the hotel grounds alone that afternoon. She had tried to find some of her fellow travellers so that she could join them for lunch, but without success. Therefore, she had gone to the hotel restaurant on her own. She ordered a platter of appetisers and a bottle of wine which she quickly consumed, and followed this with two gin and tonics before returning to her hotel room where she laid down on the bed and immediately fell asleep. She was finding that the best way to stop herself thinking about anything at all, was to drink alcohol and then there was no opportunity for unwanted thoughts to drift into her head before sleep engulfed her.

She had been sound asleep when the telephone rang to remind her about the welcome dinner taking place in the basement restaurant, but she quickly roused herself, freshened up and dressed for dinner.

She was pleased to see that the wine included with the meal flowed abundantly as she drank one glass after another, not being afraid to ask for it to be refilled, unlike the other guests who kept to one glass of wine with each course, not even finishing it if it was not to their particular taste.

Therefore, by the end of the evening she was quite tipsy, and was surprised when she looked around the room to find that her fellow travellers had left. She was now the only member of the tour party who remained at the table, with half eaten plates of food in front of her, and only the tour guide and the wine expert for company. For a while, she chatted to them incessantly until she realised that they were not listening any more. Then she knocked back the remains in the variety of glasses in front of her, announced that she was going to bed and staggered to her feet. The guide helped her up the stairs and made sure she was headed in the right direction for her room before he went back down again to continue his conversation with the wine expert.

The cool evening air helped Amy sober up enough to find her room, her key and her bed where she collapsed, but not before remembering to telephone reception to ask for an alarm call the next morning.

Surprisingly, when morning came, she was alert and ready for the second day of her adventure. She went down to breakfast bright and early, eager to join her fellow passengers for an 8.00 am departure as she was looking forward to travelling along the Panorama Route.

* * * * *

Breakfast was another wonderful eating experience for Jerry and Dawn, with plenty of fruit available as well as yogurt, crusty bread rolls, eggs, bacon, sausages and mushrooms in a barbecue sauce. The only dampener on the experience was the rudeness of a large African businessman who shouted at the waitress, demanding two slices of toast.

Dawn looked at Jerry and said quietly, "There was no need for that."

Jerry just shook his head and carried on eating, trying to ignore what was going on, and Dawn followed his example.

After breakfast, they packed and put their suitcases outside their hotel room before 8.00 am. They were also eager to enjoy the second day of their African Experience.

* * * * *

The Chinese businessmen, however, were not so eager.

Their breakfast that morning was, in their opinion, another unpleasant food experience. They hadn't bothered to enquire whether breakfast was included, or to ask anyone to wake them at a certain time. However, on the dot of 8.00 am, there was a knock on their door. When they opened it, there was nobody there, but looking down they saw that a tray had been placed on the floor. On it were two steaming bowls of what looked like porridge (this was actually 'Mielie' a mixture of corn (maize) flour, milk, salt and butter) and two mugs of very weak black tea (Rooibos Tea) accompanied by chunks of bread.

Completely oblivious to what they were eating as their stomachs were craving food after consuming so much alcohol the previous evening, they ate and drank everything provided, assuming that their associates had arranged this meal for them.

And so it was that at 10.00 am they went down the stairs and out of the hotel. To their surprise a car, two of their companions from the previous evening, and a driver were waiting for them. They were on time!

* * * * *

CHAPTER 3
'Mpumalanga'

As they boarded the bus now located in the grounds of the hotel, Brian suggested that each day a different person sit in the front seat next to the driver, as he preferred to spread out on the double seat behind Dan from where he was able to turn and face the tourists when speaking.

This was agreed and it was suggested that Amy take the first turn of sitting up front next to Dan. She eagerly accepted, and everyone settled down in his or her seat.

Even before they left the grounds, Brian picked up the microphone and turned to face them in order to announce,

"Today, we will travel to Mpumalanga, the 'Province of the Rising Sun', via Blyde River Canyon, Bourke's Luck Potholes, God's Window and Pilgrim's Rest, an unspoilt gold-mining village proclaimed a National Monument in 1986. You will have the opportunity to experience South Africa's cultural heritage and its dramatic landscapes. Then you will be staying for two nights at the Pine Lake Inn, Mpumalanga."

"A chance to unpack," laughed Dawn.

As they left the hotel and started the drive along the wide avenues of Pretoria, Brian took up the microphone again and continued his commentary,

"This is the east side of our capital city. It is the smart area of Pretoria where many High Commissions are situated."

He pointed out the Libyan, British and Nigerian High Commissions as particular examples.

Despite the fact that it was September, the coach drove past areas where they had already put up their Christmas decorations, and then suddenly they were on a main road.

As they went under the M1 Motorway, Brian commented,

"The M1 is part of the Cairo to Cape Town highway, approximately 6,400 miles (10,200 km) long. It is more

than 1,200 miles (1,930 km) from Cape Point to the northern border of South Africa. We are now travelling on the M4. The majority of the highways in South Africa were built during the 1960s and 1970s."

Then they passed some retirement villages close to the main road, where Brian explained that they were not only for South African farmers to retire to, but there was one for elderly Taiwanese people as well. Next, as they passed one new power station and several others that had obviously been in commission for some time, he announced,

"We have one nuclear power station in South Africa, situated near Cape Town. The majority of power stations use coal because there are many coalmines in South Africa. South Africa has one of the biggest coalfields in the world and is the fifth biggest producer of coal with 70 million tons being exported each year. ESCOM is the official company. We have 25 generating points and only 2 hydroelectric power stations. We do have some wind generators in the Cape and now solar power is also being used."

When they had passed industrial areas, and were out in the countryside again, the next comment was,

"We are now entering the province of Mpumalanga which was formerly known as the Eastern Transvaal."

"This is the cultural heartland of South Africa. Three point five million people live in this province; it is the fifth largest in terms of population."

"Mpumalanga is one of South Africa's top tourist destinations because of its magnificent scenery, flora and fauna. We have mountains, panoramic passes, valleys, rivers, waterfalls and forests as well as many game reserves, including of course the most famous, the Kruger National Park. All of the sanctuaries are teeming with wildlife and birds. That is why it is known as 'Paradise Country'. Also, there is historical interest as this area experienced the 1870s gold rush, plus it is a region of many interesting tribal legends. But now the streams where prospectors once panned for gold are used by anglers trying to catch trout. Steeped in the history of pioneers, hunters and fortune seekers, fascinating gold rush towns abound, such as Pilgrim's Rest where we will make our first official stop."

"To get there, we will travel through the town of Dullstroom, over the Long Tom Pass and see panoramic views going down to Lone Creek Falls and the forestry town of Sabie. The Mac Mac Falls are 13 kilometres beyond Sabie. We won't get as far as that in our travels, but they are quite spectacular as they have a drop of 70 metres."

Then as they were passing large tracts of rough scrubland and fields of stubble where maize had been harvested, and before reaching a Vanadium factory and signs for Clewer, Brian added

"This is one of the richest areas on earth for metal extraction, and there is a coalmine at Clewer. In fact, this is the place Winston Churchill (as a journalist during the Boer War) escaped to after being taken prisoner. He went to the Manager of the mine and, despite the fact that a bounty of £25 (a large sum of money in those days) had been put on his head, they hid him in the pit for six days. Then, fortunately, he made it to Durban where he made his first political speech."

Next they went past an area known as White Banks where there was a small river. Again, Brian explained that this was an industrial area where they produced chemicals, in particular the cyanide that was used in the gold mining industry, and then he said,

"White Banks used to have the highest level of air pollution in South Africa until regulations were brought in to clean up the district. Now it is a green area, planted with trees, and full of Country Clubs, Golf Clubs, Cricket Clubs, etc. Apparently, the bungalows (family type homes) at the side of this road cost the equivalent of between £70,000 and £100,000."

They passed another power station, Duva, and then a shopping mall with a casino and an entertainment centre. Brian explained that when it was only possible to have casinos in the countryside, they had been built to encourage tourism in the area, but now casinos can also be sited in cities.

Thankfully, the scenery then changed to open countryside once more, and there was a nature reserve on both sides of the road – it was the start of Elephant River.

* * * * *

The Chinese businessmen were certainly not treated to such a wealth of information. In fact, it was in complete silence that they were driven to the HSBC Bank in Johannesburg. The first words that were spoken were when they arrived at their destination and the car stopped on a busy road. At this point it was explained that cars were not allowed to park near the bank. They were instructed to quickly get out of the car, visit the bank on the opposite side of the road, and when they came out of the bank, to stand at the dropping off point where they would be met.

The Chinese saw no reason to do other than exactly what they were told. They managed to cross the busy road, went into the bank, found a cashier who understood their requirements, and obtained enough money to cover the cost of the helicopter trip and sufficient for any incidental expenses. Then exactly half an hour after they had alighted from the car, they were standing at the appointed place awaiting their driver. Everything appeared to be going to plan as they were met and driven off to their next appointment at a private airstrip.

* * * * *

While all this had been happening, the tour party were continuing to travel along the M4. They hadn't even stopped to take a break, and the commentary carried on.

"We are now entering the Highveld. Because there are so many small trees, this land is not suitable for large-scale mining operations. There are still some small coalmines, two to three hundred feet deep (that's between 61 and 90 metres), but there are open cast mines as well. You may see the resultant scars on the countryside. However, in this grassy interior of South Africa, zebra, eland and rhebuck wander freely because it is a nature reserve. Occasionally, you will also see cattle grazing; mainly the white Brahman cattle."

"We have approximately 12 million cattle in total in South Africa, and Brahman, Herefords and Aberdeen Angus are among the breeds used for beef production. We also have approximately 50 million sheep, but we don't export our lamb. We prefer to eat it ourselves!"

"However, we are the second biggest producer of lamb. Australia is in first place with approximately 250 million

sheep. Originally we imported merino sheep from Spain, but now our sheep are interbred with Dutch sheep and sent to Holland."

"There is a joke which we share with our visitors from New Zealand. In New Zealand they have 11 sheep per acre. In South Africa we have 11 acres per sheep."

Everyone was laughing as the driver slowed down. They were passing a weighbridge, but no one indicated that he should pull over, so Dan continued onto the booths ahead where he stopped and showed his paperwork to the young lady sitting there.

Brian had already explained that he spoke Zulu, but this was the first of many occasions when the tour party heard him use his language skills to smooth their journey across the northeastern part of South Africa.

"Unjani", he shouted loudly as he lent across the driver. (Unjani translates to 'How are you?' in English.)

The girl in the booth laughed as she returned his greeting and a conversation in Zulu commenced, with all three parties who understood the language, laughing at what was obviously a joke they were sharing.

Jerry had noticed some signs at the side of the road: a P and an S, both with obliques through them, and at the end of the locals' conversation he took the opportunity to ask Brian what they meant.

"No Parking and No Stopping," Brian replied.

"That must be confusing for Americans," Jerry laughed. "They will probably think they have to pay dollars to get through this checkpoint."

Everyone on the coach laughed again as they continued on their way.

As they passed fields containing white-faced antelope and some with a white rump, Brian pointed out,

"The white-faced antelope is now called a blesbok."

He added that waterbuck and pied buck also grazed in these areas; they were very popular with farmers because they did not move away once placed on a particular piece of land.

When they passed a Wattle Plantation, Brian explained,

"Wattle is used in the mining industry and for paper making, and it is also used for tanning leather. Apparently, a South African botanist sent a consignment to London for analysis, but it stayed in the London Dockyard for eleven years. Then, after all that time, the South African botanist received a reply stating that the acid extracted from wattle was outstanding for tanning leather."

"Originally the whole of this area was grassland, and all the trees you see are the result of planting. Now the wattle tree, which was imported from Australia, is causing problems in some places because it is taking all the water out of the soil. It cannot be burnt. In fact, it likes to be burnt because the seeds then spread. Also, if it is cut down and the branches are given to locals for firewood, the same situation occurs – the seeds are burnt and spread elsewhere."

"This is one of our richest geological areas with platinum, chrome, manganese, copper and lead being mined, but unfortunately, no oil. Therefore we convert coal into synthetic fuel, and now South Africa is exporting this technology to many other parts of the world – it has become very competitive because of high oil prices."

As they travelled across the Olifants River, Brian explained that it had featured in the Boer War, adding that the British troops had been advised not to cross the river, but Cecil Rhodes had decided that they would do so. If orders had been followed, the British may not have suffered the sieges of Ladysmith and Mafeking. Now the river was home to approximately 60% of the Kruger Park's hippo population.

Seeing yet more coalmines on their left, Brian changed the subject and stated,

"This area experiences the biggest thunderstorms in the world. The sheet and fork lightning is spectacular with strikes going up to 60,000 feet (18,288 metres) from the ground and one or two inches of rain can fall in just half an hour."

Then as they were passing a game park with no animals to be seen, Brian explained,

"This is a new development where they are just starting to introduce different breeds. Many wild animals have contracted bovine tuberculosis, and this dramatically *reduces their lifespan to approximately seven years so young males are taking over prides of females. The healthiest lions in Africa are found in the Kalahari so these are imported into new game parks."*

They were crossing an inland plateau rising slowly up to 6,400 feet in altitude when Brian announced that a short stop would be made on the outskirts of Belfast, the second highest settlement in South Africa. He added that the highest village stood at 6,750 feet and Johannesburg Airport was 1,000 feet lower than they were now.

When they saw a sign stating 'Welcome to Highlands Meander', their guide explained that the area had been so named because the scenery resembled the Scottish Highlands.

They were just passing large grain silos in several rows of tens where animals were grazing on the nearby stubble when Amy suddenly shouted,

"Lambs".

This was the first place where sheep with lambs had been spotted, but Brian's commentary was now on a totally different subject.

"The Dutch settlers developed lots of nurseries near Johannesburg and there are also many in this region where they grow daffodils, tulips and hyacinths in September and the bulbs are sent to Australia, China and Japan. The flowers can be cut one day and arrive in Europe on the next day. For Lady Diana's funeral, two planes loaded with crates full of flowers were sent out."

At that point they turned off the M4 and made their first stop of the day, at the One Stop & Quick Shop Service Station where Dan filled up with petrol and the passengers got out to stretch their legs, use the facilities and wander around the shop and cafeteria.

Dawn got quite excited at one point and exclaimed,

"Ooh, look at those 'Chariots of Wire'",

as she dragged Jerry across to a stand housing vehicles of various shapes and sizes, ranging from sports cars to farm vehicles with trailers and dumper trucks large enough for a small child to sit on, all very strongly made out of wire.

"Wouldn't they be lovely for the grandchildren," Dawn enthused, but Jerry stopped her dreaming by saying,

"They'd never fit in the suitcase, even the smaller ones, and I'm guessing it's the big ones you find more interesting."

Dawn had to agree, and all they ended up buying were two local newspapers and some drinks.

However, from then on, everywhere they stopped Dawn and Jerry were looking out for more examples of 'Chariots of Wire'.

Before they entered the town of Belfast, Brian explained that Belfast benefited from a wonderful deposit of black granite that they exported. Then they passed several trout farms and on reaching the town centre, saw the Trout & Tackle Shop, the Belfast Royal Hotel, and the Pig & Pickle Country Tavern.

As they went out of the town, just to verify what Brian had told them previously, there were huge granite boulders piled at the side of the road, and the swathes of green, dry brown and golden countryside that they then travelled through was scattered with even more boulders; it all looked very like English moorland as the ground was seen to rise and fall away again, far into the distance.

"Just waiting for the summer rains to make the land green again," Brian said.

When forested areas were visible in the distance, Brian added,

"Australia gave us eucalyptus trees and now we have eucalyptus plantations. Eucalyptus trees grow to a greater height here than they do in Australia because there is plenty of rain. We also have pine trees from Canada and sometimes both are grown together at altitudes of over 3,500 ft."

Then the railway line that had been beside the road for some time, branched off towards Palmer, and the road continued straight on. When the railway appeared again beside the road, Brian explained that it was Cape Gauge 3ft 6ins (106.7 cms) whereas the UK Gauge was 4ft 8½ins (143.5 cms), being the width of Roman chariot wheels.

"Because South Africa was not invaded by the Romans," he joked.

As they drove along, Dawn and Jerry worked their way through a newspaper each, reading out stories of interest to each other when there was nothing very much to see outside the coach windows.

One of the articles Jerry found was about rhino poaching, and after checking that their fellow travellers would find it of interest, he read it out loud for all to hear. It was entitled 'Double rhino kill' and headed 'Bay Organised Crime Investigation Unit now holds over 50 open dockets for poaching' before stating,

> 'The wholesale slaughter of rhinos by horn poachers continues unabated, with another two animals found dead in the iMfolozi Game Park on Monday. This means that at least four Zululand rhinos have been added to the growing list of victims in just 10 days, after consecutive weekend discoveries of carcasses at the Ndumo Game Reserve.
>
> Despite huge resources and manpower being thrown at the problem, the situation shows no sign of improving and members of Richards Bay's Organised Crime Investigation Unit are being kept running responding to new incidents. They are presently carrying between 50 and 60 open dockets related to rhino and endangered game poaching – on top of scores of cases with regard to other serious and violent crimes.
>
> Unit Commander, Lt Col . . . has appealed to members of the public to come forward with information and to contact him on 035 7808219.
>
> **Spate of killings**
>
> A black rhino carcass was discovered at Ndumo on Saturday. It had been shot dead some 10 days before and both horns had been removed – the second rhino kill found at Ndumo on consecutive Saturdays.
>
> On Sunday, field rangers at iMfolozi Park heard gunshots shortly after 6pm in the remote Makhamisa wilderness area, accessible only on foot. The following morning they found the

carcass of an adult white rhino, with horns hacked off.

At nearby Mphekwa area they came across a second dead rhino, again killed by heavy calibre gunfire. . . . said all avenues will be explored to identify and find the killers and the market, believed to be Gauteng.

"We recovered spent projectiles at all the scenes and will wait for the results of ballistics tests. We will also gather information from informers and our own crime intelligence network. Our members are currently testing weapons of rangers in public and private parks," said . . . "A logical question arises: how do poachers know and get to the exact location of rhinos in areas inaccessible by vehicles?". . .'

Attributed to Dave Savides,
The Zululand Observer

Jerry then added,

"Apparently, it's World Rhino Day on the 22 September when people all over the world take a stand against rhino poaching and the illegal trade in rhino horn. It's a global campaign initiated by the WWF who call on all concerned citizens to dress up in red, if possible, dust off their vuvuzelas (whatever they are), toot their horns, blow their didgeridoos and make as much noise as possible at 1.00 pm, as a symbolic act to send a powerful message to leaders that the time to take serious and effective action against rhino poaching is now."

Dawn took this opportunity to speak up, saying that she had read an article in a magazine that stated that a recent upsurge in poaching in southern Africa threatened to undo decades of work to protect rhinos.

Before anyone else could comment further, Brian explained that he would be speaking about this issue once they got nearer to the Kruger National Park, and as they were approaching Dullstroom, he changed the subject as he pointed out that this area was a favourite spot for a getaway for those who lived in Johannesburg. The town was named Dull after the surname of one of the first male settlers and combined with Strom meaning stream.

Sometime later, Dawn found an amusing article that she read out quietly to Jerry. It was entitled,

'Yolk on egg thief'

'An egg thief was caught by police . . . and was left with eggs that none of the king's horses and none of the king's men could ever put back together again.

On August 22, an Ezakheni resident was on his way to E-section when he drove past his aunt's house in the Emanzinabilayo area and immediately noticed that one of the windows was open. Knowing that his aunt was away from home, he went to investigate and saw someone inside the house.

Police were called and 26-year-old Bonginkozi Mbatha was arrested. He was caught red-handed . . . or rather egg-handed . . . stealing three bars of soap and some eggs. Sadly, the eggs he had stolen and hidden inside his pants' pocket broke while trying to evade capture.

On September 7, he was found guilty of housebreaking and theft, and sentenced to two years' imprisonment, of which 12 months was suspended for five years. No yolk of a sentence for sure!'

Attributed to the Ladysmith Gazette

Then, as they crossed it, Brian said,

"The Crocodile River forms the southern boundary of the Kruger National Park, but it is too cold for crocodiles. This area has many small lakes and a healthy mountain climate."

"The city of Nelspruit, the capital of Mpumalanga, lies in the fertile Crocodile River Valley and fruit has always played a vital role in the town's development; it is the centre of a vast citrus growing area. Nelspruit is also notable for its tobacco and timber industries, and is the commercial and administrative hub of the Lowveld. The streets of this large, modern city are lined with jacaranda and other flamboyant trees."

They passed a cheese factory and stone houses with gardens full of flowers before reaching shops named

The Village Angler, Charlie C's, The Historical Rose Cottage, Joe Bangles, Bo-Peep, and a hotel in the shape of a castle.

Then they crossed the Dorp River on at least four occasions as it slowly meandered 2,000 feet (609 metres) down towards the Middleveld, where they saw many different trees, including those bearing peaches and kiwi fruit. They stopped briefly in Lydenburg where Brian pointed out the first Voortrekker School built in 1847 and the Voortrekker church built in 1849, explaining that the Zionist Christian faith was the most popular religion in South Africa.

* * * * *

CHAPTER 4
'Pilgrim's Rest and Graskop'

As they headed towards the Long Tom Pass on their way to Pilgrim's Rest, they went past a huge platinum mine on the outskirts of the town.

"Platinum mines on the High Meander have a depth of between 3,000 and 4,000 feet (914 and 1219 metres) and produce 60% of the world's platinum," said Brian as they looked up at some very ugly buildings on top of the hillside on their left.

"Gold mines are much deeper. Diamond mines are the safest because they are not so deep. The deepest Gold Mine in the world is in South Africa; it is approximately 12,600 feet (3,840 metres) deep. When the gold runs out at that depth, they will need to go deeper, but the price of gold per ounce will have to be much higher to make it viable. It takes the men an hour to travel down to the current depth. They work down there for 8 hours and then they have an hour journey to get back up to the surface again. Air conditioning is used to keep them cool because the rock face can be as hot as 60 °C. At least four or five miners die every year."

"Now you are going to experience a special treat," he continued, "This will be your first opportunity to meet the Big Five; the five most dangerous animals to hunt in South Africa."

In anticipation, everyone peered out of the coach window in the direction in which he pointed, and then burst out laughing as there at the side of the road, in the garden of their creator, stood life-size sculptures of elephants, rhino, buffalo, lions and leopards.

Next Brian pointed out The Bride of the Bushveld, wild pear trees, lovely tulip trees and a laburnum that was covered with yellow flowers. He explained that the aloe had flowered during July, the tree wisteria would flower in October and the flame tree was currently displaying its flamboyant red blossom.

They passed road works where seven men were employed; three working while four stood idle, holding their chins while they watched what their colleagues were doing.

Then they were passing the Magaba Game Reserve, fields of beet, vines, and clouds of orange dust where a tractor was turning over the red, rusty coloured soil. The turn off for Pilgrims' Rest was just over the other side of the railway line; 27 km further to travel. The road narrowed where there were steep holes on both sides and groups of women were hacking back the bushes. They went up to Robbers' Pass, passing the signs to the Inn on Robbers' Pass, Misty Creek Complex, Mount Sheba and chalets at Crystal Springs (all holiday resorts) and continued to climb higher and higher.

At the very top, Brian explained that the pine forest was 1,700 metres above sea level, which was the same height as Johannesburg. There were beautiful views down the escarpment. Then, on the journey down the other side, there were road signs indicating that this was a high accident zone as the road twisted and turned to the left and right.

"Mining in this region of Mpumalanga dates back many centuries. In 1873, Alex 'Wheelbarrow' Patterson discovered gold on a farm. He had left the vicinity of Mac Mac to search for a place that was less congested, and though he tried to keep the discovery a secret, the inevitable happened. Within two months, 6,000 prospectors had converged on Pilgrim's Rest, and on 22 September 1873 it was officially proclaimed a gold field."

"The many tents and shacks soon grew into a flourishing little village complete with sturdy brick houses, church, shops, canteens, a newspaper and the well-known Royal Hotel. The prospectors named it Pilgrim's Rest because there, at last, after so many false trails and faded dreams they felt that they had truly found their home."

"However, in 1882 gold mines were discovered elsewhere and as the deposits in the area around Pilgrim's Rest were becoming depleted, many prospectors drifted away. But some of them turned to forestry, and their village, whose residents still number in the hundreds, has been painstakingly preserved as a 'living museum'."

As they got even closer to the town, Brian added,

"Pilgrim's Rest is divided into three parts: Down Town, Up Town and New Town. However, the whole, quiet,

Victorian-style town has been declared a national monument."

They crossed the Blyde River and passed a golf course with scarring on the greens providing evidence of the old diggings. Cuttings also scarred the surrounding mountainside. They saw corrugated iron houses, some with wood panelling, old petrol pumps and traditional buildings as they went through Down Town, before entering Up Town.

Dan drove the bus up the hill where the high street was situated and parked at the top. Then the whole tour party got out and strolled back down the hill, taking photographs as they went:

- white traditional buildings with intricate latticework on the verandas
- a view up the road providing many examples of the historic architecture
- Matabele Bead women selling traditional beadwork items, wearing traditional garments with high collars (*and trainers!*)
- The Royal Hotel
- The Stables, proclaimed to be the longest deli and café
- The Central Garage
- Bourke & Co, General Dealer (1895), with life-size models of animals on the grass outside the store
- The Post Office, a corrugated iron building painted light blue, with an abundance of flowers blooming in the garden at the front

When they reached the bottom of the hill, Dan was there with the bus, waiting for them to arrive and ready to take them on to the town where they would stop for lunch – Graskop.

* * * * *

Anne and Cathy were the first to reach the bottom of the hill, and seeing an opportunity to speak to Brian privately, Anne drew him to one side.

Brian was puzzled when she asked if she could have a quiet word, but he accompanied her away from the bus when requested to do so.

Then Anne explained,

"When we lived in Johannesburg we had a maid. Well, she was much more than a maid. She actually delivered Cathy because the baby arrived so quickly that there was no time to get me to the hospital. Then she acted as a nanny to the children, and we became great friends."

"Even after we went back to England, we kept in touch by writing letters regularly. Then a couple of years ago the letters stopped coming. I kept writing, but never received a reply."

"One of my reasons for coming on this trip was to try and find out why she stopped writing; has she died, or is there another reason? I was going to investigate on my own, but I don't know where to start. Is there anything you can do to help?"

Brian was silent for a moment before he replied,

"I could try and trace her, but I can't promise I'll be successful. There may be a reason she does not want to be found. However, if she has died there will be a record of that. I'll do my best."

"Oh, thank you so much," Anne sighed with relief. "Anything you can find out will be better than not knowing. Her name is Naomi Cebekhulu. She had a son who was two years older than Cathy, Thembinkosi."

Then she handed him a slip of paper,

"That's the last address I have for her."

Brian put the paper in his pocket, and they walked back to the bus to continue their long journey across swathe after swathe of the South African countryside.

* * * * *

On the way to Graskop, Brian explained,

"Traditionally, Matabele married women wear masks, copper and brass rings round their arms, legs and neck, and high collars around their necks to stop them looking at other men. A man has to give 11 cows to the father of the bride to seal the contract of marriage. Now that quantity of cows equates to 55,000 ZAR, and men do not have such a large amount of money. Therefore, many Matabele women are having children without a husband."

"If a man has plenty of cattle then they can have many wives. It follows that husbands like to have daughters because they will get 11 cows for each of them. At 11 years of age, the boys have the duty of looking after the cattle, and would then be given a calf for every year they do so; the boy would be over 20 by the time he was able to marry his first wife."

"If boys have to look after the cattle, what about their schooling?"

Jerry then asked, and Brian replied,

"When they are nine years old, all children go to school. The clever ones continue at school and when they come home, they teach their younger brothers (who have been looking after the cattle) what they have learnt that day."

Brian was in the process of pointing out that the people of this region were big producers of pulp and paper, and that the trees grew two and a half times faster here than in the northern hemisphere when they spotted a sawmill on the hillside, and passed an unusual sign stating, 'The Drinking Man Sings'.

Then as they continued down a steep, winding road, that got narrower and narrower, Brian pointed out the town in the distance and said,

"The town of Graskop was so named because of its situation on the flat top of a hill; it looked like a mop of grass on top of a person's head."

And it really did look like a topknot of grassy hair.

On entering Graskop, they saw that it was a large town where the streets were lined with bars, restaurants, cafes and takeaways with names such as 'Wrap it Up Food', 'The Loco Pub Grill', 'Tasties Take Away', and surprisingly, an establishment called 'The Elephant Dung Paper & Craft Shop'.

Dan parked in a central location. Then he stated that the tourists should be back at the same place in one hour's time because he had to move the bus quickly and leave it in a coach park.

As the tourists got down from their Mega Bus, Brian had to shoo away Africans trying to sell macadamia nuts. He then pointed out several restaurants that he recommended; one of them being Harries' Pancake

House. However, as Dawn and Jerry had already experienced that enterprise, they decided to try another pancake house, but ultimately this did not turn out to be such a good idea.

Having found an empty table inside the restaurant because there were no free tables on the balcony, they sat there for nearly half an hour trying to attract the attention of the waitress, but without success.

"Right, that's it. We're leaving," Jerry said angrily, as he got up and left. Dawn, realising that nothing she said would make any difference, followed him.

They then walked along the street looking into other restaurants which were either full, or did not look very inviting. They saw Amy sitting in Harries' Pancake House with Anne and Cathy, and Meryl and Peter were on the veranda of the restaurant next door.

As they passed a side street, they looked down and saw a coach park filled with Magic and Mega buses, together with other methods of tourist transport; that explained why all the restaurants were full.

After walking the length of the main street and also down some side streets, passing further restaurants and some dubious looking bars, they decided to get a sandwich at a supermarket.

It was easy to find one, and once they had what they wanted - two ready-made sandwiches and two bottles of milkshake - they proceeded to the till to pay. After ringing up their goods, the teller stated "Plastic".

"No," Jerry replied thinking that by asking for plastic she meant a credit card. "We will be paying with cash."

"Plastic," she repeated more loudly this time and rudely flapped a plastic bag in their faces.

"No," Jerry said again, finally realising what she meant. "We don't need a bag."

Then they made their way back to the place near a sunken garden where they were to wait for the bus. There they found Brian sitting on a wall, so they joined him, and ate their sandwiches.

Shortly, Dan arrived back with the bus and signalled to Brian that he wanted a word. They both went to the back of the bus and had a brief conversation.

Undoubtedly, the tour group would have been very interested if they had been allowed to hear what was being said, as Dan reported,

"We've got a problem. I found two thugs trying to get into two suitcases. I only left it for a few minutes in the coach park while I went off to get something to eat. When I got back, I shouted as soon as I saw what they were up to and they ran off. They'd broken the lock on the trailer to get in. One of the suitcases now has a damaged combination lock where they were trying to prise it off, and the scratched one, is now in a worse condition. What shall we do?"

We don't tell the tourists the truth about what has happened," Brian replied immediately. "We don't want to ruin their holiday by scaring them. They'll always be looking over their shoulders, thinking that everybody in South Africa is a criminal. We'll say that the suitcases were damaged while in the trailer. Make sure you hit some rough roads before we get to the hotel to make the excuse sound more plausible."

"Okay," Dan answered gloomily, "that shouldn't be a problem, but I don't like it. We should report this to the police."

"Don't worry," Brian tried to console him. "I'll take the blame if there's a problem."

As they left Graskop, Jerry and Dawn were independently thinking to themselves that they were not very impressed with the town after having discovered rundown side streets and been treated in such a shoddy fashion. It was obviously a centre for tourists as there were many souvenir shops and hotels, but although it looked nice at face value, they had found that the reality was somewhat different.

Meryl and Peter would probably have agreed if they had known about the damage to their suitcases while their transport was parked nearby.

However, the majority of the tour party had enjoyed their meals, and everybody was now ready to have a quiet snooze during the remainder of the journey.

* * * * *

Like the tour party, the Chinese businessmen were being driven around the South African countryside, but as they looked at the scenery, they were wondering about what the future would hold for them, not really enjoying their surroundings.

They had travelled out of the town centre, through the suburbs of Johannesburg and into the bush. Almost immediately, their driver had turned off the main road and onto country lanes, and although they tried to keep an eye on the road signs, it was soon obvious that they had no idea at all of where they were, or where they were going.

However, after a rough and dusty journey down roads that ultimately turned into dirt tracks, they pulled into what was clearly a small airfield. Some rusty shacks were situated close to the perimeter where some cars were parked and out on the field beyond, there were three small, light aircraft and two helicopters.

Having parked near the other vehicles, everyone got out of the car, and the two Chinese businessmen joined their companions who knocked on the door of the closest of the shacks and immediately went in. Inside, it was surprisingly light with a large plate glass window overlooking the airfield.

In the corner, a red-faced, beefy man rose from behind a desk and welcomed them, heartily shaking everyone's hand.

"I'm Herman, Herman Meintjies," he said. "I will be piloting the helicopter."

He offered them coffee and seats before settling back in his chair.

Then he spread a large map out on the desk in front of him. He pointed to where the airfield was situated and then to the Kruger National Park.

For the first time, the Chinese actually realised how large the park was and how far away; that was why a helicopter was needed to get them there and back.

"Joseph has been in touch," explained Herman. "He is on his way to Kruger. He has learnt from some friends approximately where a large herd is currently grazing and he will be entering the park this evening to check it out. He has already given me an approximate location, but by tomorrow night they might have moved on so we have to be prepared to land as near as possible to whatever location he tracks the animals to. We have some very sophisticated equipment with night-vision, and we'll dart the animals with tranquillisers first before we kill them with guns fitted with silencers."

"Isn't it a bit risky landing in the Park at night?" asked the smaller of the businessmen. "I presume you're not intending to use a proper landing site."

"Joseph knows what he's doing," replied their pilot. "He will find a suitable spot, set up some flares and guide us in. He's done it before. I've filed a flight plan for us to fly to Durban tomorrow night. A short diversion over the Kruger won't be anything untoward if anyone checks."

"If we're going to Durban, would it possible for me to call in and see the Agents regarding a piece of machinery we are going to buy?" asked the larger of the two Chinese businessmen. "I understand their offices are in the Mzansi Zulu Centre, Merrivale, which is just off the N3 near Howick West between Durban and Ladysmith."

"That would be a great idea," replied the pilot. "That's not far from the private airstrip where we are due to land, and then we will have an official reason for going to Durban. Why don't you telephone them from here and make an appointment for the day after tomorrow."

"The plan is that we'll take off from here tomorrow evening, make our short stop at Kruger, and then fly on to Durban where you'll spend the night in a hotel near the airfield. Then you will have time to visit your suppliers before we fly back to Jo'burg."

A telephone was pushed across the desk and the Chinese businessman removed some paperwork from his pocket. Then he dialled a telephone number he had obtained earlier, and asked to speak to the Manager.

After explaining that he was interested in purchasing a Gammill Long-Arm Quilter, with a computerized Statler Stitcher, the appointment was made for 11.00 am on the day after next.

This amazed his Chinese colleague, who whispered in English,

"Isn't that a bit premature? How do you know we'll have the money we need to pay for such a fantastically expensive machine?"

This questioning was, in fact, overheard and understood by Herman, who laughed and said,

"Of course, you'll be able to afford expensive machinery once we have the horns, and there is no risk. We will all do very well out of this little trip."

As everything appeared to be very well organised, the Chinese were happy to hand over the money when they were asked for payment for the helicopter trip. They then asked to be taken to see the agents in Johannesburg who would be dealing with their freight consignment once the job had been completed.

Their companions were also quite happy to act as chauffeurs, especially when the smaller man, who had now gained more confidence, suggested that perhaps afterwards they could all go to a Chinese restaurant.

* * * * *

CHAPTER 5
'The Panorama Route'

There was certainly no opportunity for the tour party to have a siesta, as it was only a short journey further along the Panorama Route before they were treated to their first fantastic experience of South African panoramic scenery. Also, even before they had reached the edge of the Blyde River Canyon, Brian started his commentary,

"The Blyde River Canyon is the third largest canyon in the world. It covers 290 square kilometres."

"From God's Window, it is approximately a 914 metre drop to the river below. Within the canyon, there is an indigenous forest and the tracks running through it are now used as hiking trails. Overnight accommodation has been provided for hikers and bikers. There are many tree plantations, and a lot of waterfalls, including the Tufa Falls of which there are two with the same name in South Africa."

On passing a rain forest, Brian explained that it was the only place in South Africa where orchids grew, and then obscurely he added,

"The mountain rhebuck has long ears like a rabbit,"

when the scenery suddenly changed to plains where they saw mountain rhebucks grazing.

Across the river, there were pine trees on both sides of the road, some of which appeared to be in a distressed condition, leading Brian to explain,

"If no trees had been planted in this area, it would be a desert. But because the trees are now consuming too much water, there is a new Government restriction that they have to be planted at least 100 yards away from a river system. Baboons have damaged the trees with the red tops. This damage means the tree dies upwards from that point. Every three years, the branches are felled to make the trees grow taller and straighter. Twenty years after planting, the fully-grown trees are ready to be harvested."

As they viewed the Treur River (the River of Sorrow), Brian said,

"This is known as the sad river because of what happened to a group of Voortrekkers who travelled through this

region. The men left all the women and children with the wagons when it was found impossible to cross the river. They were told to wait until their men folk returned, or if they did not return within one week, the women were to travel back to Pretoria. The men went off to look for an alternative route across the canyon, and when they did not return within the period stipulated, the women turned back. However, after they had travelled some distance, they met up with their men folk coming from the opposite direction. Where the two groups met each other is near Pilgrim's Rest, and from that point the Blyde River became known as the Joyful River."

Brian then sang a song in Afrikaans, which he told them was the song of the river, and everyone clapped even though they did not understand the words.

Cattle and horses were now grazing at the side of the road so Dan drove carefully in case they decided to cross, and the sight of the animals prompted Jerry to ask if there were any disputes about the ownership of the cattle. Brian replied,

"Native African people believe in common grazing. There is always a shepherd who looks after the cattle during the day and brings them back at night. The men know everything about their cattle: distinguishing marks, ages and ancestry. However, there have been disputes between native Africans and Europeans who do not believe in free grazing. In particular, there has been conflict on the Eastern frontier."

In the distance, there were numerous flat, grassy topped, conical shaped mountains with their steep sides glowing in shades of red as the sun picked them out.

Eventually, they pulled off the road at a signpost indicating God's Window. In the car park, there were stalls selling souvenirs and a modern toilet block was solitarily situated at the back of the clearing.

After everyone had got off the bus, Brian warned,

"You may see baboons nearby as they are attracted by the sweet smell of buddleia."

The tour party then followed him as he walked over rough ground to the viewing point at the edge of the canyon, passing waste bins fitted with bent pipes that had to be lifted to enable one to insert rubbish. Brian explained that this was to stop baboons raiding the bins and that baboons had already stripped the nearby trees of plums. Wild sage and wild geraniums grew everywhere, and there was even a grandfather's beard tree that Brian pointed out to them as they followed him down a winding path in order to reach the viewing point named God's Window.

Once there, they looked down over the sheer edges of the canyon to the valley far below, and in the distance they saw impressive views that appeared to stretch to eternity across the Lowveld. Lichen growing on the rock face made the sides of the mountains glow in the sun; beautiful colours (red, green, yellow and orange) could be seen. They could also see spectacular rock formations all over that section of the Klein Drakensberg escarpment.

The tourists took a lot of photographs, and Dawn even took one of Jerry as he posed on the edge of the cliff with the beautiful scenery in the background.

"Don't step back," she warned, afraid that the edge would crumble away, and he laughed.

Then they walked across to Wonder View via a path made up of flat stepping-stones, before going down some steps that had been cut into the rock face.

Again the mountain scenery and panoramic views were quite spectacular. Brian pointed out 'The Pinnacle' which rose out of the deep wooded canyon, explaining that it was a single quartzite column, and 'The Three Rondavels' (also known as 'The Three Sisters'), which were three huge pillars of dolomite rock rising out of the far wall of the canyon. Their domed tops were green (being the hairy heads of the sisters) and their sides were covered with fiery orange lichen. In the far distance, behind 'The Three Rondavels', they could see the Swadini Dam, which marked the end of the nature reserve.

After they had all taken even more photographs, they returned to the bus to go on to 'Bourke's Luck Potholes'. As they drove along, Brian explained,

"Natural erosion has formed holes in the rocks, which have become enlarged over time by the eddies resulting from the fusion of two converging rivers. The potholes

were named after Bourke, an Australian prospector who found gold in this area."

The road was lined with cabbage trees when they passed a graveyard named 'Keep Us All'.

At the entrance to the park, Dan stopped the bus to pay and Jerry noticed that, according to the sign informing visitors of an entry fee of 7 ZAR per person, there was a 100 ZAR fine if receipts were not issued. As the wording was not clear as to who would be fined, Jerry asked Brian for clarification.

"That's to stop fraud," Brian explained. "It will be the Park Manager who will be fined if people complain that they have not been given a receipt because that could mean that the money paid has been pocketed illegally by those collecting it."

Again, the car park contained souvenir stalls and a toilet block, but here they were all positioned in a central area under trees among which baboons swung from branch to branch and occasionally dropped to the ground. In fact, as they walked to the gate leading to the potholes, two baboons walked across the road in front of the tour party and pictures had to be taken because one was an adorable baby baboon.

While they were walking down a steep path together, Brian explained that this was the only place where the bald ibis was still breeding.

Then from strategically placed bridges, they looked down at the meeting point of the Blyde River and the Treur River where over many thousands of years, water erosion had created one of the most phenomenal geological marvels in South Africa. These were strangely shaped holes in the rock and peculiar cylindrical sculptures, both of which had been created by the churning water that swirled rapidly around them. The dark pools of water contrasting with the smooth light grey rocks and the white foam created by the eddies made it a spectacular sight.

Brian pointed out the scars on the mountainside that marked the places where prospectors had tried to discover gold, and as they looked down at small waterfalls where the rock faces had been eroded, he added,

"The geology and climate of this high rainfall plateau results in many beautiful waterfalls. Some of these can be visited, but a lot of them are hidden deep within some of the largest man-made forestry plantations in the world, where there are rows upon rows of pine and eucalyptus trees."

Yet again, the tourists took photographs, and then once more it was back to the bus.

Thankfully, from there it was only a short drive before Dan turned off the main road, along a country lane, and they arrived at the Pine Lake Inn; the second overnight stop for the tourists who had just undertaken an eight-hour, very tiring coach journey.

They were all thrilled to see that the hotel was an attractive traditional stone structure, built around three sides of a car park which was like a courtyard, and they were even more pleased to find that once again a welcome drink was awaiting them in the reception area. From there they could look across the extensive grounds that included a swimming pool, bowling green and tennis courts, and went down to a beautiful lake with grassy banks and attractive houses situated on the opposite shore.

While they were taking advantage of their welcome drinks, Brian disappeared to sort out the luggage. Shortly, he returned and asked Meryl and Peter to go out to the bus with him.

When they came back with the luggage, it was obvious that something was wrong, as Meryl was furious.

"Now both of our suitcases have been damaged. One has been scratched and now the other one has a buckled lock. We will need to contact the manufacturers to see if we can obtain a new combination lock locally."

Everyone commiserated with them before they were directed to their rooms.

These were once again of a very high standard and they were all very well satisfied with what had been provided for their comfort. In particular, Dawn and Jerry had a view of the lake and the grounds below through picture windows and sliding doors that opened out onto a balcony, which stretched across the full width of one wall.

In fact, they later found that all the members of the tour party were in the same wing of the hotel, with rooms overlooking the grounds and the swimming pool below. As this particular wing went in the direction of the river, it appeared to have been built into the slope of the hill so that the ground floor became a basement and the first floor was at ground level at the far end of the corridor.

Having unpacked the items they needed for their two-night stay, Dawn and Jerry stretched themselves out on the king-size double bed and had a quick nap to make up for the planned siesta that had not been possible on the bus.

Surprisingly, when they awoke in the late afternoon the sun was still shining so they decided to explore their surroundings.

Walking in the grounds, they found Brian sitting on a sun lounger next to the pool and asked him if it was possible to walk around the lake. He pointed them in the right direction, explaining that a lot of the land around the lake was private, but they could easily walk the short distance to the other side and back if they went out of the hotel via the route he indicated.

Walking round the wing of the hotel in which their room was situated and where the grounds sloped down to the river, they noticed a door at ground level that led into the corridor where their room was located on the first floor.

"An alternative way in?" Jerry asked.

"I hope not," Dawn replied, "that door should be kept locked and only used as an emergency exit. It's too easily accessible for burglars."

They actually ended up going right round and out of the back of the hotel, where there was a service entrance. There they found themselves in a field that sloped even more steeply downhill, way below the level of the lake that appeared to have been dammed at that point. However, they bravely soldiered on across the rough grass from where a flock of large white birds looked up at them briefly before continuing to peck at the ground in order to find morsels to eat.

Eventually they were able to climb up the other side where there was an entrance to a country club. Although the sign said 'Private', they walked just inside the gate and down to the water's edge from where they could see the Pine Lake Inn on the other side.

Jerry took some photographs and then they quickly left, taking the road back to the hotel's main entrance.

Since their arrival, the car park had filled up, and Jerry pointed out a large number of white vehicles with the words 'Forensic Science Department' emblazoned along their side panels.

"Perhaps there's been a murder at the Pine Lake Inn," Dawn suggested.

"I don't think so," Jerry replied. "With so many vehicles, it looks more like there's a conference of forensic scientists taking place."

They laughed as they entered the hotel, but quickly suppressed their amusement when they saw Meryl and Peter looking quite forlorn; they were enquiring at Reception if there was a WiFi network that they could use to email the manufacturers of their suitcases. When they saw Jerry and Dawn, they explained that they had had to break into one of their cases, which would never lock again, and Jerry volunteered to let them have a luggage strap, for which they expressed their appreciation.

Then Jerry and Dawn went up to their room to get ready for the evening meal. Although, they acknowledged how unfortunate it was that Meryl and Peter's cases had been damaged, they had to agree that they had had a fascinating day.

* * * * *

The two Chinese businessmen had also had a good day. They were both becoming more relaxed and starting to enjoy their time in South Africa. At lunchtime, they had eaten a Chinese meal with their companions with whom they were now on first name terms.

It was actually in the Chinese restaurant that names were exchanged with the Chinese introducing themselves formally,

54

"Please call me Feng," said the larger of the two Chinese businessmen, 'and my associate is known as Changpu. Of course, both of us would now like to be named Chaoxiang because that means 'expecting fortune'."

Feng then laughed at his own joke, even though he was not sure that anyone apart from his colleague understood.

When it was the turn of the South Africans to introduce themselves, one of them also laughed as he said,

"Me, my parents named me Mthombeni, but you can call me Beni. It is easier to shorten our given names. My friend here is Bongani, and our driver is Elphas, known as Eli."

Conversation was also much easier as the Chinese were becoming accustomed to the South Africans' accent when they spoke English, and the South Africans were now better able to understand English spoken with a Chinese inflection.

"Will you be accompanying us in the helicopter?" Feng asked.

"Oh, no," Beni replied. "Our leader, Rocky the Red will come with you, together with his second-in-command, Thembinkosi."

This statement was then clarified by Beni who explained that they were all members of the JH Branch of the ANC Youth League. In fact, he went on further to say that their branch was a member of a radical faction of the Youth League that had broken away from the main party because they believed in taking action to bring about their beliefs.

The Chinese were astounded to learn that they had become involved with members of a breakaway section of the ANC Youth League, and even more surprised to find out that their associates wanted to expel all Whites from South Africa. The Africans even thought that Mugabe had the right ideas – the policies being followed in Zimbabwe were those that should appertain in South Africa, they were informed.

At that point, Feng did just pluck up enough courage to make one comment.

"Aren't a lot of native people fleeing from Zimbabwe because they're being mistreated?" he asked.

"They are just the fools who do not believe in Mugabe," came the reply. "All Zimbabweans should follow him because they will be better off then."

The Chinese exchanged puzzled glances, but said no more. They had doubts though as they had read reports of atrocities in Zimbabwe and had personally experienced Communist rule under Chairman Mao. Later that day and during the day that followed, however, more political opinions were expressed, and they did manage to impart their views.

During lunch, the beer flowed freely once again and after drinking several large tankards of a particularly intoxicating concoction, the Chinese had to agree that it tasted good. Soon they were no longer hungry and everyone was very friendly. It was of no concern that they would be expected to pay for everything being consumed as they now knew the protocol and it didn't seem that expensive.

The conversation eventually got round to their plans for the remainder of that day and the following day. Bearing in mind that they would not need to go to the airfield until late afternoon the next day, the smaller Chinese businessman boldly asked,

"Would it be possible for us to do some sightseeing tomorrow?"

"Of course," replied Beni enthusiastically. "In fact, we can take you on a tour of Soweto today. It's full of tourists now. You'll be able to see Nelson Mandela's house and the Nelson Mandela Museum. Then tomorrow we'll take you to see our beautiful capital city – Pretoria."

Although Soweto was not exactly what the Chinese thought would be included in a sightseeing tour of Johannesburg, they readily agreed as their companions were so eager.

And so it was that after finishing their lunch, they were driven to Soweto.

Beni and Bongani had obviously personally experienced an official tour because they tried to act just like real tour guides. As Eli negotiated his way around the places of interest, they took it in turns to provide a commentary.

"Soweto stands for South Western Townships. It is an urban area on the southern side of the city of Johannesburg, bordering the mining belt where many of the population work."

As they turned off a main road,

"You can see our magnificent Soccer Stadium. Soccer City was built to host the 2010 Football World Cup, and we are now passing through an area known as Diepkloof Ext where there are some very expensive houses."

As they reached the Baragwanath area, it was explained that although this was originally an informal settlement, it now housed the largest hospital in the southern hemisphere where there were many people battling against the HIV/AIDs epidemic.

They also stopped near Bara Taxi Rank, where many small, predominantly white, mini-buses were parked and it was explained,

"These taxis have been used for many years by black people as it is the cheapest method of transport for them to travel to work, or back to their homelands. It is one of the earliest forms of a black regulated and black run business, but many accidents occur on these buses because they are often overcrowded and badly maintained."

Bongani then interrupted his friend in order to add,

"Now all these taxis have to have proper licences, and there are many police stops where vehicles are checked. This helps to ensure less accidents by making sure that the vehicles are not dangerous or overcrowded."

When Eli stopped and parked the car, Feng and Changpu were able to observe the sights and experience the smells of a colourful open-air market where all manner of food was being sold, as well as where people were having their hair cut, or styled, whilst sitting under umbrellas that shaded them from the sun.

They were then told that their next stop would be Kliptown Squatter Camp on the Old Potchefstroom Road. As twin towers were pointed out to the tourists, their guides supplied more information.

"Those towers used to supply electricity to the north of Johannesburg – you see, we have twin towers, but not quite the same as those which were destroyed by terrorists in New York. We also have a beautiful shopping mall here that was recently opened by Soweto's first millionaire, Richard Maponya."

"There are many anomalies here. Kliptown has been a squatter camp since 1903, and it is still a poverty stricken area, but we also have smart areas like Diepkloof. One day, it is our dream that all native South Africans will live in smart houses and squatter camps will disappear altogether in South Africa."

Eli stopped the car outside the Kliptown Museum where, because there was insufficient time for the Chinese tourists to go in, it was explained,

"Inside this museum, the history of this area of South Africa is explained, including apartheid which oppressed the black majority population. Kliptown is also famous because it is where the Freedom Charter was adopted in 1955, and that is what the current South African Constitution is based on."

Bongani then continued by quoting something he had obviously learnt by heart,

"The Freedom Charter has been described by the South African Nobel Prize winner, Chief Albert Luthuli as 'a document that gives flesh, blood and meaning to such words as democracy, freedom and liberty'."

Their next stop was the Regina Mundi Church, and here their tour guides voiced their commentary in tones that were full of respect making it obvious that religion played a large part in their lives.

"The Regina Mundi Church is one of the largest Catholic churches in South Africa, and it has become known as 'The Parliament of Soweto'. Many meetings took place here during the struggles of the 70s and 80s."

Then when they stopped outside yet another museum, the Hector Peterson, which again they viewed from the exterior, their guides explained,

"This is where people can learn about the student uprising of 1976 and the transition to democracy in South Africa."

Finally, they were advised that they were on their way to Nelson Mandela's house and the Visitor Centre where they would be able to alight. As they travelled along Vilakazi Street, the Chinese were proudly told,

"This is the only street in the world where two Nobel Prize Winners have lived: Nelson Mandela and Desmond Tutu."

It was quite a surprise for Feng and Changpu to see that Nelson Mandela's house had been refurbished and there was a smart Visitor Centre. At this stop, they were encouraged to walk around, and there they learnt about the Hector Petersen Memorial; a memorial erected to commemorate the death of the first schoolchild killed in the student protests of 1976.

Then it was back to the car where the Chinese businessmen were given to understand that they would now be taken back to the local headquarters, the building they had experienced the previous evening, well-known for its beer and other refreshments. On the journey, Beni became quite passionate while making a long speech,

"Nelson Mandela is a great man, but his reforms did not go far enough. When his generation are gone, it will be the time for South Africa to become a great Black Nation. We are preparing for the time when all the white farmers and the immigrants who have been stealing from us for many years, will be expelled and their lands and wealth will be distributed among those Blacks to whom it rightly belongs. God gave us great wealth in South Africa with the gold, diamonds and other minerals that are to be found in such large quantities in this country. That wealth should be used to improve the lives of Black people. It was not put there by God to make White people rich."

Again that evening the Chinese businessmen spent their time eating and drinking in what they now knew to be the headquarters of the JH ANC Youth League. Also, once more they noticed that the man who they now knew as 'Rocky the Red' was involved in angry conversations, but this time with a group of young men who appeared to be very contrite. However, the suited businessman was nowhere to be seen that night.

What the Chinese businessmen did not know because they could not understand the language was that the angry discussions were about another failed attempt to steal a particular suitcase. Two attempts having failed, a decision had now been made to hand over the task to colleagues situated in an area closer to the Kruger National Park.

After consuming a lot of alcohol, but only snacks in the way of food, the Chinese businessmen were feeling very inebriated, and being quite comfortable in their surroundings, they began to speak. In fact, they started talking a lot, explaining about their lives in China: how terrible it had been during the Cultural Revolution when under the rule of Chairman Mao the borders had been closed and the Red Army had controlled the people with an iron hand. The Government, they said, had told them how this type of Communist rule would benefit the people, but it was the people who had suffered.

It was not long before quite a crowd had gathered round to hear them tell more personal experiences that included increased poverty and hardship. They told tales of people who had joined the Red Army in order to support the Cultural Revolution.

Feng, in particular, told of his own aunt's experience. As a teenage girl, she had been an enthusiastic devotee of the Cultural Revolution and had enlisted in the Red Army. For some years, her family heard nothing from her then the grandfather received a message that she was seriously ill. Despite a lot of obstacles, he managed to find her on a farm where she had been forced to work long hours in the fields, with very little food, and where she lived in appalling conditions. Although she had been in a feeble state, he managed to get her home where Feng had met her when he was a young boy. However, she was suffering from heart disease and did not live long.

"Do not believe all the stories you are told by men who say they are working for the good of the people," Feng warned, "In all societies, there are those who are corrupt, and there will always be people who take advantage of the poor."

"In China, the only people who benefit from communist rule are those at the top; the 'Fat Cats' we call them," Feng added. "They do not care about the people. In fact, in the past they have brutally used their own people to ensure they could enjoy a luxurious lifestyle themselves."

It was, therefore, quite late that evening when Feng and Changpu were driven back to their hotel where they immediately fell into bed in a drunken stupor.

* * * * *

Before going into the Dining Room at the Pine Lake Inn on their first evening there, Dawn and Jerry joined Mery and Peter in the bar.

They had just settled themselves on bar stools and ordered Vodka and Cokes when two South African holidaymakers walked into the room.

On hearing the English group talking together, they immediately introduced themselves. They were sisters, one of whom lived in Cape Town and the other in Durban, who had got together for a holiday and were going to visit the Kruger National Park the following day. However, having recognised the English accents, they were eager to talk about England rather than South Africa.

They explained that their family could be traced back to the original European settlers in South Africa, and they had a grandfather who came from near Bath in the United Kingdom. They talked about how they had investigated their ancestry, after which they had visited England and even found the house where their grandfather had lived. However, when they had knocked on the door and explained who they were, the owners had not even invited them in.

At that point, Amy entered the bar and she was introduced to the two sisters. On finding out that one of them was a teacher, Amy monopolised the conversation with her whereupon the others turned away and conversed together.

Nevertheless, certain parts of the other conversation were overheard; in particular, Amy explaining that she had once been an Assistant Head, she had taught at a Special Needs School and was now a supply teacher.

Eventually, everyone decided it was time to go in for dinner, and Amy asked Dawn and Jerry if she could join them.

"Please do," Jerry replied as they walked into the dining room where numerous small tables were set out to accommodate groups of four.

A waitress took them to an empty table and Jerry ordered a bottle of wine. The meal was served from a carvery; a roast dinner with a selection of meats. The alternative main course was a curry, and there was a choice of entrees and desserts.

Once they had selected their first course and were all seated back at the table, the waitress served the wine, pouring it into the three small wine glasses previously laid out on the table. Amy did not decline the drink as she had now finished the large glass of wine she had brought in with her from the bar.

Conversation centred on previous travel destinations, but as soon as Jerry or Dawn mentioned places they had visited, Amy interrupted to explain her trips to those exact same destinations. Although Dawn and Jerry attempted on several occasions to speak about their experiences, they eventually gave up and concentrated on eating the main course that they had moved on to by that time.

As Amy talked, she helped herself to more wine from the bottle on the table so that before they had finished the second course it was empty. Amy then called the waiter over, and without asking Dawn and Jerry if they wanted anything further to drink, she order another glass of wine for herself,

"But not in one of those small glasses," she said. "You can fill up this big one that I got from the bar."

Dawn and Jerry were embarrassed because other people could easily overhear this conversation, so much so that they left Amy to finish her main course while they went in search of a dessert.

"This is getting too much," said Jerry. "We don't want her ruining our evening. Let's finish our meal and take our coffee in the lounge."

When they got back to the table they explained to Amy what they intended to do, and she replied,

"Good idea. I'll join you."

Luckily, when they reached the lounge, other members of their party were already there so they sat with them knowing that it would be easier if there were more people for Amy to speak to. At least then they could also have conversations with the others.

However, Dawn and Jerry excused themselves as soon as they could explaining that they were going to have an early night as they had to meet up in reception at 5.30 the next morning so that they could be at the Kruger National Park when the gates opened at six o'clock.

"What a nightmare Amy is," said Jerry as they walked up to their room. "She never stops talking."

"I think she'd already had a few drinks before she came into the bar," Dawn added. "Have you noticed that she talks more if she's had a lot to drink."

"You can't get a word in edgeways once she starts," replied Jerry. "Perhaps you're right. At least when you meet her at breakfast time, she's not quite so talkative."

Then he continued,

"It's funny how more information is emerging about her life. Now she is saying that she has worked as teacher. Therefore, she has not been looking after a disabled husband full-time since she left university as she first stated."

"She could have done both," Dawn tried as always to add logic to the argument.

When they reached their room, Jerry set two clocks for a 4.45 am alarm call before they went to bed where, just like those unknown Chinese businessmen who did not have to wake up so early in the morning, they fell into a deep sleep. Jerry did not even get a chance to point out to Dawn, an article he had been reading in the local paper entitled,

'Possible reduction in the speed limit'

"Cruising at 120km/h on the country's roads could be a thing of the past if a review of the current legislation governing the speed limits on our roads is approved by Cabinet . . . This after visiting the scene of yet another horrific accident on the N2 between Empangeni and Mtubatuba, and survivors at Ngwelezana Hospital and

Netcare The Bay Hospital. The accident, involving a mini-bus taxi and a van towing a trailer, claimed 10 lives.

The deceased were among 18 passengers (including two children thought to be under the age of 4) travelling from Durban to Mtubatuba on Monday evening.

> 'People cannot be treated as luggage'
> – Transport Minister Sbu Ndebele."

Attributed to Ronelle Ramsamy,
The Zululand Observer

* * * * *

CHAPTER 6

'The Kruger National Park'

As planned, Dawn and Jerry were awake and out of bed before sunrise the next morning.

When they walked into the reception area just before 5.30 am, they found individual brown paper bags containing a packed breakfast awaiting them. These were distributed, but nobody checked to see what was in their paper bag before walking quietly out to the waiting bus; they were barely awake enough to care and would save that revelation until later.

* * * * *

Feng and Changpu certainly did not wake up early that day. In fact, they were still sound asleep when at 8.00 am a knock on the door indicated that once again their breakfast had been left outside the room.

Luckily, Changpu just managed to register that there had been a knock, and after waking Feng, endeavoured to walk unsteadily over to the door thinking, quite logically, that if their breakfast were left to go cold, it would taste even worse.

Unexpectedly, however, they were getting used to mielie and rooibos tea, and they had now decided that they were just the right thing to eat and drink when one was suffering from a hangover.

* * * * *

Apart from greeting Dan, none of the tour party spoke on the bus that left the car park of the Pine Lake Inn at 5.30 am, possibly because they were still sleepy. However, they were all excited as Day Three was one of the main reasons they had all come on this trip; to see wild animals in their natural environment.

En route, they passed a broken down logging lorry near a sign directing travellers to the Mac Mac Falls. When they encountered further logging lorries with men sitting on the back, it was even more obvious that they were going through a big forestry area. There were a variety of small and large trees everywhere, together with some black stumps that Brian said indicated that trees of more than 40 years of age had been removed.

Brian also pointed out that Sabie was a base for painters and expeditions as well as a centre for forestry. When they saw enormous eucalyptus plantations on both sides of the road, the tourists were told that as these trees grew taller than pines, they were ideal for mine shafts. Then as they passed the TombFu Tomb Stones, Brian explained that a lucky gold discovery had been made there.

They were at an altitude of 4,000 feet (1,219 metres) when they turned off the road in the direction of White River; the town of White River being only 15 minutes away from the lodge where they would be entering the park.

Brian explained that with approximately eight hundred small farms in this area, it was the most densely farmed region in the whole of South Africa. On crossing a river, they saw macadamia, pecan and cashew nut orchards.

Then they passed the "White River Country Club" which advertised 'Cricket, Hockey, Squash, Tennis and other Clubs'.

Next they saw a development of small brick-built bungalows and then a wide area of small shanty properties. Brian pointed out that this was a homelands village, saying that the majority of the population were elderly people who looked after young children while the parents worked in the towns and cities, only returning at weekends, or on public holidays. With that situation and the AIDS/HIV crisis, grandparents were raising seventy-two per cent of black children.

After passing another similar village and going under a railway line, they arrived at the Numbi Gate less than half an hour after leaving their hotel. They were the second bus in the queue waiting for the gates to open at 6.00 am when Brian began his commentary,

"So this is what you have all been waiting for - a morning open vehicle game drive in the Kruger National Park. Over four million people visit the Kruger Park each year. It is one of the biggest botanical gardens on earth. In the early 1960s, malaria was eradicated here. This is a unique place; animals come first and homes come second."

"A park ranger will take you for a drive of approximately two hours and then he will stop at a picnic area where you

can eat your breakfast. We need to obtain permits from the office and then we will link up with the Ranger. At about 12.00 noon, you will return to the reception area where Dan and I will be waiting for you with the bus. Then you will have the afternoon at leisure; you will probably want to take a nap then because I can assure you that you will be exhausted."

"Hopefully, you will see a wide selection of the 'Big Five' this morning as well as many other animals and birds that reside in this beautiful area. You are likely to see White Rhino rather than Black Rhino. The White Rhino is not really white; that was a misinterpretation of a native word that means 'wide-mouthed', not white. There are between 11,000 and 12,000 White Rhino in this park. They can weigh up to 2,500 kg. The Black Rhino is only two thirds of the size of the White and there are only approximately 4,000 of them. They are both extremely dangerous animals, but it is the Black Rhino who is the most vicious. The only animal which is more aggressive than the Black Rhino is the Honey Bear."

"The White Rhino young run in front of their mother so they are protected by the big horn, but the Black Rhino babies run behind and are easy prey for predators. The Black Rhino lives in thick, dense areas of the park not like the area you are visiting today, which is open savannah."

"Now that it is the end of the dry season, it might be a good time to find animals at the watering holes. Also the grass will be dry and flattened, so the animals cannot easily hide."

"Lions are poor hunters so they hunt together to make it easier and that's why they form prides. Young male lions form brotherhoods to hunt."

Then Jerry asked,

"Is there a poaching problem in this park?"

"There are sporadic outbreaks of poaching, and rhino horn poachers now use helicopters. Rhino horn is much sought after for use in Chinese medicines. It is also desired by Arab Sheiks who want it for the handles of knives to be presented to their sons and now some people believe powdered rhino horn is a cure for cancer. An anti-poaching unit has been formed, consisting of military personnel and security is becoming much tighter now. It is a similar situation on other reservations where they are *losing rhinos. Nevertheless, over 270 rhinos have so far been killed this year. This is because the poachers are willing to take risks when they can obtain approximately £50,000 per kilo for rhino horn."*

Once inside the park, Brian jumped down from their vehicle saying that he was off to find the Ranger who was going to be their guide. Dan also disappeared after parking the coach, but nobody saw where he went.

The tour party got out of the bus and stood about aimlessly while other buses entered the car park and their passengers hurried away, following people dressed in the official uniform of the Park Rangers.

Eventually, Brian returned accompanied by a small, spritely man of indeterminate age, with a face under his Rangers' hat, which was as brown as a brazil nut and just as wrinkled. However, he had a sparkle in his blue eyes and a broad grin on his face as he greeted the party and Brian introduced him,

"This is Ted. He is the most experienced Ranger in the park, and if there are animals to be found this morning, you can rest assured that he will make sure you see them."

Then Ted spoke to them,

"Well, folks, I'll try to make the morning as enjoyable as possible. Our vehicle is waiting for us over there. If you see any animals, make sure you let me know so that I stop, but don't shout too loudly or you'll scare them away, and maybe cause me to have an accident," he laughed at this own joke as he led the group across the car park. As they walked, he added that early mornings in August and September were the best times for seeing animals because they would not be hiding away in the shade, out of the sun.

It was agreed that Amy should travel in the front with him, and the three couples spread out on the three bench seats situated at a higher level behind the driver, so that each person was seated next to an open window in order to be assured of a good view.

As they clambered aboard and settled into their allotted positions, they were all able to overhear Ted's conversation with Brian:

"You probably won't see me here again, Brian. I'm retiring in a few days' time. Bought a place down south near Knysna. Much kinder climate near the Cape. Better for these old bones of mine."

"You'll certainly be missed, Ted. You've taught all these young trackers everything they know. Won't you miss it?" replied Brian.

"Oh, I don't know. I'll probably find some work on a game reserve down there. A lot of private ones are starting up. It's big business now."

Ted then leapt agilely into the driving seat and started the engine.

"This is not going to be a 'Ferrari Safari'," he told the tourists. "I won't be driving that fast. I can go faster if you want, but then you won't see anything."

Everyone agreed that he shouldn't go too quickly and so they set off.

Almost immediately someone shouted and there, hiding underneath the trees, were a pair of water buffalo. Pictures were taken and Ted drove off again along a rough dirt track.

Soon he and Amy were deep in conversation – well, perhaps truth be told, Amy was the one doing most of the talking only stopping when Ted decided that it was necessary to provide a commentary that the other occupants of the vehicle needed to hear.

"Kruger National Park is a wildlife sanctuary like no other. Being the largest game reserve in South Africa, it provides the ultimate safari experience. It is larger than the state of Israel, with nearly 2 million hectares (20,000 square kilometres) of land that stretches for 352 kilometres from north to south along the Mozambique border. The Kruger National Park lies across the provinces of Mpumalanga and Limpopo in the north of South Africa, just south of Zimbabwe and west of Mozambique. It now forms part of the Great Limpopo Transfrontier Park - a peace park that links Kruger National Park with game parks in Zimbabwe and Mozambique, and fences are already coming down to allow game to freely roam in much the same way as it would have done in the time before man's intervention. When complete, the Greater Limpopo Transfrontier Park will extend across 35,000

square kilometres, 58% of it South African, 24% in Mozambique and 18% in Zimbabwean territory."

"Today, I will try to ensure you see as many different animals as possible, but we might not be lucky enough to see leopards or cheetahs as they are rarely seen where there are lions. However, there are numerous other animals you might see as we have more species of mammals than any other African Game Reserve."

"We have good-sized herds of elephant; the latest estimate being that as many as 9,000 reside here. We also have herds of kudu, impala, giraffe, buffalo, zebra, and white rhino."

As Ted drove carefully along the bumpy track, the weather was cold and it was raining at times, but this did not stop anyone from enjoying themselves. They were all well wrapped up with layers of clothing as Brian had suggested, and they draped the blankets that they found in the jeep, over their laps and around their legs. Initially it was Dawn and Jerry who bore the brunt of the rain as they were seated on the first bench seat above and behind the driver, where without the protection of the windscreen, the sharp, icy rain blew straight into their faces.

The vehicle stopped again and again to allow the tourists to look at small herds of kudu (females with pretty faces below their large ears and groups of young males), impala with their distinctive markings, giraffes and zebras in groups of two or four. There were also some smaller animals: duiker who always seemed to be alone and were quite squittish, a single hyena who stared at them for some time before moving off and a warthog who only stopped for a second before disappearing into the bush. Then there were the elephants: the first two were thought to be two-year old males, then there was a very old bull elephant, and just when everyone started thinking those were going to be the only ones they would see that day, there were several more – more bulls either in pairs or alone and some females. They saw just one fully-grown male kudu which had two twists in its fine antlers, and Ted pointed out unusual birds sitting high above in the branches of the trees: a wallbeck eagle, a crested frankolene, a yellow-billed hornbill, and wandering along at the side of the road, several helmeted guinea fowl. At one point, there were vultures circling overhead and near the water hole, there was a white-breasted fish eagle.

The whole party were amazed that so many of the animals showed no fear of the tourists and did not scurry away in fright. It was almost as if the tourists were providing entertainment for them as they looked up occasionally from the more important task of grazing in order to pose for photographs to be taken.

The water hole was a disappointment as there were no animals drinking there, but although Jerry and Dawn could not see them, some of their fellow travellers thought they could see hippos out in the water in the far distance. All Jerry and Dawn saw were the numerous large termite mounds around the lake, and Ted explained that the different middens were the droppings of either rhino or elephant; black indicating that it was rhino, and yellow being from an elephant.

However, afterwards the tourists had two absolutely thrilling and marvellous experiences. The first was when Ted stopped the vehicle and pointed to a group of trees in the far distance under which there were several lions. As they watched, three females got to their feet and strolled across to the vehicle. As Ted moved forward slowly, they walked alongside, but did not get too close. Then he stopped again, and all three of them walked across the road in front of the tourists. They followed each other and disappeared into the bush on the opposite side of the road.

The second experience began when another vehicle stopped and the occupants explained to Ted that rhinos had been seen in a certain location. The driver gave Ted directions and they set off to look for them. The first sighting was of a small group asleep some distance away from the road, again under some trees. It was difficult to see them at first as they blended into their surroundings, but after a while they started to move and it was possible to ascertain that some animals were much larger than others.

Then Ted drove off, and just a little further down the road, there were three more: one large female standing nearby watching two young males playing in the road, pretending to charge each other and playfully knocking horns. Several vehicles drew up from both directions and all stopped so that the occupants could watch. In any event, it wasn't possible for anyone to drive on as the rhinos were blocking the road.

After everyone had had time to take photos and have a good look, Ted joked,

"You might be interested to learn that the collective noun for a group of rhino is a crash, and a crash is exactly what I will attempt to avoid now,"

as he carefully drove over to the right of the two young rhinos who got the message and moved back off the road to join the female in the bush.

All the drivers of the other vehicles (some of which were private cars) gave Ted a grateful wave as they drove off.

They met quite a few more private cars driving down the dusty roads and Ted had to stop on one occasion when in front of them he saw a woman outside her vehicle taking photographs. By the time they reached her she had got back into the car, but as Ted drew up beside them, he still leant across Amy to speak to the two occupants. He was extremely polite, wishing them a good morning and hoping that they were enjoying their visit to the park. He then said that he had seen one of them outside the vehicle, pointed out that in the park this was an offence and that it was extremely dangerous. He asked for assurances that it would not happen again, and obtained their agreement before driving off.

Ted explained that during the World Cup there had been many such incidents.

"With so many visitors to the park it was difficult to control what they got up to and many people did not even consider that while they were out of the car taking photographs of one animal, there was always the danger that another could come up behind them."

As promised, approximately two hours after they started out, Ted pulled into a picnic area where there were souvenir shops, cafes, toilet blocks, and tables and chairs laid out in the shade of trees overlooking an attractive canyon.

The tour party found some seats near the edge of the canyon where there was a marvellous view and opened up their breakfast bags which contained a cold drink, ham sandwiches and an apple. They had to be careful not to put anything down as there was a troop of baboons walking around, sitting on fences, or swinging from the branches of trees, watching them.

After consuming their 'hearty' breakfast, Jerry went off to find a baboon-proof bin and then decided to purchase hot drinks from the café. These had dual functionality; not only did they warm up their insides, but it was possible to warm their hands by placing them around the outside of the cups containing the hot liquid. After this they were ready for another session within the open vehicle, and were able to take off some of their layers of clothing as the weather was becoming warmer.

On the second part of the tour they went through slightly different scenery with large rocky outcrops and burnt off grassy areas, many of which were inhabited by very large troops of baboons.

They also saw many more of the animals mentioned previously, together with a dwarf mongoose who caused some excitement.

When they got back to the starting point of their journey through the Park, Jerry asked approximately how far had they travelled that day, and Ted replied,

"About 40 miles (64 km) in each direction."

Everyone thanked Ted for looking after them so well, and shook his hand after getting down from the jeep.

The majority of the members of the tour party then went in and out of the souvenir shops situated near the entrance to the park while they waited for Brian and Dan to turn up with the bus. Only Amy did not join them; she and Ted were seen by the others sitting at one of the picnic tables, conversing intently as they drank beer.

When Brian and Dan arrived, everyone clambered aboard the bus, including Amy who waved goodbye to Ted as they drove out of the park.

Then it was time for a review of the animals and birds they had spotted during the day, and Dawn read out from the list she had been keeping,

"Impala (too many to count), two duiker, at least eight elephants, seven kudu with one of them definitely being a male, more than eleven zebra and more than eleven giraffes, three female lions, one warthog, one hyena, seven rhino, baboons (too numerous to mention), one dwarf mongoose, a white breasted fish eagle, a yellow-billed hornbill, a crested frankolene, five helmeted guinea fowl, a wallbeck eagle, and several vultures circling overhead."

Brian laughed, "That sounds like a good score. Did you enjoy your day?"

"Oh yes," everybody enthusiastically agreed. "It was amazing."

"You do realise, don't you," he continued with a joke, "that you can tell the difference between male and female zebras; the male zebra has black stripes and the female has white ones."

They all laughed merrily, and happily sat back in their seats reminiscing on their experiences.

* * * * *

Feng and Changpu had also experienced their best day yet during a sightseeing tour of Pretoria.

At precisely 10.00 am they had come down the stairs to go out of their hotel and there, once again, a car was waiting for them, with Beni and Bongani standing next to it, and Eli in the driving seat. This morning, the greetings were much more convivial – it was a meeting of old friends and they were all looking forward to the day ahead.

Feng and Changpu were definitely beginning to feel like tourists, and they put out of the minds the fact that they would need to get back to their hotel early that afternoon, so that they could rest before undertaking a helicopter flight that evening.

It was only a short, one-hour car journey to the outskirts of Pretoria. Like the British tour party, the first stop for the Chinese tourists was the Voortrekker Monument, but the commentary they received was completely different to that given to the English tourists. In fact, they were told,

"Inside this monument, you will find out about the first people who came to steal our lands. If only the Zulus had

been victorious on that occasion, perhaps our history would have been different, and we would still control Zululand."

As they entered the Voortrekker Monument alone, the Chinese businessmen commented on the radical views of their companions who had decided that it was time for them to enjoy a nap and a quiet cigarette in the shade of some trees.

Inside, the Chinese spent some time looking at the exhibits and even joined a tour party whose guide was speaking Mandarin, which they could understand. It made it so much more interesting when the history of South Africa was being explained in their own language.

Then it was off to the Union Buildings where once again their companions wandered off into the gardens, and the Chinese were left to their own devices while investigating the purpose of the grand buildings.

It was only when they reached the centre of Pretoria itself that their companions became more animated.

As they drove along wide avenues, the different districts were pointed out, and then they drove right into a busy shopping area, heaving with people. Eventually, a parking space was found near what they were initially told was Market Square. However, it was not directly into the square that they were first taken, but down a nondescript side street where the Chinese learnt why their companions were so excited.

They had led them to a Chinese Restaurant. It appeared that their new friends had really enjoyed their meal the previous day, and were eager to sample more Chinese food, especially as they knew they would not be paying for it.

Feng and Changpu both laughed and slapped their companions joyfully on the back as they entered the dimly lit premises.

Once again, they all enjoyed a delicious Chinese meal before the visitors were given a tour of all the historic buildings in what they were now correctly told had been renamed Church Square.

When they got back to the car, the Chinese tourists were then taken to places not seen by their British counterparts; they saw the National Zoological Gardens in the heart of Pretoria (known to locals as 'the zoo'), the State Theatre, the Pretoria Art Museum and the National Cultural History Museum. They didn't get out of the car to go into any of these establishments though, just stopped as close as possible while their colleagues explained what the buildings were. They even went up to the University buildings and the Loftus Versfeld Stadium, one of the most famous sports stadiums in South Africa.

After these short stops, it was back to their hotel where arrangements were made to collect them that evening for the trip to the airfield.

Throughout the day, however, Feng and Changpu had provided their new friends with details of how Communist rule had affected the Chinese people. They had pointed out that it was slowly getting better now, although there were still problems with farmers losing their lands and not receiving the compensation that they were entitled to.

Beni and Bongani listened with interest to the tales that their new friends were telling them, and started to wonder about the future of South Africa.

Was following the ideas of Mugabe the right thing to do?

* * * * *

CHAPTER 7
'A Night Safari'

When the tour party got back to their hotel that afternoon, everyone went straight up to their rooms for a rest, exactly as Brian had prophesied. In fact, some of them were so exhausted that they slept as soon as their heads touched the pillows.

However, there was a shock awaiting Meryl and Peter as they walked into their room. After noticing that the lock had been forced, they discovered two burglars going through their suitcases.

On seeing the tourists coming in the door, the burglars fled through open patio windows that led out onto the balcony from where they dropped down into the grounds of the hotel. By the time Peter reached the balcony, they had disappeared around the corner and the next thing he heard was a car engine starting. Then there was a screech of wheels skidding on rough gravel and the cries of a flock of disturbed birds who rose into the air with a great flapping of wings as a car drove off at speed.

Peter turned back into the room and faced Meryl.

"I think it's about time that we stopped thinking like tourists, and put our professional training back in gear," he said. "There have now been three incidents involving our suitcases, and taking that into account, as well as the fact that there was a salesman in London very eager to sell us a particular suitcase, it's all getting rather suspicious."

Meryl could only agree, and asked,

"Do you think this is anything to do with our professional lives, or are these incidents unconnected?"

"We won't know until we investigate further, and the first thing we need to do is take a good look at the suitcases. We packed really quickly, and haven't had a minute since. Now a full inspection is called for."

Many items from their suitcases had already been strewn about the room, and therefore, they only had to remove a few more things before both cases were completely empty. Then they compared the suitcases with each other. It was immediately obvious that one was deeper than the other.

"I thought it was just because you were bringing too many clothes that your suitcase filled up so quickly," laughed Peter, "But that doesn't seem to be the reason. There is definitely a false bottom in this one."

"And that could explain why our luggage weighed so much more than we anticipated," Meryl added. "We even paid a surcharge as we were over the weight allowance. Why didn't we notice that one suitcase was heavier than the other when they were empty."

"We wheeled them everywhere," Peter continued. "When you're rushing to catch a plane, comparing the weight of suitcases is not something you consider."

Meryl agreed that they had been in a hurry to get to the airport, and then went on to say,

"We need to think this through if we want to catch those involved. What should be our next step?"

"I think we should contact Brian first," Peter continued, "Have you got the mobile telephone number that was included with the itinerary?"

Meryl had it programmed into her phone and dialled it immediately. Brian was still downstairs in Reception when his phone rang and he agreed to come up to their room.

When he arrived, they put him in the picture; not only did they explain about the burglary, but they also confessed that in the UK Peter was actually an Officer with HM Customs & Excise and Meryl worked as a Police Inspector at New Scotland Yard.

Brian then had to reveal the fact that the previous damage to the lock on their suitcase had also actually been part of an attempt at theft, and apologised for covering up the matter as he could now see that something more serious was going on. Perhaps even the incident at the airport was connected.

He agreed with Meryl and Peter that they would have to be very clever if the thieves were to be caught because this was obviously not just an instance of petty crime. Then he had an idea.

"A friend of mine is speaking at a conference for Forensic Scientists in this hotel. He's now a Lieutenant Colonel in the South African Police Force, but I have known him from the time when we both served in the South African Armed Forces. I'll contact him, but first we should just report this as a petty burglary, which did not succeed. Cover up the fact that you know about the false bottom in the suitcase. If we don't report it, it would look suspicious, but the police won't take it any further."

With that Brian contacted Reception and reported an attempt to steal from their room. Shortly after this two policemen knocked on the door. They took down the particulars, and after being told that nothing had been stolen, they left without even making arrangements for fingerprints to be taken. Seeing that Meryl and Peter were not impressed, Brian had to explain,

"There are so many cases of attempted petty crimes that they are only taken seriously if items of value are stolen, or injuries are involved. However, I can make sure that this case is taken seriously."

With that he made another telephone call, and found that his friend was available. Arrangements were made for the Lt Col to visit their room by a roundabout route so that no one would see him arrive.

* * * * *

Upon receiving the call to Reception reporting an attempted robbery in one of the guest rooms, the Hotel Manager had immediately telephoned the police, but he had not realised that his conversation was being overheard.

Prior to the telephone call, a well-dressed businessman had been drinking coffee in the lounge situated between the Reception area and the patio from where it was possible to see both wings of the hotel and the balconies attached to the guest suites. He had observed two young men leaving a first floor room by an unusual method; they had jumped down from the balcony before running off round the corner to the service area. However, he had said nothing.

He did change his seat though, and moved closer to the Reception area so that he could observe if anything happened next. Luckily from his point of view, he was not disappointed, although from the look on his face it was obvious that he was not happy.

He was slightly cheered, however, when two young policemen returned to Reception after visiting a guest room, and reported that no action was being taken.

"We don't want any more crimes added to our statistics and risk upsetting the South African tourist industry," they stated and the Manager agreed.

However, the businessman would not have been so happy if he had known about the plans being discussed in Room 147 shortly afterwards.

* * * * *

When another hotel resident arrived in room number 147, Brian introduced him.

"This is my friend, Lieutenant Colonel Pieter Du Plessis."

The situation was then fully explained once more and the suitcase was thoroughly inspected. After this, it was agreed that it would be left to experts to deal with the false bottom; they would not tamper with it.

A plan to catch those involved was then discussed.

"I'll arrange for the contents of the false bottom to be removed and replaced with something similar, and tracking devices to be fitted to both suitcases," Du Plessis explained before continuing,

"It just so happens that there's a man staying here at the moment who is very skilled in this respect – he's speaking at the Conference like myself. If you let me have your spare room key, he'll let himself into your room while you're out this evening and nobody will be any the wiser."

The arrangements were confirmed, together with the fact that what had occurred and was about to occur would be kept a secret; nobody else was to be informed. However, as the tourists were scheduled to visit Swaziland the next day, it was pointed out that no rushing around was necessary.

"Nobody will try anything while you're in Swaziland," the Lt Col explained. "Their treatment of criminals is much harsher than ours. A South African would think twice about committing a crime there, and there are border controls. I'll still make sure your suitcases are watched at all times, but it is more likely that a further attempt will be made when you are in Zululand."

Therefore, Meryl and Peter agreed to be patient, and carry on acting like carefree tourists until the trap could be set at the Ghost Mountain Inn where they would be staying in two nights' time.

However, after all their visitors had left, Meryl had to remark to Peter,

"It's so unusual letting someone else deal with a crime. Are we doing the right thing by not getting involved?"

"We're in a foreign country, Meryl," Peter replied. "We don't know enough about procedures here, and we have to be careful not to tread on anyone's toes. They appear to know what they're doing. Let's just try and enjoy our holiday."

* * * * *

Dawn and Jerry had slept through all this intrigue. They had just intended to take a short nap when they reached their room, but instead managed to sleep for three hours. What actually woke them was a telephone call from Reception. Despite the fact that they had put the 'Do Not Disturb' notice outside their door, on seeing the sign the housemaid had asked Reception to ring the room to ask how many clean towels were needed.

"So much for relying on 'Do Not Disturb'," complained Jerry as he went to the door to let in the maid who went through into the bathroom before he could stop her.

Dawn disappeared under the bedclothes at this point and stayed there until the maid had left.

"No privacy," she said as she emerged when she heard the door close. "I could have been stark naked. You should have stopped her coming into the room."

"No way," said Jerry. "She was a large lady. I wasn't going to argue with her."

"Traditionally built, as Brian would say," laughed Dawn.

Now that they were wide-awake, they realised that they were feeling hungry. Having missed lunch, the only option was to go down to Reception and see if they could arrange for a snack to be served while they sat out in the sun at one of the many tables arranged around the swimming pool.

Before sitting down at a suitable table, Jerry went over to test the temperature of the water in the pool. As a result, he decided it was too cold for him to take a dip, but there were a lot of other people doing so.

In fact, they sat watching a group of young people splashing each other and laughing hilariously until a waitress came across to take their order. The only food available turned out to be homemade apple crumble, which they ordered together with a pot of coffee.

A well-dressed man was seated at the table next to them, reading a newspaper. Occasionally, one or two of the group of young people came up to talk to him, and eventually all of them left the pool and sank down onto the chairs that surrounded him.

"That's better," Jerry spoke quietly. "Slightly more peaceful now."

"I'm sure I recognise that man," Dawn whispered. "Isn't he the one who complained about the toast when we were in Pretoria?"

Even though Jerry took a surreptitious look, he wasn't able to agree, and just at that moment, Brian walked past.

"Would you like to join us for coffee," Jerry asked him. "We have a potful here."

Brian was only too pleased to sit down and enjoy a cup of coffee. Jerry signalled to the waitress and she brought over another cup.

They spoke together about plans for that evening and the next day until eventually Dawn could not stop herself from asking,

"That man over there. Is he someone well-known?"

"That's Robert Goodnuf Xulu." Brian replied. "He's some sort of leader in the ANC Youth League. Aspiring to be a politician, but he's a bad lot. Woe betide South Africa if he ever gets to occupy a position of power."

Having finished their coffee and apple crumble, Dawn and Jerry left Brian sitting by the pool, and went up to their room to get ready to go out to the special Barbecue Dinner that had been organised to take place at the Greenway Woods Resort that evening.

* * * * *

Surprisingly, when the tour party met in Reception, Amy was not there.

"I received a phone call earlier," Brian announced. "She's not feeling well. Too much bouncing about on uneven roads, I understand."

The others muttered "What a Shame" as they climbed aboard the bus to travel to the hotel just a short distance up the road, where the BBQ was being held. Despite being told, none of them were really convinced that it was the bumpy roads that had made Amy feel ill. More likely, they thought, that she had been drinking alcohol all afternoon.

* * * * *

Amy's fellow travellers had been partly right in their assumptions. The bumpy roads had not made her feel ill, but she was also not suffering from an over-indulgence of alcohol. In fact, she was travelling along a bumpy track at that precise moment and she did not feel at all ill; she was actually feeling happier than she had felt in a long time.

Ted had picked her up at the hotel earlier that evening, after having arranged to take her on a special night safari.

"You won't believe how wonderful the park is at night, and this might be my last chance to see it. Some of the animals have fantastic night vision. The cats, for instance, can see eight times better than we do at night and they sleep for most of the day," he had said in order to convince her. However, she had not needed much convincing. It sounded just like an adventure she wanted to be involved in, especially if it meant spending more time with Ted whose company she was enjoying.

Now, they were travelling along in total darkness as he had not even put on his headlights, and for once Amy was quiet. Although Ted seemed to know exactly where the track was, she wanted him to concentrate on the road ahead, and she just looked out of the window intently as she had been instructed.

"Keep all windows closed, and doors locked," he had told her, after they had transferred to his safari vehicle parked on the other side of the park gates. Although the gates had been locked at 6.00 pm, Ted had a key that opened them and they had driven through in Ted's car. Then he had locked them again.

"They'll be no Rangers patrolling this area this evening because they've received a tip off about poachers on the other side of the park. We're going to stop near a water hole, out of sight, and then when the moon comes out from behind the clouds, you'll be able to see everything. Believe me," he repeated, "it's amazing. Much better than seeing the animals during the day."

However, before they reached the steep track leading down to the water hole, Ted came to a halt.

"What is it?" asked Amy.

"I saw a light," Ted replied as he leant over to the back seat for his rifle. "You stay in the car. I'm going to investigate."

He got out of the vehicle and set off down a track on the right. It only took a few seconds for Amy to decide that she was not going to stay in the vehicle alone, before she got out and trotted quickly along behind him.

As Ted got nearer to a clearing, he saw more flickering lights and realised that there was a line of beams illuminating the area. He had seen this arrangement of lights before and knew exactly what it meant – it signalled the imminent arrival of an aircraft; a small plane or a helicopter landing illegally in the Kruger National Park meant only one thing – poachers.

With eyes that were accustomed to the darkness and knowing the layout of the area, he quickly spotted the person who had laid out the lights, squatting down in the bush ahead of him. As he approached, he was vaguely aware of the noise made by the rotor blades of a helicopter, but he did not look up. He was concentrating on moving swiftly and silently. Angrily, he raised his rifle butt, swung it at the side of the man's head and knocked him sideways, whereupon he fell to the ground.

What Ted hadn't realised, because he had approached from behind, was that the squatting man had a rifle ready to fire, held in front of him. As the man went down, the rifle swung upwards and his finger must have depressed the trigger because he fired off a shot. The first thing that Amy heard was a loud noise as the bullet hit an unintentional target, "bang".

It was at that moment that both Amy and Ted looked up and saw a helicopter coming tumbling down out of the sky. It was out of control, with its front windscreen shattered and its pilot injured, it was spiralling haphazardly before it crashed into the ground. Pieces of metal flew off in all directions and then there was a roar as the helicopter immediately caught fire and was engulfed in flames.

Ted turned and almost bumped into Amy standing directly behind him.

"What are you doing here?" he asked. "I told you to wait in the jeep."

"I couldn't stay there without you," she muttered as if in a daze, with her eyes fixed firmly on the blazing helicopter immediately in front of them.

"Well, we've got to get out of here fast," Ted said urgently; at least all his senses were alert. "We can't do anything for them and this place will be swarming with Rangers shortly. An alarm call will go out when the blaze is spotted. It will easily be seen from miles away, and I don't want to be here when the Rangers arrive. It's the first time I've broken the rules of the park and there is no way I want to get involved in an official enquiry. I might lose my pension."

So taking Amy by the elbow he forced her to move back along the path to their waiting vehicle, which he reversed, turned round and then drove at a much faster speed than when they had been coming in the other direction, until they reached the edge of the central compound near the gate. Ted pulled in around the back, and parked his safari jeep near to where he had hidden his private car, as he thought to himself,

"Thank goodness, I put that out of sight,"

because there was already some activity in the compound.

Orders were being shouted to men who had obviously just arrived and they were being directed to board vehicles that were leaving the compound via the route that Ted and Amy had just driven.

They were back just in time.

Ted helped Amy down from the jeep and into his private car as she still seemed to be rather stunned. Then he told her to stay there while he investigated how they could get out without being seen. This time he knew from her face that she was not going to argue, but was going to do exactly as he asked.

Ted approached the control room where his boss was stationed,

"I came in with the others when I heard the alarm," he announced. "Do you need me?"

"Thanks, Ted," came the reply. "But as you finish this week, I don't think you need to get involved. You'll be writing reports until next month if you do," he laughed. "You get off home. There are plenty of others who'll deal with it."

So Ted went back to his own car, told Amy to lie low in the front seat and then drove out of the park gates, waving to his boss as he did so.

"Whew, that was a close shave," he said as Amy sat up beside him.

* * * * *

Meanwhile, Amy's fellow travellers were all enjoying what had not actually turned out to be a barbecue after all.

There had been some confusion about the booking, but they had all eaten well from another buffet, laid out in a similar way to the one they had participated in the previous evening with the difference being that there was a larger selection of dishes to sample.

Also, another difference on this occasion was that the tour party had all been seated at a long table where Brian and Dan had joined them. Discussions had been lively and entertaining, and the evening passed quickly.

Nothing more had been said about Amy that evening, but without her being there it was so much easier to have light discussions, with politics, schooling and the problems South Africa had faced, and would possibly face in the future, not being mentioned at all.

As a result, they had all returned to Pine Lake in an excellent mood, and went straight up to their rooms.

Sleep came easily to those members of the tour party that night, but in the early hours of the morning, Dawn was woken up by the sound of peacocks screeching.

"That's funny," she thought to herself. "I didn't know that there were any peacocks here. We'll need to investigate tomorrow."

Then she went back to sleep.

* * * * *

It was actually Amy who had disturbed the peacocks when she returned to the hotel at 2.00 am. She was lucky to get back in, and only did so because the night porter recognised her.

Ted had taken her back to his house after leaving the park and there she had consumed several stiff drinks. He had also had the sense to make her eat a meal that he had cooked, realising that she was drinking alcohol on an empty stomach.

Then they had discussed the events of that evening and their future plans, discovering to their mutual joy that they had both already independently decided that they enjoyed each other's company.

* * * * *

CHAPTER 8

'Matsamo Cultural Village'

On Day 5, Dawn and Jerry met the rest of the tour party in the Dining Room where they enjoyed a wonderful, enormous breakfast (so different from the previous day) before they left the Pine Lake Inn at 9.00 am on a lovely sunny morning.

Today, it was Dawn's turn to sit in the front seat next to the driver, and as they drove off, Brian picked up the microphone and announced,

"Today we will travel south to the mountain kingdom of Swaziland where we will enjoy an educational show at the Matsamo Cultural Village, view some local homesteads and eat a traditional lunch prepared by our hosts. Tonight will be spent at the Tum's George Hotel in the beautiful Swazi Highlands."

Dawn noted that they took Route 569 to Hazyview and then turned off at a junction where the trees were covered in purple bougainvillea.

They passed a small airfield as they drove through the Crocodile Valley with its many farms. Nelsburg could be seen in the distant mist and white orange blossom covered the trees leading Brian to inform them that this area was a major exporter of Outspan oranges.

Then when they saw a macadamia plantation and an avocado producing area, Brian explained,

"Avocados and bananas are grown in rotation. Because of its shape, the Avocado was originally named testicle fruit; āhuacatl in Nahuatl (the language originally spoken in Mexico). Then it became aquacate in Spanish."

They crossed the Crocodile River, the southern boundary of the Kruger National Park, on several occasions as they continued through the valley.

Then suddenly a lorry pulled over onto the hard shoulder to allow Dan to pass. Soon it was evident why as the motorway narrowed to only one lane in each direction, and police checks were taking place. Dan was not pulled over, however, and the tour party continued through the Crocodile Gorge where Brian informed them,

"We are passing the oldest rock on earth; it dates back 3,700 million years. I do recommend that you read a book (Earth & Life) that tells the story of the geological formation of South Africa. Many archaeological remains have been found near Johannesburg and in some other South African World Heritage Sites."

After a sign stating,

> 'Welcome to The Wild Frontier'.

they found themselves once again travelling through a very fertile valley, with sugar cane growing on one side and many different species of mangoes on the other. Then paw paw trees and orange orchards.

When they stopped at the Malelane Shopping Mall with shops named Woolworths, Sheet Street, Cell Shop, KFC, Spar, Vodacom, Discom, PaperWork, CAN, and an abundance of clothing outlets, Jerry visited every suitable shop to buy a replacement memory chip for his camera, without success.

Then they drove past the Inkwazi shopping centre where fever trees were growing in the grounds all around and along the avenue leading out on to the main road. Brian explained that originally these were named fever trees because it was thought that the trees caused malaria. This did not prove to be the case; fever trees just thrived in swampy areas.

With the Kruger National Park on their left as they progressed along the north side of Crocodile River, they passed sugar cane lorries transporting a crop to the mill with smoking chimneys that they could see set amongst a range of foothills.

Suddenly, Brian asked Dan to stop the bus. Jumping out, he purchased a bag of oranges for just two South African Rand, saying as he got back on the bus,

"I bought these to prove to you how good they taste."

The tour bus then travelled along via Jeppé's Reef, where buffalo were being imported onto the range because of the problem of bovine tuberculosis in the game reserves. Giraffes could be seen feeding off the trees in the distance, and game lodges and private farms abounded. Then they saw their first flowering Jacaranda tree in South Africa.

"Spring is here," Brian announced.

When they passed a banana plantation, he explained,

"There are three generations of trees – grandmother, mother and daughter. The small bananas growing here are not those that are exported to the UK. Bananas are picked when they are green for transport purposes and then put in gas chambers to turn them yellow. The blue bags you can see covering the bunches are full of insecticide and they also protect the banana from the sun which can cause black spot."

Then more sugar cane fields, before they discovered huge trees full of lychees which, Brian informed them, made a wonderful fruit juice.

As they crossed yet another river (the Sperkspruit) orchards and plantations covered the valley floor and cows grazed on the grass verges at the roadside.

Shortly, Brian gave them their instructions:

"When we get to the border with Swaziland, Dan will have to obtain a licence for the bus to enter the country and all passengers have to go through passport control. In the passport control office, you will see a picture of the king on the wall with his mother on one side and his father on the other."

"We will walk across the border to visit the Matsamo Cultural Village. The people who live in the villages around Matsamo follow Swazi customs and traditions; they have a well-preserved and rich cultural heritage. A group of young people (nearly all under 30) now use their resources in a unique and responsible way to earn an income through tourism. They have formed a company in which all the staff own shares. You will be given a guided tour of the village, introduced to their customs and traditions, and have an opportunity to join in the singing and dancing," he laughed. "Afterwards, you go up to the restaurant for a typical Swazi meal."

Just as they passed a school on the left, Dan slowed down to allow a cow to cross the road.

"Cow crossing," Dawn warned.

"It's not children running across the road, you have to be careful about here," Jerry commented. "It's the cows. Thank goodness we don't have them wandering about in England."

"Perhaps they should have cow crossings in South Africa rather than zebra crossings," Peter joked, "with black and white blodges similar to cows rather than stripes like zebras."

Brian then started his commentary again,

"The dam on the Samati River to your left was built ten years ago to bring water to this area, and the old road was obliterated when the dam filled up."

As they drove down the hill, there was a superb view of the lake created by the dam, and then it was back to seeing scrubland with beautiful views of the river on their left.

Shortly after this, Dan drove into an intersection of streets lined with houses, which he manoeuvred the bus up, down and around via a circuitous route before eventually they were in a road lined with lorries. Dan parked the bus on a corner and everyone got out. They had reached the border.

The group then joined the queue waiting to enter the passport control building. Once inside, sure enough, there were three pictures on the wall; one of the King, one of his mother and one of his father.

After they had all had their passports stamped, it was time to take the short walk across the border and meet their hosts at the Matsamo Cultural Village.

Arriving there, a young woman dressed according to Swazi custom, led them through a forested area until they reached the entrance to a clearing. Here she halted the party and explained that a greeting had to be shouted very loudly to announce their presence. They would then receive a reply confirming that they were allowed to enter the village.

She then demonstrated the words that had to be shouted, and when the tour party did so, replies were received from various places around them, although no one could be seen.

Then they all walked into the clearing that contained several round huts of assorted sizes and in various stages of construction. Each comprised a wattle frame.

Some frames were partially covered in woven wattle, whilst others were completely encased. In further examples, the finished wattle structures had then been covered with a mud and straw mixture.

The young female guide explained, as Brian had done previously, that they had formed a group to entertain tourists,

"The fact that about seventy-five per cent of us are woman was not planned," she laughed, "but women certainly play a significant role in tourism and community development in this country."

She then provided an insight into the history of the cultural village and Swaziland.

"The cultural village first opened in 2001. We receive many visits from school children and invitations to perform at various venues, as well as undertaking the role of entertaining tourists here. Matsamo enjoys a lot of support and we are proud to be South African."

"Before this area became Swaziland it was inhabited by various different ethnic groups of people for a very long time. In fact, in eastern Swaziland human remains have been discovered that date back 100,000 years; these have been confirmed as belonging to the oldest homo sapiens. The first inhabitants were Bushmen, as is evident from the large number of cave paintings that have been found in this region. The Swazi arrived much later."

"In 1922 King Sobhuza II was the paramount chief of Swaziland and King to the Swazi nation. He took over from his grandmother Gwamile, who had been Queen Regent whilst he was underage. King Sobhuza died in 1982 after 60 years on the throne; he was our longest reigning monarch."

"King Mswati III ascended to the throne in 1986 at the age of 18; he was then the youngest reigning monarch in the world."

"Matsamo Cultural Park is named after Chief Matsamo, a prominent Shongwe Chief and contemporary of King Mswati II. He was the first Swazi Chief who resided permanently in the area and established thirteen rural villages between 1840 and 1925. Today this area is under control of the Matsamo Tribal Authority."

"Although today the residents of the thirteen villages are still predominantly Swazi in custom and traditions, we are part of the South African Nation."

"This area has been designed to simulate a typical Swazi village, or community, where the men would have several wives. The first wife would always receive the most respect, and would have to give permission for her husband to take more wives and approve them. Contrary to common belief, the first wife is generally happy for her husband to take more wives because they would take on the household chores that she would prefer not to have to do and there would be more women to share the workload. Also, they would be a very sociable group."

"The wives would occupy one hut with their babies, or very young children, and take it in turns to sleep in the husband's hut; husbands and wives do not sleep together even in the husbands' hut. If the husband wanted the services of the particular wife who was sleeping in his hut, he would bang with his stick to indicate that the wife should join him in his bed, or perform other tasks."

"The stick sounds like a good idea," Jerry laughed and the other men in the party agreed. "Would it be possible for me to take one home with me?"

"Of course," agreed the girl jokingly. "It will be arranged."

Then she carried on,

"Toddlers and infants sleep in the same hut as their grandmothers, but once they are old enough the boys move out to sleep in other huts."

"Another custom that is different in our country to your own is that men always go first, especially when leaving or entering the huts. This originates from the time when the men were warriors and had to protect their women from danger. Also, for defence reasons, the hut entrances are low so that those entering have to stoop or enter with a bowed head."

The tour party were then invited to go inside one of the huts, with the men going first, of course. After they had made an inspection, the guide then led them to another clearing where there were some burnt out huts, which she explained,

"While we were away from the village, performing during the World Cup, our village burnt down and this is all that is left."

The tour party commiserated, but none were at all sure whether this was true, or an attempt to obtain more money in donations.

The guide then walked on, and the tour group followed, until they reached another entrance similar to the one encountered previously.

"Now we are entering another village," she said. "Do you remember the words you must chant?"

Laughing, the whole group shouted the words they had learnt previously, even though they did not know exactly what they were saying. However, once again they must have got it right because from close at hand this time, they received loud replies verifying that they could enter.

On walking into yet another clearing, they found that this one was laid out differently. In the centre, in between some trees, there was a clear area resembling a stage in front of which were a group of tree stumps arranged like seats. At the back of the clearing, there was a fenced area from behind which voices and giggling could be heard.

The tour party were invited to sit on the tree stumps, and then a performance of singing and dancing began. At the end of the formal entertainment, members of the audience were invited to join in the dancing, and it was ultimately only Peter and Jerry who were left sitting on the tree stumps; the only ones who had not been asked to participate.

Jerry was secretly pleased that he had not been asked to make a fool of himself, but Peter had been quite eager and was disappointed at being left out.

Then it was all over, and members of the dance troupe circulated amongst the audience, trying to sell CDs of their songs and pointing to containers situated in the dust where donations could be placed.

Jerry and Dawn were among those who purchased a CD, and put a small contribution in a container, not knowing whether the performance had actually been paid for by the tour company and was part of their inclusive package, or not.

Then the whole group followed their guide along dusty paths through the trees until they reached the restaurant where the performers were waiters and waitresses. Having arrived before the tourists, they had already changed out of their traditional costumes and were now wearing jeans and T-shirts.

The tour group sat at a round table and ordered drinks. Then they were invited to help themselves from a buffet comprising of pots of what appeared to be a chicken stew accompanied by vegetables, or salad, and a very attractive display of desserts involving bananas and a wide variety of fruits.

After enjoying their lunch, the party gathered together for Brian to explain where the coach could be found.

As they strolled along the road, Amy rushed up to Dawn and Jerry, and gushed,

"Wasn't that wonderful?"

Dawn tentatively agreed, while Jerry, ever the sceptic, muttered,

"I thought it was all a bit contrived."

But his comment was lost on Amy who by then had hurried away to share her enthusiasm with the rest of the group.

* * * * *

While the tour party were enjoying their introduction to Swaziland, Ted had been at work as usual, taking a group round the Kruger National Park. However, the morning had been particularly fraught after the drama of the helicopter crash the night before. The police were interviewing all the Rangers who could not stop discussing the matter amongst themselves at every opportunity.

Ted had endured all the conversations with a steadfast resolve not to let anyone become aware of what he knew; he was keeping his own counsel and had not mentioned his involvement. It was hard, but he knew that if his future was to be assured, it was necessary to keep quiet, but he so dearly wanted to do something to help solve the mystery of who was behind so many attempts to steal rhino horns; he was absolutely certain that there was more to the situation than met the eye. The question he kept asking himself was 'How could he help stop such attempts happening in future?'

There was one thing that came out in the conversations which surprised him, however, and that was that he had personally trained the man he had hit with his rifle butt. In the dark, he had not recognised him, but the Rangers who found the unconscious man afterwards, had done so. They kept repeating his name throughout the day, questioning why Joseph Ntombela had been involved.

Ted also wanted to know the answer to that question, even more so than his colleagues. After all, he had got to know Joseph well whilst training him, and he was the one who had knocked him unconscious. Ted knew that Joseph had had money problems, and every Ranger in the station knew he been dismissed from the Ranger Service because of petty pilfering. But to be desperate enough to kill animals that he had previously sworn to protect – how had that happened?

As the day wore on, Ted became more and more desperate to find out, and eventually he decided to approach the policeman in charge of the case who was, in fact, Lt Col Pieter Du Plessis.

After explaining his relationship with Joseph, Ted asked if it would be possible to visit him in hospital, and the Lt Col eagerly agreed, realising that this 'old timer' probably had more chance of getting Joseph to tell him the truth than the police. Therefore, they arranged to meet in the hospital reception area the next morning.

* * * * *

CHAPTER 9

'Swaziland'

On reaching the bus, the tour party clambered aboard, Dan drove off and they left the border behind. They crossed yet another river and once again there were goats running across the road proving that the farming methods in Swaziland were very similar to the rest of South Africa.

Brian then began another commentary,

"Swaziland gained Independence in 1968, which is celebrated annually together with the King's Birthday. According to Swazi custom, the son who is to become the next King is not the first-born son. The next son (the second-born son) is the King's successor and he undergoes an initiation ceremony at the age of 19. The Swazi have their own coins, but these have no value outside the country. However, they can be exchanged one for one for South African Rand at the border, and South African Rand will be accepted in Swaziland. If you receive any Swazi coins in your change, let me know and I will arrange for you to exchange them before we leave the country."

"Swaziland is approximately the same size as Wales in the United Kingdom, and has a population of 1.5 million people. While South Africa had the Sunday Observations Act, the Immorality Act, and no television until 1976, Swaziland did not have to conform to South African legislation. There were casinos in Swaziland when they were not allowed in South Africa and tourism used to be big business; South African tourists came to Swaziland to gamble, and enjoy other pleasures that were not available in South Africa. However, now that there are casinos in South Africa and much of the restrictive South African legislation has been revoked, tourism in Swaziland has reduced to only approximately 200,000 visitors each year and it is no longer so profitable."

"In Swaziland, they grow pineapples, grapefruit and oranges. They did have a vibrant canning industry, but with more and more fresh fruit being exported with the advent of improved transport arrangements, income from this source has also declined. Therefore, they have now established a forestry industry and they also grow sugar cane."

To reinforce this statement, Brian pointed out that they were travelling through what had previously been a treeless area, but now trees were being planted.

The road twisted and turned as they went uphill, passing the Piggs Peak Hotel and a sign for Phophonyane Falls, until high above they reached another thickly forested area and a sign saying,

'Welcome to Piggs Peak'

where Brian joked,

"You might be amused to learn that Thomas Pigg married Valerie Hogg."

Then they turned off towards the Maguga Dam and the Komati River where there was a beautiful view looking down into the valley below with the sun picking out the golden colour of the fields of corn stubble against a background of red soil and the dry black road surfaces gleamed as though they were wet. Soon there was yet another river where signs stated,

'Beware of Hippos'

When they stopped at a viewing point with even more spectacular views across a lake and valley, Brian explained that the enormous dam they could see before them was just five years old.

Everyone then got down from the bus and took photographs.

After leaving the viewing point, they travelled down to the dam where there were further signs, but this time they stated,

'Beware of Crocodiles'

This prompted Brian to add,

"A few interesting facts about crocodiles: they can walk ten to twelve miles (over 19 kilometres) during the night; a crocodile lays approximately 60 eggs; the gender of the newborn crocodile is determined by the temperature during incubation; the female keeps guard and after they hatch, the babies climb into her mouth to be transported to the river; a Nile River crocodile can live up to 160 years."

Then they drove across the top of the dam at the far end of the lake where there was a picnic area, vast botanical gardens and cows standing aimlessly in the road. The scenery was wonderful with undulating green hills interspersed with wattle plantations.

In some places it was possible to imagine how the villages had developed with some round buildings from the traditional setting remaining in amongst the new square structures that had been added.

Seeing this the tourists joked among themselves and asked the question, "Was the husband still using a stick to call his wife to his bed?"

Brian laughed when he heard them, but he did not answer. Instead, he said,

"Behind the lake on the left is the King's residence,"

and at that moment they actually passed a sign that stated,

'To the Royal Residence'.

They were now on a busy, new road with two lanes of fast traffic in each direction. Many bridges and overpasses crossed this main road. Smart bungalows were situated on the hills all around, and Mbabane, the administrative capital and largest city in Swaziland, could be seen in the distance.

Then they turned off the motorway, passing huge hoardings on both sides of the road advertising such delights as African Bohemia flooring and the Royal Swazi Hotel, Casino & Spa containing a Hot Spring known locally as a Cuddle Puddle.

After driving down a road lined with hotels, they arrived at a craft market. This was actually a dusty square surrounded by a host of huts in which people were selling exactly the same souvenirs and bric-a-brac as each other. Dawn discovered some wonderful carved wooden animals that again were too large to be transported, and in the end it was only Amy and Brian who purchased anything at all; Amy bought a woven, brightly coloured plastic shopping bag, and Brian displayed the traditional blanket that he had obtained to cover a worn chair in his home.

On leaving the craft market, they passed many new developments and a recently built commercial centre, together with a sign stating,

'Twiggs Garden Pavilion – these guys are good!'

After travelling for such a long time through the bush and open countryside, it was a shock to find parts of Swaziland were very commercial, modern and almost European.

Then it was on past the sports stadium, the Independent Stadium, with Parliament on their right and the National Football Association of Swaziland on their left before they took the road leading down to the Manzini motorway. At that point, Brian pointed out that Manzini meant a marshland area, but there was certainly no sign of any marshes – it was a well-developed, built up area now even if it had been marshland in the past.

As they passed yet another industrial estate and the Msapha Airport, Dawn commented,

"There's a wealth of amusing signs around here," as she quoted,

'Speed up Your Social Life.'

'Christmas has come early – put some colour in your life.'

'Time is a non-renewable resource'

'Mini Skirt Party – Big Fun'

Then they were passing a plethora of churches of many different denominations, and driving through a bustling area with shops, cafes and street vendors being visited by crowds of people. They had reached the town of Manzini and suddenly they arrived at their hotel – the Tum's George Hotel. It was 4.00 pm.

After a short discussion with Dawn, Jerry decided to once again try to find a replacement memory chip for his camera at one of the shops they had just passed. He went off even before the luggage had been unloaded, and it was left to Dawn to check into the hotel with the rest of their party and enjoy a welcome drink without him.

* * * * *

The layout of the hotel was slightly confusing, as the hotel rooms appeared to be back to front. In fact, there was no front entrance to any of the rooms. All the rooms were entered via patio doors looking out onto gardens, and there was a brick wall where you would expect the main door to the room to have been.

The large, clear glass patio doors were covered with curtains to ensure privacy when required, and therefore, it was quite difficult to get the door opened, deal with curtains, and take in the suitcases that had been left outside. Then, if you wanted privacy, you had to leave the curtains drawn meaning the lights had to be on. Alternatively, if you left the curtains open, everybody could see into the room.

Dawn managed to find some of the light switches, and by the time Jerry returned from his shopping trip, she had unpacked everything they needed for their overnight stay and was ready to go into the shower. However, before she did so, she listened to Jerry's account of his experiences in the town.

"In total, I have visited six cell phone, computer and photographic stores," he said. "The first one I found was run by two Canadians. Although they were very friendly, they could not help apart from pointing me in the direction of two other shops where suitable chips might be available. I then went from shop to shop, each time being directed to somewhere else until I achieved success in the sixth establishment. This was actually in a shopping mall that I would never have discovered if I hadn't been shown where it was."

"Did you see many other white people in the town?" Dawn asked to which Jerry replied,

"Not a single one. Apart from the two Canadians in the first shop, everyone was black. But they were all friendly; a lot of people greeted me with 'hello' or 'good afternoon', and all the shopkeepers could converse well in English. I didn't feel at all intimidated, and in fact in the last shop, the man there had to sort through lots of odd bits and pieces before he found something to fit. Then he put it all together, and the charge was minimal."

Dawn then went and had her shower, but as she was drying herself she felt something bite her foot. Looking down, she discovered a large ant actually walking across her toes. She killed that one, but then let out a loud scream as she noticed that the floor all around her was covered with ants and they were definitely not like the small ones to be found in England.

Jerry immediately rushed into the room, and killed a lot more by stamping on them, but as quickly as they were killed, more were emerging from a hole behind the toilet.

"Something has to be done about this," he said. "I'm going to report it to Reception."

They both left the bathroom, closing the door behind them, and while Dawn got dressed, Jerry went to the Reception Area.

"They're sending someone," he reported on his return, and soon afterwards that 'someone' arrived; a young girl who was obviously a cleaning maid, with a bucket and mop.

"Haven't you got anything to kill the ants with and destroy the nest?" Jerry asked.

"I clean them away," she replied.

"That's not good enough. They'll just come back," Jerry angrily stated before adding, "I'm going back to Reception. We want to change rooms."

The young girl then stood uncertainly in the room, watching Dawn pack all their belongings back into the bags and suitcases.

This time Jerry returned with another room key that he waggled in front of him.

"We're moving to a new room," he said.

The girl then sprang into action.

"I'll help," she said.

"No need," Jerry replied as he picked up their suitcases and marched out of the room. "We've got everything."

Dawn was not so sure, and carefully opened every drawer and cupboard to make certain they were empty. She even went back into the bathroom, checked that she had left nothing behind in there, and took a final look around the room to make certain that all the surfaces were clear before she picked up the remaining bags. She then gave the young girl a knowing nod and followed Jerry.

After giving their new room a complete inspection and finding no evidence of any small intruders, Jerry and

Dawn settled in. That evening they decided to have dinner in the hotel, and in fact, it was a very romantic meal with just the two of them seated at a small table. They didn't notice whether any other members of the tour party were also in the restaurant; they could easily have been, but they did not see them and nobody came across to talk to them.

It was, therefore, not until the next morning that they discovered that Anne and Cathy had found more than ants in their room.

* * * * *

Although Ted had made the arrangements to visit Joseph, he still found it difficult to concentrate on his work during the remainder of the day as Amy was regularly on his mind. Never before had there been any possibility, or an opportunity for a woman to occupy his thoughts during his working day, or during his evenings. He'd never married. He'd never found anyone he wanted to spend the rest of his life with. There had been girlfriends, of course, especially when he had been younger, but his work had been his life and when the girls had drifted away, he had been quite happy to let them go.

Now it appeared to be different. He was just about to retire and he had to admit that he was getting on a bit, but could it be that he was proving that no one was too old to fall in love; that it wasn't just young people who experienced these unusual thoughts - unusual as far as he was concerned at least.

He couldn't wait to see her again, to hear the sound of her voice, and see her smile.

Then just as he was drifting off to sleep, it came to him – the way to help finding those involved in killing rhinos for their horns. Instead of retiring, he could become a trainer. Then he would have an excuse to spend time in different safari parks and try to discover if there were people working there who were involved as it was obvious that the poachers needed inside information.

However, the problem was how could he combine that role with his desire to keep seeing Amy.

Before he went to sleep, he decided that he would telephone Amy soon, but he would go and see Joseph first.

Perhaps the answer would come to him.

* * * * *

News of the accident in the Kruger National Park had reached Beni, Bongani and Eli who were drinking as usual in the JH ANC Youth League Headquarters on the outskirts of Johannesburg. However, they were not their usual jovial selves as they were in mourning, not only for their South African compatriots, their leader and the second-in-command of their group, but also for the two Chinese businessmen, Feng and Changpu, both of whom they had come to regard as friends.

* * * * *

And so it was that while the tour party had been enjoying their visit to Swaziland (well, for most of the time that is), and were happily looking back on their safari in the Kruger National Park, others were sadly contemplating issues connected with the disaster that had so recently happened in that same park.

What would be the future for a breakaway branch of the ANC Youth League without a leader?

What would happen to Feng and Changpu's families?

How was Joseph faring in hospital?

How would the helicopter crash be explained?

So many questions without answers.

* * * * *

One member of the tour party was slightly anxious that evening. Amy was worrying about Ted. As a result, she was also asking questions, but not the same ones as the South Africans. Her questions comprised:

Was Ted all right? Had the police questioned him?

Would he be implicated in what had happened in the Kruger National Park?

* * * * *

Having now got into the routine of getting up early, packing and putting their suitcases outside their rooms before going to the dining room for breakfast, all the tour party had eaten their first meal of the day, assembled in Reception and were on their bus by 8.00 am ready for departure on Day 6 of their South African experience.

However, unusually, the discussions among the tourists had already begun before Brian had a chance to start on his commentary for the day. It was then that everybody learnt about Anne and Cathy's horrendous experiences with cockroaches which nobody else could quite equal. Jerry and Dawn told the story of their ants. Even Meryl and Peter explained that they had had to change rooms because their original one was not clean. The only person not to have requested a room change had been Amy, but even she had not been happy with her room. She said that she hadn't felt safe because the patio door did not lock properly.

"You should have asked for a different room," everyone advised her, all of them being well aware of how Amy was always flashing around large amounts of money in clear plastic bags making it so obvious that she had a lot of cash just waiting to be stolen. Combined with the fact that she was already vulnerable being a woman travelling alone, the whole tour party were actually amazed that she had not been targeted already.

Brian apologised for all the problems they had experienced and explained that in future the company were proposing to use a new hotel positioned high in the hills above the dam they had seen the previous day, but it was not ready yet. He then added,

"There is a problem with ants because the farmers are killing the aardvarks (we call them baby hyenas). They think they are destroying the crops, but it is the aardvarks who eat the ants and now we have plagues of ants."

It was Peter's turn to sit next to the driver that day as they drove off with the low-lying mist not stopping them from spotting signs containing peculiarly interesting statements such as,

'Kae Kae Butchery at the Kae Kae already operating'.

Then Brian announced,

"It will take us two hours to get to the border. We will be passing the fourth largest dam in South Africa. The Gessini Dam was built to prevent floods because as much as ten inches of rain can fall in half a day up at Gessini. Now the famous South African tiger fish can be found there."

"After crossing the border, we will continue to Zululand, home to one of the most famous tribes of Africa. A short time later we will arrive at the Ghost Mountain Inn, which is your next overnight stop. Then this afternoon, you will transfer to another bus and a different guide for a visit to the Pongola Nature Reserve (in Zulu it is called uPhongolo Nature Reserve) and a cruise on Lake Jozini. Your guide will take you on a scenic drive along the Lebombo Mountain Range from where there are wonderful views over the water and across the valley below, and you will be able to experience the local Zulu communities."

Gradually the mist cleared, and the tour party were once again able to see beautiful views of Swaziland, while Brian provided them with more snippets of information such as,

"Ladies visit South Africa for face lifts, and many people come for heart and eye operations because it is so much cheaper than Europe."

Then he proudly told the story of Christian Barnard, the first surgeon to perform a heart transplant.

As they went through a market town, he added that in Swaziland unemployment was only 28% which was much lower than in the rest of South Africa.

On crossing a small river with a Big Band Branch on the bend, Brian announced,

"Sugar cane is planted every four years and three crops can be obtained from each plant. The fields are burnt to get rid of the snakes, but this does not harm the sugar cane. Soil with high clay content is good for sugar cane."

He then changed the subject completely and said,

"South Africans were asked to design their new flag, but they liked the interim flag so much that it ultimately became the new national flag. The colours are very symbolic: black represents the struggle for equality, the yellow area symbolises gold, green stands for agriculture and crops, red is for the blood that was shed, blue signifies water, and white stands for a pure future."

"Orange is a colour which is detested by Africans because it is the colour associated with apartheid. That is why the Orange Free State has been renamed the Free State."

"The flat top thorn tree that you can now see all around, is the logo for the National Party, and it is known as the umbrella tree."

At that point, Peter shouted, "Ostrich behind the fence",

and everyone quickly turned in the direction he was pointing as this was the first ostrich they had seen on this trip.

Then Brian described their surroundings.

"On the left you can see the Lebombo Mountain Range that was the former boundary between countries. Ghost Mountain is part of that range and was so called because it houses a cave that was previously a sacred burial place and is now said to be bewitched."

As they passed some traditional huts, Peter shouted again,

"A woman walking along balancing a Singer Sewing Machine on her head."

On this occasion, it was impossible for the tour party not to laugh as they observed such an amazing sight.

Eventually they reached the border where sisal (agave) trees were growing on both sides of the road throughout the towns of Lapladusa on the Swazi side and Golela on the other side of the border.

Dan negotiated his way through another crazy road system until he found a space for the Mega Bus in amongst hundreds of haphazardly parked lorries.

However, this border station was different. Unlike the wooden hut they had encountered on entering Swaziland, it comprised a newly built, contemporary building with air conditioning, automatic doors and modern counters faced with glass. Nevertheless, once again the members of the tour party had to take their places in queues, and on reaching the officials sitting at the desks, they had to have their passports examined and stamped before they returned to the bus.

* * * * *

CHAPTER 10

'The Pongola Nature Reserve'

As they drove across the border, Brian explained,

"We are now entering the province of Maputaland in northern KwaZulu-Natal. KwaZulu-Natal is the most densely populated area in South Africa. With the states of Zululand and Natal having been combined, eleven million people now live in this province."

"As KwaZulu means 'The Place of the People of Heaven' and 'Natal' being 'Christmas' or 'The Birth of Christ', I would now like to welcome you to 'The Place of the People of Heaven and Christmas'. Pietermaritzburg is the capital of this region, but Durban (originally named Port Natal) is home for the majority of people."

Travelling through the Pongola Game Reserve, they crossed the Pongola River and saw trees covered in magnificent blooms including red flowers on the Weeping Farmer's Bean Tree and an assortment of flowering wisteria, where Brian stated,

"This is an area of prolific bird life, as well as wild game such as giraffe, rhino, wildebeest, kudu, impala, nyala, burchell and mountain zebras, buffalo and elephant. In the shallow lake there are many hippos and crocodiles, and a lot of fishing takes place there."

Almost as soon as he finished speaking they rounded a bend in the road and there was a beautiful view of a lake with a range of mountains behind it. Then as they crossed the Mkuze River, Brian pointed out the magnificent Ghost Mountain in the distance – shaped like the top of an ice-cream cone with a cloud above.

Fever trees covered in yellow flowers lined the road to the Ghost Mountain Inn, and just as they saw a spectacular Jacaranda tree in flower, they arrived at their hotel. It was 10.50 am, and as Brian had foretold, the journey had not taken long. Regardless of this, the group were all glad to alight from the bus and enjoy the cool mountain air.

On entering the Ghost Mountain Inn, they were shown into a central courtyard where a magnificent cold buffet had been laid out especially for them.

All the members of the tour party tucked in as though they had not eaten anything previously that day. The Manager came over to welcome them and she was complimented on providing such a delightful repast. Then in answer to a query, she explained that the bright yellow birds flying around were weaverbirds, who were peculiar in that it was the responsibility of the male to build the nest. The female would approve it. If she did not like it, she would peck at it until it fell down.

The tour party thanked her for providing this information, and continued to watch the activities of the yellow birds with interest.

* * * * *

Early that same morning Ted had met the Lt Col of Police outside the local hospital, as arranged.

As they made their way up in the lift to the floor on which Joseph's room was located, Lt Col Du Plessis explained the progress they had made so far with questioning him and that a policeman was standing guard outside his room. He added that when Joseph had regained consciousness, he had said that he had lost his memory and had no knowledge of how he had come to be in the Kruger National Park. The police, however, were finding this hard to believe and Du Plessis hoped that Ted would manage to talk some sense into the young man.

They were just getting out of the lift when a smartly dressed man pushed past them, obviously very eager to get in. Ted only caught a brief glimpse, but at the back of his mind he thought that he recognised him.

"Perhaps it will come back to me," he said to himself, "but now it is more important to prepare myself for meeting Joseph."

Suddenly, Lt Col Du Plessis let out a shout,

"Where's the man on the door?"

Ted looked down the corridor in the direction towards which the Lt Col was running, and saw an empty chair outside one of the rooms. He then quickly caught up with the policeman just after he had entered that room.

There was a figure lying prone on the bed, surrounded by various pieces of equipment from which the tubes had been disconnected; these were now in a tangled mess on the floor. The patient's face was covered by a pillow, which the Lt Col quickly removed.

"Get help," he shouted, but Ted had already realised that action was necessary and was pressing every call button he could find before he went out into the corridor and added his voice to the commotion.

Very quickly, various medics arrived in the room, and went into their practised routines. They tried their utmost to revive Joseph, but it was too late. They pronounced him dead at 09.26 am that day.

The senior officer vented his exasperation on a young Constable who he recognised just as he and Ted were leaving Joseph's room. The young man was strolling along the corridor as if he did not have a care in the world, carrying a cardboard carton of coffee, which he hastily threw into a nearby bin when he saw his superior approaching.

"Where the hell have you been?" the Lt Col asked angrily.

"I, I, I" the Constable stuttered and gulped, before he managed to say,

"I received a message that you wanted to see me in Reception so I went down, but you weren't there."

"You idiot," his boss continued to chastise the young man. "Your instructions were to stay here at all times, until your replacement arrived."

"But, but . . ." the man was still stuttering.

"There are no buts," Du Plessis continued. "Get back to the police station. I'll deal with you later."

The young man scuttled away immediately, without a backward glance.

"Now we've lost our only witness to what actually happened in the Kruger National Park," the Lt Col confided as he and Ted made their way out of the hospital.

But even though Ted obviously knew that this statement was incorrect and that there were two other witnesses (himself and Amy), he said nothing.

"I'll have to break the news that he's died to Joseph's wife. How am I going to explain that even though her husband was making a good recovery the last time we spoke, he's now dead?"

Ted realised that Du Plessis was not expecting him to answer his last question, but he did want to help and therefore suggested,

"Would you like me to come with you to see Joseph's wife? I do know Sabatha Ntombela quite well."

"By all means," agreed Du Plessis with a slight sense of relief. "You might be able to assist."

* * * * *

After lunch, all the members of the tour party went to their rooms to freshen up before embarking on their afternoon excursion despite the fact that their guide, Mary, had introduced herself when they arrived and was waiting for them

Dawn and Jerry were the first to appear back in Reception, and they browsed in the souvenir shop until the rest of the tour party arrived. While Dawn was quite happily looking at the delightful South African baby clothes that would be ideal for their grand-daughter, Jerry bought a local newspaper and sat in the Reception area reading it.

Eventually, Dawn purchased a small outfit with "Safari Queen" emblazoned across its front, and went in search of Jerry.

On seeing her approach, he exclaimed,

"There's something interesting on the front page. Listen to this," as he went on to quote,

"Poachers in Kruger National Park meet their Death in a Helicopter Crash?"

He then provided a précis of the article:

"The report says that forensic experts who are still looking into the crash landing of a helicopter in a secluded area of the Kruger National Park on Tuesday evening, have got no further in their investigations despite the fact that the man found unconscious at the scene is recovering in hospital. Apparently, he has 'lost his memory'. He is going to be charged with trespass while investigations continue into whether or not this was an attempt to obtain rhino horns. In total, five people lost their lives on that fateful trip – according to the flight plan the pilot was accompanied by four passengers, and investigations are taking place into their identity."

"That must have happened the evening after we left the park on Tuesday," Jerry surmised before continuing reading from the article,

"Some will say that the accident was poetic justice as it's believed that the party were intent on killing rhino to make money by selling their horns. In fact, the spot where the helicopter crashed was very near the site where a large group of rhinos, including several youngsters, had been seen earlier that day."

"Perhaps it is justice," Jerry concluded.

What neither he nor Dawn had realised was that while Jerry had been talking, Amy had arrived and was standing nearby. She had overheard what Jerry had been saying, and although she had suddenly come over very cold, she calmly asked if she could read the report.

"Sure," said Jerry as he handed over the newspaper.

Both Dawn and Jerry were then surprised when Amy not only read the front cover of the newspaper, but also quickly scanned through every single page before returning it, saying brusquely,

"Nothing more in there."

As she walked away, Dawn remarked,

"Did you see her face? She looked quite grey, almost as if she'd seen a ghost."

"Don't be silly," Jerry replied. "You're getting carried away because we're staying at Ghost Mountain Inn. She's probably just concerned about the rhinos. You know how enthusiastic she was about preservation when we were in the Kruger."

Soon everyone was assembled, and ready to climb aboard Mary's land rover. It was suggested that once again Amy should sit in the front next to the driver, and soon she and Mary were getting on really well together.

"Like a house on fire," the British would say.

As they drove towards the entrance to The Pongola Nature Reserve, Dawn borrowed Jerry's newspaper and discovered the Zululand Roll of Dishonour.

"Listen," she said to Jerry. "This method of shaming people must act as a good deterrent. There's a list here giving the names of those sentenced this month in Richards Bay District Court. Some of the crimes listed are what you would expect, ie robbery, theft, assault with intent to commit grievous bodily harm, but some of the other charges are more peculiar: for instance, negligent loss of a firearm, negligent discharge of a firearm, housebreaking with intent to commit a crime unknown to the State, possession of dagga . . . Isn't that a drug?"

Jerry confirmed this as he looked over at the Zululand newspaper, and read about the sentences imposed.

"Perhaps we should have something similar in the UK," he suggested.

As they drove through sugar cane plantations, taking regular diversions off the main track to avoid the lorries transporting the crop and the dust they created, Mary explained,

"Our first stop will be Lake Jozini which winds its way down from the Lebombo Mountains above us. The lake is used by anglers who delight in catching the tiger fish, known as the "Striped Water Dog". This is a freshwater fish, which is indigenous to rivers and lakes in many parts of the African continent. The fish is an excellent fighter with its strong jaws and very sharp teeth. There are fishing competitions on this lake in September and October, because it takes a skilful angler to catch these fish. However, they almost always fish from a boat because of the dangers of hippos and crocodiles lurking near the banks."

"We will take a boat cruise on the lake ourselves because it is a watering hole for many animals. You might see hippo, elephant, buffalo and crocodile from the boat."

"Lake Jozini is part of the Pongola Nature Reserve which lies on the northern and eastern banks of the Pongolapoort Dam. The dam was built in 1970 to stem the flow of the Pongola River and to irrigate the region's sugarcane plantations. Approximately 17,000 hectares were flooded,

and a section of the original reserve was declared a nature conservation area in 1979."

"Just to explain some of the history of this area. It was originally declared a nature reserve in 1894 by the then President, Paul Kruger. At that time large herds of elephant, antelope, zebra, rhino, buffalo and giraffe were roaming the African savannah, together with lions and other big cats. However, during the Boer War the farmers took the land over and killed most of the game in the erroneous belief that this would eradicate the Tsetse fly, the carrier of sleeping-sickness."

"Now we once again have game living in the park where there is acacia bushland sloping down towards the lake."

"When we get off the boat we will take a drive up into the Lebombo Mountain Range where you will see some wild animals as well as traditional Zulu dwellings."

Mary had timed her introduction well as just as she finished speaking they turned off onto a steep dirt track leading down to the lake.

As the group got down from the land rover, it was obvious that the crew were ready and waiting for them as they stood lined up alongside a boat moored at the jetty. The boat was fitted out with rows of seats accessed via a central aisle, and all the members of the tour party eagerly took up good viewing positions. The weather was not favourable for those sitting in an open-sided boat however, with drizzling rain and a chilly wind blowing across the lake. Everyone buttoned up their kagoules, or jackets, and those with hoods put them up. Then they all gladly accepted the blankets that were distributed after the anchor had been raised and they started to 'putt-putt' across the lake to a point on the far side where Mary had spotted a group of elephants that she thought were sleeping. It was hard to tell, however, as they were standing up as usual and were in a close group with little space between them, but definitely none were moving. Mary further explained that there were probably baby elephants in the middle of the group and that was the way they were protected from predators.

"We can stay here for a while and see if they come down to drink," she suggested.

Then the loud noise of an outboard motor disturbed the peace and quiet, and Mary angrily looked in the direction of a small boat working its way speedily towards them. The men in the boat did not cut their engine until they were much nearer to the shore than the tourist craft, and when they did so, they set about casting fishing lines.

The noise had also upset the elephants who were now walking in different directions while they surveyed what the fishermen were up to.

"I hope this doesn't mean the elephants will go back into the bush," Mary complained. "How I would like to give those fishermen a piece of my mind. They think they own the lake."

However, the fishermen did not stay for long, possibly because they were receiving bad vibes from all the tourists looking at them angrily, or perhaps it was just because the fish weren't biting. Whatever the reason, they soon reeled in their lines, and with a lot more loud engine noise, they roared off across the lake.

The elephants watched them go and then to the joy of the tourists, they approached the water's edge.

There were three baby elephants in the herd, which the adults made sure were always surrounded and protected when the games commenced, with elephants taking water into their trunks and spraying their companions.

The tourists watched entranced as these large creatures played in the water, took long drinks and then moved back towards the shore where they split up into three groups, the first of which moved off in single file up the hillside.

Then Mary suggested that the boat move to another location on the lake where she believed hippos would be found and there, sure enough, with their heads just above the water, the tourists spotted them.

"We can't go in too close," explained Mary, "or they'll just move away. You'll be able to see better with binoculars."

Binoculars were then distributed so that everyone aboard was able to get a better view of the hippos watching them as they were being watched.

"I wonder who is being entertained here," Jerry observed, "them or us?"

After another circuit of the lake, with no sightings of crocodiles, it was time to return to the jetty. Everybody confirmed that they had really enjoyed the cruise, and it was only Brian who had had two bad experiences while on board. On both occasions this was when he tried to use the toilet facilities. On opening the door of a small room situated at the back of the boat, he was greeted with loud screams as there was already a lady in residence.

The tourists thanked the crew as they got off the boat. Then it was back aboard the landrover to travel up into the mountains.

Once they were on the main road again, Mary explained that the Lebombo or Lubombo mountain range was approximately 500 miles (800 km) long with the average height being 1,970 feet (600 metres) above sea level.

Then she added,

"The name of this mountain range comes from a Zulu word, Ubombo, which means 'big nose'. These volcanic rock mountains form the boundary between the province of KwaZulu-Natal in South Africa and Swaziland, between Swaziland and Mozambique, and between Mozambique and the South African provinces of Mpumalanga and Limpopo. The vegetation is mostly tropical forest and in the narrow ravines, the tree growth is dense. Otherwise, as you will see, it is mainly savannah."

As they turned off the main road once more and started up a dirt track leading upwards, she said,

"I'm known as Grandma Mary hereabouts because when I bring tourists this way, I sometimes bring presents for the children. I don't bring presents on every visit though because they would come to expect it. Today, we have pencils to distribute."

She then handed a quantity of pencils to Amy and asked her to hand them to the children.

"The children will come out to get them. You'll see," she added mysteriously.

Sure enough when they stopped, a group of excited children emerged from some houses and ran down the hillside to the four-wheel drive vehicle where they were given a pencil each.

This same situation occurred every time they came to a halt as they travelled along the road. It was almost as if a bush telegraph was functioning. When the vehicle stopped, children seemed to cascade out of the houses. At first, there were just small groups of delightful children; occasionally just one, but more often, twos and threes. Then as they journeyed further into the bush, the numbers increased. With more children tumbling out of houses and running towards the vehicle, it was like a waterfall of children. At one point, there were at least twenty children around the car, pushing and shoving to get pencils for themselves as well as their brothers and sisters.

"That's enough," said Mary sternly at one point. "There are plenty. You don't have to fight to get them. Just one each mind."

This calmed the children down, and each time the vehicle drove off they left behind groups of children clutching pencils, smiling and waving happily.

Higher up, there were quiet locations where Mary stopped to point out places of interest.

On the first occasion, it was to invite those in the bus to climb up the hillside for a spectacular view of the lake. Only Jerry and Peter accepted the offer as the climb was very steep and over rough ground. Mary offered to lead the way, but they were both determined to go it alone, and strode off.

Unfortunately, thorn bushes blocked the route they had chosen, and every time they moved amongst them, they became attached to thorns. The remainder of the party laughed as they watched their antics as they tried to avoid getting scratched to death. When they reached the top, however, they decided to follow Mary back down the path she pointed out so that they did not get attacked again.

The next stop was to take pictures of a Nguni cow; a beautiful white and light brown creature with a docile look in its eye.

"That's a traditional South African cow," Mary explained. "It's not all skin and bone like the Brahmans."

It was after this that they passed children carrying containers full of water weighing at least 25 kgs on their heads, and groups of traditional houses spaced out along the long winding track.

Then Mary stopped alongside a plot of land with a derelict house and a garden of grave stones.

"That's the burial place of some ancestors," she explained. "It is a tradition to allow the house to fall down after the parents or grandparents die."

It was cold, wet and windy during their journey up the mountainside, but it was a wonderful experience to see the traditional dwelling places of the Zulu people and so many beautiful children.

Just when everyone had begun to think that the rough dirt track was going on and on forever, and Dawn was worrying that they would have to drive back along it and contend with all the potholes again, they went round a bend and suddenly they were on the main road once more.

Within minutes they arrived back at their hotel, surprised to find that it was only 5.30 pm after what had been a very full afternoon.

Once again, Dawn had done a tally of animals seen which totalled 5 nyala, 3 impala, 2 warthogs, 6 hippos and between 30 and 40 elephants.

* * * * *

By this time, Ted was back home in his cottage on the outskirts of the Kruger National Park.

Du Plessis had been right about the problems that they would encounter during their meeting with Sabatha Ntombela, and even now Ted was sadly thinking about the injustice of it all. Poor Sabatha, her only crime had been to fall in love and marry Joseph, a weak man who had been easily led by others promising him wealth.

When they had reached the tumbledown hut where the couple had lived with their children, it was obvious that they were poor, but it surprised Ted that it was Sabatha who answered the knock on the door. Where were the relatives who would normally be supporting her in times of trouble?

Sabatha had looked directly into the eyes of Du Plessis before suddenly remembering her manners and inviting them in. She was very obviously pregnant, and balanced a small child, not more than a year old, on one hip. Two other small children clung to her skirt, making it difficult for her to move.

Then she had recognised Ted and greeted him warmly.

"I'm sorry," she'd said. "I don't have anything to offer you to drink."

"That's all right," Ted had replied, and then on an impulse he had taken her in his arms and hugged her.

Sabatha had broken free in surprise, saying

"What's the matter?"

As it was now Du Plessis' turn to speak, he had told her, without going into details, that Joseph had died.

The wail that had emitted from Sabatha's throat had been loud enough to be heard in the next village, and she would have fallen to the floor but for the fact that Ted caught her and carried her to a chair. By this time the children had started to cry, and the men had stood there, not knowing what to do next.

Then an elderly woman had rushed in.

"Get out, get out," she had screeched in Afrikaans as she hustled the two men out of the door.

Outside, Ted and Du Plessis had looked at each other, but it was left to Ted to speak,

"I think that woman is her grandmother," he had explained, "but I can't understand where the rest of the family is. It's not normal for someone here to be left alone in such circumstances."

"I can explain that," Du Plessis had replied. "Sabatha told me the last time I saw her that she was being shunned because of the crimes Joseph has committed. They are ashamed of him. Even his own parents have disowned him."

"I hope that situation changes now," Ted had added. "With Joseph gone, Sabatha is going to need all the help she can get."

Just at that moment Du Plessis' mobile phone had rung and he had turned aside to answer it. After a short conversation, he turned back to Ted saying,

"I've got to get to Pongola quickly. Do you want a lift somewhere?"

"I left my car at the hospital," Ted had explained. "If you could drop me off there it would be appreciated."

At first, Ted had said nothing as Du Plessis drove at speed to the hospital because he could sense that Du Plessis now had other things on his mind.

However, he had soon realised that this might be the only opportunity he would have to explain his proposal of working undercover in various safari parks in future in order to find out who was supplying information to poachers.

Du Plessis had been surprised at Ted's suggestion, but it was exactly what he wanted to hear. He had replied that he had already been thinking of setting up a team of undercover operatives to work in safari parks for that specific purpose, and he would truly appreciate it if Ted could make a start on recruiting suitable individuals.

With this agreed in principle, it was left that the details could be discussed later.

Du Plessis did thank Ted, though, as he dropped him off, and promised to keep in touch.

However, Ted was right about Du Plessis' thoughts being elsewhere; he had been concentrating on his next appointment.

* * * * *

CHAPTER 11

'Ghost Mountain Inn'

When the tour party walked into the hotel lobby of the Ghost Mountain Inn after their interesting afternoon, the Manager beckoned to Peter and Meryl indicating that she wanted them to join her in her office.

"I wonder what that's all about?" Jerry queried. "I hope it's not another problem with their suitcases."

But little did Jerry know how close he was to the truth.

When Meryl and Peter entered the office, they found the Lt Col they had met previously, sitting there.

Du Plessis got up immediately, and after closing the door behind them, said,

"One of your suitcases has gone."

"You mean it's been stolen," Peter asked.

"Yes, but the men who did it were seen as they broke into your room. They got in via the patio doors from the grounds that go down to the lake, and they made their exit that way as well. It was a close thing. We were worried that if they were allowed sufficient time, they would just take the contents from the false bottom of the suitcase, rather than the suitcase containing the tracking device."

"However, we arranged it so that an undercover policewoman dressed as a maid would go into your room a few minutes after they arrived in order to disturb them. She was supposed to be turning down the beds in that corridor, and she nearly left it too late. They had emptied both suitcases, and had started on opening up the false bottom; bits of which we found on the floor. But when they heard her fiddling with a key trying to get into the room, they just grabbed the case containing what they wanted and made their escape."

As instructed, she reported it as a robbery to the Manager immediately, who reported it to the local police so that it appeared to be a normal robbery. The local police were told to take no action, and were not even aware that my men had taken over their role and ensured nothing was disturbed until forensics moved in. We didn't want the robbers to be aware that anything untoward was happening. But your room is a bit of a mess. You'll need to check if anything else is missing other than the suitcase," Du Plessis explained at length.

As Meryl and Peter had been expecting something like this to happen, they weren't surprised, but they were eager to see their room.

The three of them then made their way to the room in question where there were fingerprint experts at work.

The Lt Col was certainly right about it being a mess. Their clothes and other belongings were strewn all around the room, as if they had been pulled frenziedly from both suitcases, one of which had also been tossed at a mirror that had shattered.

"It's a wonder nobody heard them breaking that mirror," the Lt Col commented. "Also, they must have had some inside information as they knew which was your room and that you were going to be out all afternoon. We're working on that."

As the forensic people started to gather up their equipment, he then asked,

"Do you need any help clearing up?"

"We'll manage with our things, but we'd appreciate it if you could ask the Manager to deal with the broken mirror and fix the lock on the patio door," Peter replied. "We don't want the fuss of having to change rooms."

By this time, the majority of the other members of the tour party were in their rooms, but Amy had stopped off in the souvenir shop. She was just walking along the corridor as the police were leaving Meryl and Peter's room, and hurried over to enquire what was wrong.

Meryl decided to take her into their confidence, and said that their suitcase had been stolen, but she asked Amy not to say anything to the other members of the tour party so as not to ruin their holiday.

Then poor Meryl and Peter were left alone to sort out their belongings as best they could.

"I think we need to get two new suitcases as soon as possible," said Peter. "It might be possible to repair this one, but I think they're jinxed. They'll have to go."

Meryl agreed wholeheartedly with this suggestion.

* * * * *

That evening the tour party experienced another superb buffet at the Ghost Mountain Inn, where several unusual dishes were on offer:

Potato and Bacon Soup
Mussels with Coconut and Lemon Grass
Kudu Sausages (which tasted like beef)
Yellow Potatoes with a red curry sauce
Chicken and Nyala (tasting like tender venison or pink beef) Kebabs
with sweet corn, crispy potatoes and vegetables,
followed by
Chocolate Gateau, Crème Caramel, or Banoffee Tart.

After the meal, Meryl and Peter spent the remainder of the evening with the other members of the group on the end of the jetty, drinking wine as they watched the sun go down over the lake. It was a spectacular sunset with the red and orange glow spreading over the mountains in front of them and being reflected in the lake below.

Meryl and Peter didn't say anything about the state of their room when they'd returned to it, the time they had had to spend sorting it out, or the disappearance of one of their suitcases.

The only unusual occurrence was that Peter made a slight diversion before joining Meryl back in their room afterwards. He visited the Manager's office where, despite the late hour, she was still available. Without any hesitation whatsoever, she agreed to obtain two new suitcases on Peter's behalf. She also would not hear of them being charged to the room as she was truly embarrassed that such an incident had happened in her hotel. She promised that they would be delivered to Meryl and Peter early the next morning.

* * * * *

However, not such a peaceful evening was being experienced elsewhere in Zululand.

The tracking device had worked exceptionally well, and a large number of police officers were positioned outside a building on the outskirts of the town of Pongola where the suitcase was currently located.

As instructed, they were waiting silently in the shadows, with all vehicles hidden out of sight, until their boss arrived. Luckily, no one had left the building since their arrival otherwise they would have had to quietly apprehend them. Also, it was fortunate that the very ordinary-looking tin hut did not have many windows. In fact, the Chinese businessmen would have said that it was strangely similar to the one in the suburbs of Johannesburg.

They did not have long to wait. When Lt Col Pieter Du Plessis' car drew up quietly, all his senior officers gathered round him, Captains and Majors included.

"I don't want anyone currently inside that building to escape," he said. "Make sure you have men positioned outside every door and window, and that when we go inside, some Constables stay outside ready to catch those trying to escape. We don't know how many people are inside so I have ordered plenty of vehicles to take away those captured, but in particular there are going to be a group who are involved with stealing a suitcase. It might be mayhem in there, but I want them specifically identified and caught. Have you got that?"

His officers nodded, and made their way back to their designated positions in order to instruct their men.

Then, on a signal, a squad of armed police officers broke down the main door and entered the building. As forecast, it was mayhem with people running in all directions trying to escape, but the Lt Col had briefed his officers well and people were being handcuffed left, right and centre. Those who tried to get out of side doors and windows were captured, and even those who hid in unexpected places were found. They were all escorted to the waiting vehicles, ready to be transported to the cells that awaited them in the local police station.

Unfortunately, though, there was one person who was not captured. Possibly in the light of future events, it might have been better for him if he had been. If he had spent some time in a police cell, he might have avoided his fate.

Robert Goodnuf Xulu happened to choose to arrive at the exact moment when his supporters were being escorted to the police vans. He saw the activity from a distance and without a second thought he stopped, reversed his car into a field and drove away without anyone spotting him.

* * * * *

The other members of the tour party were surprised when a gentleman joined Meryl and Peter for breakfast the next morning, but it was only Amy who was even close to guessing what he was doing there.

"Well, did you arrest them?" Meryl quietly asked as he sat down at their table.

"We certainly did," Du Plessis replied with a smile. "We found four men in a back room in the process of removing the contents from the bottom of your suitcase."

"And what was in there?" asked Peter.

"In total, the haul amounted to a value equivalent to eight million of your UK pounds, including six hundred thousand South African Rand; a substantial amount of money as far as those who had been ordered to steal it were concerned. In addition, there was a large quantity of Bearer Bonds destined to help a dishonest politician bribe his way into power."

"Really," Meryl and Peter were shocked at the amount of money involved.

"How do you know what the Bearer Bonds were going to be used for?" Peter could not help but continue to question.

"Ah, that's something I can't explain right now," Du Plessis replied mysteriously as he got up and left them.

* * * * *

The story the Lt Col Du Plessis had told Meryl and Peter at breakfast was completely different to the one that appeared in the newspaper the next day, which stated,

> 'Cops crack down on 163 crooks'

> 'Two nights ago, crime prevention operations were carried out on the outskirts of Pongola by the Provincial Taxi Violence Task Team, Officers from the local Police Force and Police Reservists. 163 arrests were made during the operation.

Arrests for serious offences included two for murder, two for attempted murder, two for housebreaking, three for assault, seven for possession of dagga, three for copper theft, five for possession of stolen property, six for theft, two for fraud, one for possession of an unlicensed firearm and one for possession of counterfeit goods.

Liquor related offences were also targeted, as they often form the root causes of crime in the area.

Arrests for liquor related offences included five for those who had previously been observed driving dangerously whilst under the influence of alcohol, 12 for gambling, 33 for drunkenness, and four for selling liquor without a licence.

In addition, 14 people were arrested for being illegal immigrants, and the police recovered large quantities of South African bank notes, liquor, dagga and copper. Several knives were confiscated, along with counterfeit cigarettes, DVDs and CDs. Other recoveries included computer equipment, a firearm and a phone.'

* * * * *

Once again, it was an early start the next day; up at 6.00 am for a 7.00 am breakfast and 8.00 am departure. However, every single member of the party was ready and waiting in Reception when Brian and Dan joined them.

Only Dan noticed that the damaged Samsonite suitcases had disappeared and that two different suitcases had joined those of the rest of the tour party. However, he just put it down to the broken locks, and that tourists had plenty of money to spend so . . .

It was Meryl's turn to sit in front next to Dan who smiled at her as she joined him.

On leaving the hotel, they travelled towards the town of Pongola on the N2, and as they crossed the Mkuze River, Brian started his commentary for Day 7.

"During the next two days you will be covering wars that have taken place in South Africa, visiting battlefields where a specialist guide will explain the dramatic events that took place there, and where you will gain a further insight into the history of this great country."

Brian paused at his point as Dan pulled in at a petrol station on the outskirts of Pongola in order to fill up with petrol and where the tourists noticed a shop with the sign,

'JUNK = Your One Stop Shop'.

As they drove off through the town of Pongola they saw that it was very smart with a large shopping mall, neat houses and blocks of flats. In the surrounding fields, jets of water were being sprayed over the sugar cane, and Brian explained that watering improved the sugar content.

Then he imparted another snippet of information that he had obviously gained from the newspaper he had purchased while they waited for Dan to refuel the bus.

"At animal auctions yesterday the highest price was paid for an animal in South Africa – a buffalo bull sold for 18 million ZAR. That's 1.4 million of your UK pounds at today's exchange rate."

* * * * *

Lt Col Pieter Du Plessis travelled from his breakfast meeting with Meryl and Peter to the Kruger National Park. He was there, ready and waiting to speak to all the Park Rangers when they returned from their morning safari drives shortly after noon.

Standing in front of his audience, he announced,

"I have come here today to provide an update on the situation regarding the recent helicopter crash in the Park and to ask for your assistance."

There were murmurs from the audience, but nobody said anything and so he continued.

"From the information given to Air Traffic Control via the flight plan it was easy to determine the starting point and destination of the helicopter and its pilot. The pilot had even been more helpful in listing the names of the passengers and the purpose of the flight, probably to cover his real purpose which had obviously been to land in the Kruger National Park because flying over the spot where the helicopter crashed would not have been on the direct route to their destination."

Du Plessis paused again to look round at his audience, but again there was no reaction so he added,

"The pilot was Herman Meintjies who operates from an airfield on the outskirts of Johannesburg and two of his passengers were Chinese businessmen. We have been checking up on these two people. We know when they entered the country. There are no records of them visiting the Kruger, and we can't find any information on where they spent their time before the crash, although by that time they would have been in South Africa for three days. Apparently, they had a legitimate purpose for visiting Ladysmith; they had an appointment to meet the Agents for Gammill Long-Arm Quilting Machines whose offices are situated at the Mzansi Zulu Centre, Merrivale, the day after the crash. Would any of you know anything about them?"

Not expecting an answer, Du Plessis continued quite quickly this time,

"No, well now I'll explain where I really do need your help. The other two passengers were listed with false names, but we have been led to believe that they were both Black South Africans. As they are now deceased, it should follow that somebody will report them as being missing, but so far we have nobody reported missing who meets their descriptions. Therefore, if you know of a male Black South African who has not been seen recently, I would appreciate it if you speak to me, or one of my officers."

This time there were further murmurings amongst his audience, but realising that nobody was going to single himself, or herself out, Du Plessis confirmed,

"I'll be available here for the remainder of the afternoon, or you can telephone if you wish to remain anonymous."

He then supplied a telephone number, which he also wrote on a whiteboard in the room. Then he quietly left them to talk amongst themselves.

* * * * *

Ted took the opportunity of speaking to Du Plessis that afternoon. It was his last day working at the Kruger

National Park and he was pleased to learn that Du Plessis had taken his offer seriously.

Du Plessis informed him of where his first assignment would take place and stated that it was hoped he would be able to start work in approximately six days' time. Arrangements had even been made for accommodation for him in the vicinity.

Ted confirmed that he would be available.

Now all he had to do was explain the situation to Amy. He had a proposal to put to her, but what would be her reaction?

Now it was more important than ever than he contact her. He could not put it off any longer.

* * * * *

CHAPTER 12
'Anglo-Zulu War'

As they continued with their tour, Brian provided the tourists with an outline of the history of South Africa.

"You already know (from your visit to the Voortrekker Monument) that the Voortrekkers experienced problems with the Zulus - the Battle of Blood River took place in 1838. However, it was not until 1879 that the Anglo-Zulu War with the 4th King of Zulus, Catcheyo, took place. Later today, you will visit the battlefields of Isandlwana and Rorke – you will probably know from the film 'Zulu' all about the battle at Rorke's Drift."

"However, between the two encounters with the Zulus, some other important events took place with regard to the Voortrekkers. As you know, the Voortrekkers left the Cape Province because they wanted to get away from British rule, in particular the British were trying to put a stop to slavery and the settlers needed their slaves to work on the farms. In 1842 when the British annexed Natal because coal was discovered in the area and they wanted control of the port at Durban, the Voortrekkers who had settled in this area then moved to the Transvaal and the Free State."

While Brian listed some noteworthy dates, the tourists listened politely whilst staring out of the bus windows at the Pongola Valley surrounded by hills covered in short trees; it was now looking less like open savannah and more like a cultivated valley although some areas were obviously game reservations as they were surrounded by electric fences to stop animals getting out and humans getting in.

"1652 – the Dutch East Indian Co founded a shipping station at the Cape of Good Hope. The settlers who then came to this area were mainly Dutch Calvinists, German Protestants and French Huguenot refugees who resented the way they had been treated in Europe. They all spoke a version of Dutch which later became Afrikaans. They had black or coloured servants and relied on slaves to undertake manual labour."

"1806 (during the Napoleonic Wars) – Britain took possession of the colony because of its strategic position, and imposed Imperial rule."

"1835 – 5,000 Boers (mainly poor farmers) plus their servants travelled to the north-east, crossing the Orange and Vaal rivers, in order to settle in the areas that became known as the Transvaal and the Orange Free State."

"1843 – the British created a second colony in South Africa by annexing Natal."

"1852 and 1854 – the British recognised the independent republics of the Transvaal and the Orange Free State. However, in 1877 the British annexed the Transvaal, but then reversed that decision in 1881. So you can see that there was a lot of inconsistency with regard to free republics."

"However, what really influenced events was the discovery of diamonds on the outskirts of the Cape Colony in 1870 (leading to the founding of Rhodesia to the north of the Transvaal) and gold in the Transvaal in 1886, which lead to a Gold Rush."

"People (mainly of British origin) flooded into the Transvaal to mine for gold and these immigrants became known as Uitlanders. There was then a peculiar situation as the majority of the population in the Transvaal were British being ruled by Afrikaans and the majority of the population in the Cape Colony were Afrikaans being ruled by the British. There was a lot of unrest in the Transvaal where the Uitlanders were being encouraged to rise up against the Boers, and atrocities against Uitlander women and children committed by the Boers were being publicised, even though they had not actually occurred."

Jerry interrupted at this point, saying

"Wasn't Cecil Rhodes involved in stirring up the situation? Didn't he mastermind an attack on the Boers in Johannesburg in 1895?"

"Yes, and it failed," Brian replied.

"Cecil Rhodes denied his involvement and blamed it all on Dr Jameson who was sent to Britain to stand trial. However, as a result, Rhodes resigned as Prime Minister of the Cape Colony. He was already a multi-millionaire by this time, and decided to concentrate his activities in Rhodesia."

"1899 – the British Government agreed to intervene in the Transvaal and President Kruger sent a message to Joseph Chamberlain (in charge of the Colonial Office at that time) *on 10 October 1899 asking for certain steps to be taken. When they weren't, the Boers declared war on 12 October 1899."*

"And that's what lead to the Anglo-Boer Wars, which you will be given more information about by the expert guide who will take you to some battlefields tomorrow, but today it is all about the Zulu War."

"During the troubles between the Boers and the Uitlanders, the British colonial officials decided that the independent Zulu Kingdom situated along the Tugela River was a threat to the British colony of Natal. The Anglo-Zulu war began on 11 January 1879. After heavy losses and many battles, the Zulus were ultimately defeated on 4 July 1879 following 5 months, 3 weeks and 2 days of fighting. The consequence was the end of the independent Zulu nation."

While Brian had been providing his potted history of South Africa, the bus had turned off the main road in order to head towards Louwsberg where they passed a macadamia orchard with sheep grazing in amongst the trees and jacaranda trees in flower in the distance – a mantle of purple.

The bus had climbed higher and higher going from a dry parched long grass landscape to short green grass, with spectacular views when one looked back down into the valley below. The sun was now picking out the bald patches of brown earth and circles of white stones where religious services had taken place.

To complete the history lesson, Brian sang the National Anthem of Natal in Afrikaans and then in English. Everyone on the bus clapped in appreciation, before he settled back in his seat for a well-earned rest.

There was a change in the scenery as they entered the area of the Natal Coal Fields where the roads were lined with trees. Then they came to Freheit, which was a centre for agriculture as well as the heart of the coal mining region of Natal. Here they passed a large railway junction, and Brian pointed out that with some trains being over a mile long (that's over 1.6 km), South Africa had the longest trains on earth.

After following the railroad for some time they turned off towards Dundee and Newcastle.

Unexpectedly Brian then joked,

"In South Africa we have a population of approximately 50 million people and over 30 million cell phones. Guess what's replaced the bush telegraph?"

After this Dan had to work his way along a road that was in the process of being built; as a result only one-way traffic was allowed and as they bumped along it was impossible for Brian to speak.

There was then a long drive along roads flanked by flat fields of short tussets of green grass, or longer spikes of dry stubble or corn. Occasionally they saw cattle, but more often it was fields of burnt stubble; there was nothing much else in this wilderness.

As they travelled along, Brian spoke about his background, how his family had arrived in South Africa, his father had worked in the coal mines and learnt Zulu from those working alongside him. When they crossed the Buffalo River where they passed a sign directing people to the site of the Battle of Blood River (1838), he reminded the tour party that 2,000 Zulu warriors had died there turning the river red.

Suddenly they were entering the town of Dundee, passing the Tilana Museum with trains on display in the gardens in front and modern, bright, brick-built bungalows all around; one even had a traditional round house in the garden. Then it was over yet another river before they stopped at traffic lights and passed through a busy shopping street that included a Harrods store, at the end of which they pulled up outside the Royal Hotel Country Inn.

As they entered the lobby they were greeted by their Battlefields Guide who was waiting for them to arrive. He explained that the hotel had provided a packed lunch for them to take to the Orientation Centre at Isandlwana. They were instructed to leave any belongings that they did not need to take with them, in the Reception Area with their suitcases, which would be taken to their rooms.

They were then all hustled outside again where they climbed aboard a small 4x4 minibus; the smallest they had encountered so far on their trip. As Meryl had spent less than half a day in the front seat, she was persuaded to sit next to their new guide, Paul. It was quite cramped in the back with just two rows of seats, each being designed to accommodate three people.

Waving goodbye to Brian and Dan, they were driven to Isandlwana 40 miles (64 km) away.

Nobody spoke as they sped along narrow roads that stretched across the plains. Then they were in a village at the centre of which they pulled in to the car park of what looked like an early schoolhouse.

They were shown into a lecture room where tables and chairs had been pushed aside. While Paul distributed the picnic boxes, the tour party made themselves comfortable on the tables and chairs at one side of the room, ready for the official introduction to the Anglo-Zulu War Battlefields.

Paul began by saying,

"Nine battles actually took place during the Zulu Wars of 1879," and he pointed to a map on the wall as he named them,

"Inyezane, Intombe, Hlobane, Kambula, Eshowe (this was actually a siege), Ulundi, Gingindlovu, Rorke (which you probably already know about) and Isandlwana (the first battlefield that we will visit)."

"The battle at Isandlwana was a victory for the Zulus which stunned everyone; a whole British Battalion being lost in a fight with natives was quite unexpected."

"Facing invasion, Cetshwayo had amassed his warriors (approximately 24,000 men armed with a few guns but mainly with spears) to meet British Battalions fortified with heavy artillery and rifles. But unlike the British, the Zulus knew the terrain well and were able to move around, using the hills to disguise their presence and enable them to strike when least expected. In contrast, the British wore bright red battledress that did not blend into the surrounding countryside, rode horses and moved about in columns (with ox carts carrying supplies), which caused the dust to rise alerting the Zulus of their whereabouts. When we go up into the hills, you'll see what I mean."

"The British troops' progress was slow because there were no roads; they had to travel across hilly scrubland, with oxen that had to be fed and watered regularly. There was heavy rain that caused the rivers to be swollen, and they

had to send out scouting parties to set up look out posts on the hills around to ensure that they were not ambushed."

Again, Paul pointed to the map indicating the routes that the columns had taken.

He concluded by saying,

"A particular fact that you might find of interest, especially those of you who are travelling on to Cape Town, is that after the defeat at Ulundi, Cetshwayo (the Zulu Chief) was captured in August 1879 and imprisoned on Robben Island."

After a quick look round the Museum, the tour party got back on the bus to visit the site of the Battle of Isandlwana.

When Paul stopped, the tour party got out to see a field full of white cairns backed by a flat-topped hill shaped like a crouching lion.

"Each of the cairns marks a British grave," Paul explained, "and it could be that several soldiers were buried together."

"The British Forces consisted of three columns; one went into the north of Zululand, one into the south, and the Centre Column crossed the Tugela River at Rorke's Drift. Leaving a company of the 2nd Battalion of the 24th Foot (comprising approximately 100 men) there as a base for the column, they headed to Isandlwana Hill where they camped on the lower slopes."

Then he indicated the slopes in front of them.

"The next day a mounted reconnaissance unit was sent out, but they encountered Zulus and a fight ensured. The Commander of the Centre Column, Chelmsford, received intelligence about the attack and decided to advance against the Zulus in order to bring about a battle. Just the 1st Battalion of the 24th Foot were left behind at the encampment which was not well protected as the majority of the men were engineers with little fighting experience. By the time Chelmsford reached the reconnaissance unit, the Zulus had disappeared."

"Several mistakes were made with orders to reinforce the camp being ignored, and with commanders whose duty it was to do so preferring to go up into the hills to attack the Zulus there where they were overwhelmed. The camp was

attacked by a 'horn' of the Zulu Army with the majority of the British soldiers who remained there being killed. However, a few managed to escape and tried to make their way to Rorke's Drift, but they were cut off by the Zulus who forced them into the hills where they were hunted down and met their death."

"Fifty-two British Officers and eight hundred and six non-commissioned ranks were killed, and at 2.29 pm that day the Battlefield of Isandlwana was plunged into darkness by a total eclipse of the sun – a fitting end to such a terrible situation."

Then, it was on to Rorke's Drift, a twenty-mile (32 km) journey along bumpy dirt track roads, during which Jerry remarked,

"I don't how our friends, Don and Molly, managed to walk between these two battlefields, and then Don waded across the river pushing Molly on a raft. I certainly would not like to do it."

Dawn agreed.

When they arrived at Rorke's Drift, the scenery was quite different. Here there was a scattering of small homesteads spaced out in amongst fields where lambs, goats and cows were happily munching away on rich green grass.

First of all, Paul led them across to the back of a group of buildings backed by a hill, where there was a cenotaph and a walled, well-kept graveyard with memorial stones listing the names of the soldiers who had lost their lives during the Battle of Rorke's Drift.

He then asked everyone to gather round while he began his commentary,

"Originally, there was a Trading Post here run by a man named Rorke which is how this place came to get its name. The location being at the crossing point of the river meant that travellers passed this way. Later it became a Mission, and then it was requisitioned by the British Army as a base camp with that building over there being the hospital."

"You will probably know from the film 'Zulu' about how the men escaped from the hospital by breaking their way through from one end of the building to the other while being pursued by Zulus who had set fire to the thatched roof. Of course, what stands there now is a replica."

"During the heroic defence of this place many men lost their lives and 11 VCs were awarded."

* * * * *

At that moment Amy's mobile telephone rang.

"Sorry," she apologised. "I have to take this. It will be a call from home."

Amy moved well away from the group, making sure that she was not overheard when she said,

"What is it, Ted? Is there a problem?"

"No," Ted replied. "I just wanted to tell you that I went to see the man I knocked out in the Kruger."

"Are you mad," Amy said more loudly than she meant to, and then whispered, "Why did you do that? Won't that look suspicious?"

"No, it's okay," Ted tried to comfort her. "All the Rangers have been talking about him. He was recognised. They knew him from when he worked here as a Ranger; in fact, I trained him. It was reasonable that I went to see him, and I needed to find out what was going on. Anyway, perhaps we can meet tomorrow, and I'll tell you all about it."

After such a long speech for Ted, he was quite breathless and then he became worried when Amy remained silent for some time. However, it was just because she was thinking before she replied,

"I'm already bored with battlefields," she said. "I don't fancy another day tomorrow trekking round the sites. Can you take me out for the day?"

"Yes, of course," Ted was finding it hard to disguise his delight. "It's my last day today. Meeting you tomorrow would be great. Can I collect you from your hotel?"

They discussed times and a pick-up point just down the road from the hotel, before Amy said good-bye, and returned to the group who were about to move on.

* * * * *

While Amy was taking her call, the rest of the group had inspected the gravestones and noticed that some of the names did relate to those portrayed as being killed in the film 'Zulu'.

"The setting's not at all like the film though," Jerry remarked quietly to Dawn. "It was filmed in a wide open area with hills in the background, not nestling at the bottom of a hill."

"It's also much more built up now," Dawn laughed, "with all these little farms around. I'm also sure the whole community benefits from tourists visiting such a famous site."

Then Amy joined them again.

"Everything okay at home?" Jerry asked.

"Yes, that was my daughter just letting me know how she was getting on looking after my husband," Amy lied.

"I thought you had a carer looking after your husband," Jerry forever the inquisitive one continued, "and your daughter was at University."

"Oh, she's just come down for a few days," Amy quickly covered up for her mistake. "The carer needs a break."

Paul then indicated that he wanted them to follow him as he walked across the site towards a brick built chapel.

"The buildings are used as a school and chapel now, but here in the grass you will notice rows of stones. These indicate the lines which the British defended, and show how they were forced to move back until the final line is just in front of the chapel."

"Cetshwayo's triumph at Isandlwana was what actually led to his downfall. He didn't bother to send a great army to capture this outpost. He was over-confident. With such small numbers of soldiers billeted here, he thought success would be easy, and went back to Ulundi leaving his followers to carry out the slaughter without his guidance."

"And he was very nearly correct in his assumption that the soldiers would be beaten as they were down to their last ammunition when the Zulus noticed a column of soldiers approaching."

"The Zulus panicked at this point, thinking it was a large army, or the ghosts of the men killed at Isandlwana. But it was only the men Chelmsford had sent on to Rorke after having returned to Isandlwana with depleted forces to be surprised by the carnage that had taken place there."

Paul then pointed,

"Isandlwana is over there, and Chelmsford could see smoke rising from the location of Rorke's Drift which is why he sent men to assist them. However, even after Isandlwana, and the near disaster at Rorke's Drift, he was still confident of success."

"The British forces learnt a lot from these two battles, and it served them well in the forthcoming encounters. They were not going to leave base camps so poorly defended in future, and rush into fights with Zulus on unknown terrain. They would strike at the heart of the Zulu Nation using military strategies to ensure they achieved the right outcome."

Then the tour party were left to their own devices, strolling around the site, visiting the gift shop and small museum before they returned to the 4x4 for a rough, bumpy ride back to the Royal Hotel Country Inn, Dundee, for a welcome two-night stay.

The Royal Hotel Country Inn had a certain amount of charm with its dark wood panelling, memorabilia decorating all available spaces on the walls, and 'olde worlde' appearance, but as Dawn remarked,

"It does need some tender loving care."

It was a colonial style hotel where the rooms had been built around a dark, central courtyard. Bathrooms had been added to the rear of each room, probably in the 1950s judging by the style of the fittings. The bedrooms were small and packed with all manner of dark, heavy wood furniture such that it was only just possible to walk around the double bed. It was also extremely cold in Dawn and Jerry's bathroom where there was no heating. This was not helped by the fact that the extractor fan appeared to blow out cold air, and draughts gushed through the gaps under the doors. However, the bed linen was beautiful, crisp and white, and the setting had charisma.

Also, the food was excellent with a three-course meal being included in the cost of the tour on the first night.

That evening Amy got exceptionally drunk, even by her own standards, ordered a three course dinner and ate very little of it, but kept asking for her wine glass to be refilled. At the end of the meal, she staggered to her feet, and on meeting the waitress as she was leaving the dining room, gave her a hug, saying

"This Big Mama is my best friend."

The waitress did not seem at all shocked, and with their arms around each other they left the room together to the astonishment of the rest of the party who just looked on until Jerry broke the silence by saying,

"I wonder if there was more to that telephone call than Amy is admitting?"

This made the rest of the party turn to look at him in surprise.

"Do you know something we don't?" Peter asked.

It was then that an exchange of the stories Amy had told each member of the group took place.

"I feel really sorry for her," said Anne, "she can't have had much of a life looking after an invalid husband all the time, no children to help her and not much money coming in."

"She told us she had two children," Jerry clarified, "one at University and another disabled child in care. In fact, the phone call today was from the one at University."

"She's also not poor," Peter added. "She told us she inherited a lot of money which is how she pays for travelling around the world. She's been everywhere."

"We've been paying for bottles of wine to share," Cathy was stunned, "thinking she could not afford it."

And so it continued, with the couples exchanging the details they had been told only to find that a lot of the accounts Amy had provided about her life were contrary to what she had told other people.

When they eventually decided to retire to bed that evening everyone was confused, and was asking themselves questions such as,

"When had Amy actually been telling the truth?"

However, it was only Jerry who put it quite bluntly as he said to himself,

"Amy obviously lives in a fantasy world."

* * * * *

CHAPTER 13
'Anglo-Boer War'

The next day, again after a superb breakfast, it was on with the walking boots in preparation for a 7.30 am departure from the hotel and another day exploring battlefields.

However, when the tour party assembled in the hotel lobby, there was no sign of Amy. This was pointed out to Brian before they all boarded the small 4x4 vehicle that was to take them out again with Paul.

"Amy's not feeling well," Brian announced. "She's going to spend the day in the hotel."

There was a smatter of muttering amongst the group after this announcement and comments could be heard suggesting possible reasons for this – perhaps she had too much to drink last night and was hanging over, or as battlefields were not really of interest yesterday, perhaps today would be boring for her. Nevertheless, no one came close to guessing the real reason for Amy's absence.

Once again, Amy was not feeling ill at all, but was planning to meet Ted. She just wanted to make sure that nobody saw her that morning and so she was staying in her room until the tour party had left. She watched from the window of her hotel room as the bus drove off. Then she slipped downstairs, walked past the reception desk and out of the hotel without anyone seeing her. Ted was waiting for her at the next road junction, as arranged. He's so reliable and handsome with it, she thought to herself as she climbed into his car.

He drove out of the town, up into the surrounding mountains from where the views were spectacular, and when they found a suitable spot, he pointed out the hills that had seen so much military action in the past. To Amy, he made it so much more interesting than anything the guide had told them the previous day and she listened, enthralled. They talked for hours about South Africa. He told her about his love for the country, and she could only agree that she found it all absolutely wonderful too.

Eventually, it was her turn to tell him more about herself, and she found it so easy to tell him the truth about her life in England. He seemed to understand her predicament and did not criticise. In fact, he became more loving, and 'out of the blue' he asked her to become his wife.

However, before she could say yes or no, he wanted her to consider what he had decided to do in future.

She was puzzled, but not for long. Ted handed her a copy of the Zululand Observer, open at the page from which Jerry had read the article entitled 'Double Rhino Kill' and pointed to the bottom of the same page. The article (again attributed to Dave Savides) stated,

'Project Rhino to be launched'

'KZN's leading conservation agencies are joining forces in an attempt to combat the escalating poaching of White and Black rhinos.

'Project Rhino' will be officially launched . . . at iMfolozi-Hluhluwe Game Park, where a Memorandum of Agreement will be signed by the founding members. They include . . .

'The need to pool resources and co-ordinate rhino conservation interventions have resulted in fast-tracking KwaZulu-Natal's leading conservation agencies in joining forces,' said a spokesperson for the project.

This association of like-minded organisations allows for co-ordination of rhino conservation interventions aimed at eliminating rhino poaching and securing the rhino populations in KZN.

The members of Project Rhino also recognise that the work in conserving and protecting rhinos from poaching is symbolic of the threat faced by all wildlife, and will benefit from actions taken by Project Rhino.

Project Rhino has been fully endorsed by . . . one of the world's foremost conservationists and co-founder of the Magqubu Ntombela Trust.

Project Rhino has identified the following key intervention areas – increased intelligence (information gathering), surveillance, ranger competence (training), communication sharing and improving public awareness and education.'

When Amy had finished reading, Ted said,

"I have decided to forget about retirement. After our experiences at the Kruger National Park and recognising that an ex-ranger was involved, I'm going to get involved with trying to stop the illegal trade which is threatening endangered species in South Africa."

"Go on," Amy whispered.

"I've already contacted the Lt Col in charge of the local Organised Crime Investigation Unit, and suggested that I work undercover for them. After all, who's going to suspect an old timer like me? He's agreed that it might be a way of finding the 'inside people' – those who are giving information on where certain herds can be found. I'm intending to work as a trainer of Rangers at various national parks (which could be situated anywhere in South Africa) just for three to four months at a time. I know most Rangers are dedicated, but there are others who might be doing it for money, especially when such large amounts can be earned. You have to realise that South Africa has many poor people, and it is difficult for them to see why they can't have what others have – after all they see rich tourists all the time. You can't blame them for being jealous, but at the same time, I feel it is really important that we protect our wild life."

"I agree," Amy said with a lot more certainty in her voice now.

"Will you join me then," asked Ted. "Will you become my wife and travel round South Africa with me? You might have to change a bit so that you are less noticeable. After all, we don't want anyone questioning why an old codger like me has a beautiful blond wife."

"I could dye my hair," Amy stated as she laughed at his compliment.

"You might need to dress differently as well; possibly in not such outstanding colours. Then you could mix with the other wives, find out who has money problems, or who is expecting to receive large sums of money. A bit underhand, I know, but absolutely necessary."

"Oh, I agree, I agree," said Amy. "I would love to become your wife, and undertake such an important role. Nothing would please me more. Dressing down won't be a problem."

"That's settled then," Ted smiled. "I know exactly where we can get married quietly, no questions asked, and in that way you change your surname legally. The records they keep at this place will be illegible anyway and no one will be able to trace you in future. Is that what you want?"

"Oh, yes," Amy was now in the mood to agree to anything, anything to get her away from her old life and the problems she might encounter in the future as a result of it.

"Now," Ted went on more seriously, "we need to do this very carefully. You should carry on with the tour exactly as you planned until I have everything in place, and then you can disappear."

"I can't wait," said Amy happily, "but please take me away as soon as possible."

Then she remembered,

"You haven't told me what happened when you visited that man in hospital."

"That's what really started me thinking," said Ted as he went on to recount how Joseph had died in mysterious circumstances.

"There are certainly bigger issues involved in the current outbreaks of rhino killings than we realise. It's not just a few locals trying to make money. It's bigger than that. I now realise who it was I saw rushing away from the hospital after Joseph was killed - a dangerous man who wants to become a celebrated politician. I need to find out exactly what's going on."

* * * * *

Paul was ready and waiting for the tour party outside the hotel that morning, standing talking to another young man who he introduced as a trainee guide who would be joining them.

It was Jerry's turn to sit in the front seat that day, but seeing that there would be two guides, he offered to sit in the back as there would be a spare seat with Amy not joining them.

"No," the trainee guide replied, "you can sit up front. I'll follow behind in my own car and then I won't have to come back here afterwards."

So it was that they all took up their seats in the bus and Paul drove off after first making sure that he had sufficient picnic lunches for them all.

As they travelled he explained that the first stop would be at a Museum in Ladysmith Town Centre before they went on to Wagon Hill and Spioenkop.

Ladysmith was a very busy town even at that early hour in the morning, but Paul eventually found a parking space in a car park near the back of the Siege Museum and the tour party followed him down alleyways to make their way to the entrance.

Once inside, they gathered round Paul while he provided a commentary,

"I understand Brian has given you some idea of the events that led up to the Boer War and you know about Dr Jameson's failed raid on Johannesburg on 29 December 1895. Well, that made the Boers realise that they needed to be well armed in order to fight a war with the British and Kruger took steps to ensure that they were; he ordered rifles and artillery to make certain that he would be able to mobilise an army of 25,000 men from the Transvaal and 15,000 from the Orange Free State. This army proved to be four times the size of the British Army in those two states alone as well as being the largest in the entire sub-continent."

"Britain, on the other hand, despatched just 15,000 troops to Natal under the command of Lieutenant General George White who was 64 years old at that time, was suffering with a leg injury and had little experience of South Africa."

"When the Boers advanced into Natal with 21,000 men, White deployed his forces around Ladysmith and Dundee where the battles of Talana Hill and Elandslaagte took place. The Boers then surrounded Ladysmith. When the British forces tried to capture the Boer artillery during the Battle of Ladysmith, they were driven back into the town

and 1,200 men were killed, wounded or captured. The town was then besieged for 118 days from 30 October 1899 to 28 February 1900. The first relief attempt was defeated at the Battle of Colenso and the Boers first tried to storm the town on the 5 January 1900. However, by that time, the Boers were suffering from lack of food, many of the fighters had gone home, and they failed to break through."

"To the south of Ladysmith, the British formed a line of defence. This was on Wagon Hill (or Platrand) which is where our next stop will be."

Then the party were left to explore the Museum and the large guns mounted on display outside.

While they stood waiting for Paul at the front of the Museum, Jerry noticed a café advertising itself as the 'Chirpy Chick where Price is King'. They were offering 'Bunnie Baps' for sale and Jerry asked the trainee guide what these were.

"Oh, that's a piece of bread with curried chicken inside," he replied knowingly.

Their next stop was actually at a petrol station, and while Paul filled up with fuel, the tour party watched a man pumping up his tyres by passing the hose over three other cars.

Then they travelled through land that was signposted as being part of Ladysmith Military Base. Certain areas were surrounded with barbed wire and fences. In fact, Paul had to stop the 4x4 and open gates to get in.

"All those defences don't stop the goats, though," Jerry laughed as he saw a herd of goats scramble in under the fence. "The defences might be good at keeping people out, but you can't stop the animals."

Then they got out of the bus to walk to the top of Wagon Hill where there was a look out station at Wagon Point from which you could view the whole length of Wagon Ridge.

"As you can see," said Paul, "this is an ideal strategic position with views down onto Ladysmith and all around. The Crow's Nest is where the King's Royal Rifles were positioned, and the redoubts are where the Manchester Regiment set up what was known as Caesar's Camp on the Platrand."

At that moment two warthogs broke out of the nearby bush and ran off making everyone jump. Then as they followed him along the edge of the ridge, Paul continued,

"The Boers attempted to attack this position on two occasions. Once they tried to sneak up at night, but they carried weapons that clanked noisily as they scaled the side of the hill and dogs came with them, so that even though it was dark, the British were forewarned of their approach. On the second occasion, they reached positions where British soldiers were dug in. One hundred and seventy-five British soldiers were killed and two hundred and forty-nine wounded, with 52 dead Boers left in British trenches. Then it rained (luckily for the British) and the Boers withdrew."

"Finally, General Buller broke through the Boer defences surrounding Ladysmith and the relief column rode into the town on 28 February 1900. Both sides had suffered from malnutrition and disease, in addition to heavy losses from the fighting. As a consequence, not only are there monuments here commemorating the British War Dead, but a memorial has now also been built for the Boers."

With that the tour party walked over to the Boer Memorial – a modern edifice with names inscribed on the walls.

"Four VCs were awarded after the siege, three of them to men who fought on Wagon Hill," Paul added as they walked back to the 4x4 by way of the British Memorial.

"Now we know why all the hills and mountains have flat tops," it was Peter's turn to joke and try to lighten the mood, "so that they make good strategic battle positions".

When they reached the vehicle, Paul commented,

"There's just one more interesting fact that may be of interest. At the beginning of the conflict around Ladysmith, the leaders of both sides agreed that a neutral hospital be utilised. Intombi Military Hospital was 5 kilometres outside Ladysmith and one train a day transported the wounded there. Initially set up with 100 beds, this soon increased to 1,900. Eventually, the hospital treated a total of 10,673 casualties from the armed forces on both sides."

Then the party were driven on to Spioenkop where picnic lunches were distributed and they were advised to rest on the rocks to enjoy their food and drink because a long trek awaited them.

When the tour party followed Paul along a steep, rough, dirt track up the hill, he pointed out that there would have been no trees up there during the Boer War.

Eventually, somewhat out of breath, they reached the top and were grateful to rest on some other rocks while Paul explained,

"The Battle of Spion Kop (Spion meaning spy and kop being hill) was fought over just two days, 23 and 24 January 1900, when General Buller's forces were trying to reach Ladysmith."

"General Buller had already suffered that defeat (mentioned previously) at the Battle of Colenso, and had decided to attempt a two-pronged attack on the Boer's defensive line which was stopping them from reaching Ladysmith some 24 miles (38 km) away."

"Spion Kop was the highest hill in the area and as it was positioned in the centre of the Boer's lines, he felt it would be helpful if the British commanded this strategic position."

"During the night of the 23rd, under cover of darkness and fog, a company of approximately 1,000 soldiers and some sappers scaled the hill and surprised the small contingent of Boers who were billeted there. The sappers then dug a trench on what was thought to be the top of the hill, but the next morning they discovered Boer positions on higher ground on three sides of them; they had built on a false summit. The Boers shot down on them and many British soldiers died in the trench, with others being mown down later as the Boers attacked."

"Meanwhile, battles were taking place elsewhere because both sides wanted to hold, or capture, the advantageous positions on the surrounding hills (kops), but there was disarray in both camps with orders not being followed and lack of communication."

"By the time the Boers realised they had regained Spion Kop, they were too weak to follow up their success and allowed the British to retreat across the Tugela River."

Paul then took the tour party on a circular route across the top of the hillside via memorials consisting of crosses indicating where soldiers had been buried and asterisks representing those who had died there but been buried elsewhere.

The blackened, burnt grass was crispy to walk on and there was a chill in the air when they eventually reached the position of the flawed British trench, which was now a communal grave surrounded by a low, white wall and covered with white stones.

Before Paul left the tour party in that location, he asked Jerry to crouch down below the far wall of the trench and then told the others to move to the other side of the plateau. From there it was easy to see Jerry even though he was crouching behind a wall because although it appeared to be a flat plateau on top of the hill, it wasn't. This proved how easy it must have been for the Boers to look down on the British soldiers huddled in the trench.

After walking around the memorials listing the names of soldiers who had fallen on 24 January 1900, the tour party made their way back down the hill from where they could view the Spioenkop, until they found Paul waiting alone by the 4x4; the trainee guide having driven off in his own car.

On their way back to Ladysmith and Harrismith, they passed an AstroTurf football pitch that had been completely destroyed, ripped to shreds, leading Paul to explain,

"The Astroturf was donated to the village by a benefactor, but you know all about the local's views on communal grazing land in South Africa. From the hill above, a farmer spotted what he thought to be green grass and brought his goats down to feed off it. Now there's nothing left."

Then as they drove through Ladysmith, which was crowded with people and cars, he had to add,

"Ladysmith is one of the towns in South Africa where old and new cultures meet. There are large supermarkets and shops, but also stalls on the pavements selling everything imaginable. In fact, sixty-four hairdressers have been counted just on one stretch of road in Ladysmith – they are in those little huts."

Now that the tourists realised what they were looking at, they inspected the huts more carefully and realised that it was possible to see people having their hair cut, or styled, in virtually every hut they passed. In fact, on one corner, the hairdresser was also selling car tyres.

It was an exhausted tour party that eventually reached their hotel rooms late that afternoon where some of them actually managed a short nap before dinner.

* * * * *

While Ted and Amy had been enjoying their picnic and the tourists had been exploring battlefields, Robert Goodnuf Xulu (or RGX as his followers had named him) had decided to visit the JH ANC Youth League Headquarters on the outskirts of Johannesburg in order to give them a piece of his mind. He wanted to remind them all that because of their inefficiency he had been involved in a lot of extra work, but he was not prepared for the reception he was about to receive.

On arriving in the building early that afternoon he gathered all his supporters around him to deliver his speech, but on this occasion it was not the usual rousing speech that he gave. He was complaining. He complained about their inefficiency, saying that as they had not been able to undertake the simple task of stealing a suitcase, others had had to undertake that role in Zululand.

Then he said that it was their fault that the helicopter had crashed in the Kruger National Park.

"How can that be our fault?" bravely asked Beni, one of the men who had acted as a guide for the Chinese businessmen. "We had nothing to do with the helicopter crash."

"You were the ones who employed the pilot, Herman Meintjies, and Joseph Ntombela was one of you. It must have been one or the other of them who was responsible, and now we will not have the income from the rhino horns to go towards our cause."

Now it was Bongani's turn to bravely interrupt.

"We are sad that our leaders, Rocky and Thembinkosi died in the helicopter, together with our friends, Feng and Changpu, the Chinese businessmen, but it was definitely not our fault," he repeated.

"Never mind about the Chinese businessmen," RGX interrupted him rudely, "They would have had to die anyway. Do you think we would have let them take away the rhino horns and make a profit out of them for themselves. No, all the profits from South African animals stay in South Africa."

These words shocked many of those present who had not realised that murder would be involved in furthering the cause.

"And what about Joseph? Have you heard how he is?" one of audience asked.

"Joseph is no more," RGX replied. "He did not do his job well, and therefore, I had to deal with him in exactly the same way as I will deal with others who cross me."

"You mean he's dead," someone quietly whispered the words, but RGX heard well enough.

"Of course, he's dead," he stated angrily. "He had to die because he could have given us away."

This was just too much for Beni to bear. What right had RGX to talk to them in this way as though they were worth nothing? Joseph had a wife and children. How could this man kill him without a second thought?

Before anyone could stop him, Beni walked towards RGX, pushing him backwards as he yelled at him,

"You are not fighting for a better future for the Black South African people. You do not care for anyone but yourself. You just want to become a famous politician."

Too late, RGX suddenly realised that he had got himself into a situation he could not handle. These people were supposed to be his followers, his disciples. They were meant to do everything he asked without question. They were not supposed to act with such aggression towards him. However, it was only aggression that he could now see in the faces of the men around him. Nobody moved forward to help him, and Beni continued to push him while shouting further harsh words, words that were lost on 'the great RGX' as he was beginning to panic.

He was their leader and he deserved respect. Yet when he commanded it, and he tried to shout out orders now asking for them to stop this man, he was ignored.

Everyone of them just stood there in silence as if stunned, but even in the silent atmosphere, they appeared to be encouraging their fellow countryman in his exhibition of anger.

And Beni was angry. He was extremely angry. He was seeing red, seeing RGX for what he really was for the first time. The sorrow he had felt for those who had lost their lives in the helicopter crash, and now for his friend, Joseph, had changed into rage, and he was not able to stop pushing, shoving and shouting at this man who was the cause of it all.

With each push, RGX was losing his balance more and more. He staggered and tried to right himself, but it was no use as the pushing continued until finally he felt himself toppling backwards.

His last thoughts were why? Why hadn't he brought some of his more loyal supporters with him to save him from these savages? There must still be some who had not been captured by the police. Then his head cracked loudly as it hit the corner of the snooker table, and he crumpled and fell to the floor with blood pouring from his skull.

He was unconscious, and the whole group of people in that room just stood there and watched him bleed to death. Nobody attempted to help him. In fact, nobody moved at all. Even Beni was now stunned into silence.

It was only when a latecomer opened the main door with a crash, and on rushing into the room, asked what was going on, that the silence was broken.

Then someone went up to RGX and confirmed that he was dead.

"What do we do with his body?" Bongani asked.

"Let's feed him to the lions in the Kruger National Park," Beni replied. "I think that would be what Joseph would want."

* * * * *

That evening, the tour party were surprised to find it was a very quiet Amy who joined them for dinner.

In answer to enquiries about her health, she only muttered,

"Feeling much better now."

However, even though she ordered a three-course meal, she ate even less than she had the previous evening, and appeared to be lost in her own thoughts, not joining in the conversations about their experiences that day. She continued to drink well, of course, but did not make a fuss when the "Big Mama" suggested that perhaps she'd feel better if she had an early night.

But there was a self-satisfied smile on her face as she wished them all "Good Night".

* * * * *

CHAPTER 14
'Return to Jo'burg'

It was Anne's turn to sit in the front of the bus next to Dan on the final day of their tour of the northern region of South Africa, and Brian spoke to her quietly before she climbed aboard.

"I have a surprise for you," he said. "I have arranged for Naomi Cebekhulu to meet you at a shopping mall on the outskirts of Johannesburg where we will stop for lunch."

"Oh, how wonderful," she gasped. "I was too afraid to ask if you had any news, in case it was bad. I knew I could trust you to let me know, but I was so worried. Thank you so much."

There was not even time for her to pass on the good news to Cathy as everybody was aboard the bus ready to set off on Day 9 of their South African experience.

It was actually a later departure than normal that morning as the coach did not leave the hotel until 9.00 am, and then there was a short stop at a mall so that Meryl and Peter could visit a shop to buy straps for their new suitcases that everybody had remarked upon when the bus was being loaded. Brian had been assured that the local mall would be open, even though it was a Sunday, but it was closed. Therefore, they were behind schedule when the tour party began following the Drakensburg Route via Laing's Nek Pass in order to get back to Johannesburg.

As they drove along, Brian informed them of other tours on offer such as one in the Kalahari Desert where it was possible to see even more animals in the wild, as well as trips to Zimbabwe, and he told of the successes in Botswana.

He also pointed out that approximately 20,000 murders occurred each year in South Africa. As it was a tribal custom to extract vengeance, most of the murders and rapes were committed by members of the family or local community. Then he went on to say,

"The South African Brewery is the second biggest in the world. The Eastern Cape farmers are very heavy drinkers and can hire hit squads for a fee. In the Afrikaans' culture,

it often happens that a man will kill his wife and children. Firearms have to have a licence, be kept in a locked case and inspections are carried out every five years. There was a drive to reduce the number of firearms. However, only one percent are registered; the rest are illegal and are readily available on the black market."

"The majority of fatal accidents on the roads involve taxis and buses; around 10,000 people die on the roads each year. So the statistics for mortalities in South Africa are high."

This distressing news was imparted as they travelled through beautiful grasslands with lovely views such as when they looked down on the Chelmsford Dam with mist over the hills in the background.

It was proving to be a lovely warm and sunny day, with not a cloud in the beautiful blue sky, when Brian pointed to a Longtailed Widow (a beautiful black bird with flashes of red and white in its plumage) hovering just above the grass, and explained that their tails fell off in winter, but they were now in full plumage which was a sign of summer.

The fields all around were full of lambs as they entered a pretty forested area with a small homestead where they came upon signs stating,

'My Home My Newcastle'

'Blackrock Casino Resort'

"It's so incongruous," said Jerry, "seeing such a monstrous casino in amongst such wonderful countryside."

Then with Mount Mujaba ahead they went through the centre of the small town of Newcastle.

"Bit different to Newcastle in the north of England," Jerry stated as they viewed shops mainly owned by Indians, "More like Bradford, although I don't think you'd find a business named 'Price 'N' Pride' even there."

* * * * *

When Beni arrived at the JH ANC Youth League Headquarters on the outskirts of Johannesburg mid-morning, he found Bongani and Eli looking as tired as he felt.

"Busy night for all of us," he said as he greeted them. "Ten hours' driving takes it out of you. It was lucky that we weren't stopped for a vehicle check."

Then he sat down at the small table where his two friends were looking down miserably into the mugs of beer in front of them.

"A committee meeting's taking place," said Bongani eventually, nodding towards the room at the back of the building where Rocky the Red had first been introduced to the Chinese businessmen.

"We weren't invited to join in. They're talking about damage limitation. If Rocky and Thembinkosi are eventually identified, the police will swarm all over this place. Everybody's been told not to even mention that they're not around any more, but that can't be kept a secret forever. There's been all sorts of ideas: say they've left the country to explain why they're no longer here; say that they worked alone, the Branch were not involved; say we know nothing about their activities – as if the police are going to believe that. They are still deciding what we will be told to say; we will have to wait and see."

"Same as usual then," Beni remarked, "we do the work while others make the decisions."

"Yes," Bongani agreed. "I think they're also making arrangements for us to be accepted back into the mainstream ANC Youth League so that we are politically protected."

"No more crime to raise funds for the party then," added Eli. "I suppose that must be a good thing."

"The best thing is no more exploitation by Robert Goodnuf Xulu," Beni concluded although there was no spirit in his voice as he said this.

"Sabatha Ntombela's expecting twins this time," said Eli, suddenly changing the subject.

"I know," Beni answered, "and she needs help. None of the family are talking to her because of what Joseph was accused of doing."

"They'll come round when the babies are born," it was Bongani's turn to add.

"How's she going to cope in the meantime, though?" Beni expressed his concern and then came up with the answer.

"We need to resurrect the airport scam. That should raise some cash."

The others nodded in agreement, and once again it was Bongani who added,

"We'll need to get the official uniforms out again then."

"Let's get started today," Beni suggested and they all agreed.

"I've just got one errand to run first," Eli said, "I'm taking Thembinkosi's mother to the East Rand Shopping Mall to meet some old friends. Somebody else is taking her home so I'll see you at the airport at lunchtime."

* * * * *

As the tour party crossed the Ncandu River, they saw Asians attending an open-air religious service, and Brian explained about the migration of Indians to South Africa.

He then added that this was a fertile, basalt soil valley because of volcanic action, and the rainfall was high with it being surrounded by the Drakensburg range of mountains.

As they approached Botha's Pass, there were impala on their left and a large tower on their right.

Then Anne who was usually so quiet, shouted,

"Blesbuck crossing with the cows,"

and Brian explained that they were passing through an outstanding cattle farming area where the cattle were taken to feed lots for finishing; as a result some of the best beef in South Africa originated from this region.

He was then interrupted again by Anne, who pointed out,

"Merino sheep in a line"

so that everybody's attention was drawn to the fact that there were now sheep on both sides of the road.

"They look like happy sheep," commented Dawn.

"I don't think the black cattle you can see being rounded up ahead, are so happy," added Jerry. "They're probably on their way to the slaughterhouse."

Then it was through the small town of Memel with a Dutch Reform Church at its centre.

Suddenly, for the first time, Dan joined in the frivolity by shouting,

"African Spa," as the road became extremely bumpy.

"Looks like the termites have started to build in the road," Jerry joked, as it was obvious that there were termite mounds in the grass all around them.

Brian did not understand the joke, however, and just said that termite mounds were good manure for the ground, before adding,

"There are now over 30,000 farmers in the Free State Province."

They passed field after field of scrub grassland and maize stubble where farmers had cut small impressions into the ground, some of which were still full of water and surrounded by birds. The indentations have been made so that they fill up with rainwater during the winter, Brian pointed out.

As they went up a hill, it was Peter's turn to joke,

"They'll be 20,000 Zulus on the other side."

However, all they saw were the grain silos of a famous co-operative on the outskirts of the town of Villiers, before they left the Free State and entered Mpumalanga in the Transvaal.

"Just a bit more information," Brian said as he explained,

"The Vaal River is the second largest river in South Africa. It joins with the Orange River to form the boundary between Namibia and South Africa."

When they stopped at a service station with yet another Wimpy Bar (much more popular in South Africa than McDonald's), there were Periwinkle Trees all around. These were known as yesterday, today and tomorrow trees because they flowered white, purple, and pink in succession.

After crossing the Moddenfontein River, they went through tolls and were pulled over for a police check.

Then they neared Heidelberg with a golf course on the left, a private airfield on the right and Sugar Bush Ridge in the distance.

They crossed the Blesbok River before they went through Boxburgh with nice houses on one side of the road and shanties on the other.

When they could then see the high-rise buildings of Jo'burg and White Waters Ridge ahead, Brian explained,

"At the time the South African currency changed to decimal coinage it was decided to use the word Rand for currency in recognition of the White Waters Ridge (Witwatersrand) upon which Johannesburg was built and where most of South Africa's gold deposits were discovered."

As they neared Johannesburg, the scenery changed dramatically, with no more fields of crops or animals to be seen. Instead, they viewed the Germiston Major Industrial Site with over 2,000 factories.

Continuing on the route signposted for O R Tambo Airport, they turned off at the East Rand Mall, just after a sign stating 'Truck Busters for used and new parts'.

Then before they all got out of the bus Brian announced,

"We've covered approximately 1,200 miles (1,920 km) on this trip. If we'd gone straight to the Kruger and back, it would only have been 514 miles (822 km). We made a few detours to see the sights."

He then laughed and added,

"It is important that you are all back here by 2.30 pm at the latest. Can you check your watches now – it is 12.30 so you have exactly two hours to have a bite to eat and look around. But you definitely need to be here by 2.30 because, although Amy, Dawn and Jerry's flight is not until 6.40 pm, Anne, Cathy, Meryl and Peter's flights are much earlier.

Surprisingly, Amy was first off the bus after this announcement, and she quickly disappeared into the shopping mall carrying her multi-coloured, woven plastic bag that she had purchased at the craft village in Swaziland.

Brian asked Anne and Cathy to go with him, while the others strolled slowly into the Shopping Mall. Dawn and Jerry, in particular, were looking for a nice restaurant where they could celebrate their 40th Wedding Anniversary.

The shopping mall was a maze of shops and fast food outlets situated down many branches off the main artery that twisted and turned as it weaved its way around the complex.

As they walked along, Anne surprised Cathy by explaining that they were going to meet Naomi Cebekhulu and then suddenly there she was, sitting at a table in the restaurant Brian directed them into.

As Naomi rose from her seat, Anne rushed over and then there were hugs all round. Tears were streaming down Naomi and Anne's faces as Brian silently disappeared, and Cathy looked on happily.

"Why did you stop replying to my letters?" Anne asked as they all sat down.

"I couldn't," Naomi replied. "I was too ashamed."

"What do you mean?" Anne was full of questions.

"It was Thembinkosi. He was such a good boy. Then he got involved with a breakaway faction of the ANC Youth League and all he could talk about was ridding South Africa of White people. I couldn't agree with him, but I felt like my family were betraying our friendship," Naomi explained.

"What nonsense," Anne continued. "Nothing can destroy our friendship."

"Now Thembinkosi is dead," Naomi added as her voice nearly broke. "Well, they tell me he's dead, but it's not official yet. I knew it would all end badly."

"My goodness," Anne exclaimed. She was shocked, but she still managed to ask,

"Is there anything we can do?"

"Nobody can do anything," Naomi stated resignedly. "He's left a wife without a husband, and three children without a father. I've lived with them for some years now, ever since I became too old to undertake paid employment. Now his wife will have to find work to support the family, but she is not strong."

"I might be able to help," Anne tried to be positive. "Although my husband's retired, he still has contacts in South Africa. Perhaps he could find her a job."

"Oh, if only that was possible," Naomi doubtfully replied. "She's an intelligent girl. She speaks good English as well as Afrikaans and Zulu. She should have gone to University, but she married my son instead. They started a family straightaway."

Anne agreed to do what she could and that appeared to lift Naomi's spirits. Then a meal was ordered, and they all conversed more happily, with Naomi being so surprised to learn that the daughter who accompanied Anne was Cathy, the baby that she had delivered.

* * * * *

Eventually Dawn and Jerry had found an unusual eating establishment – a Portuguese restaurant with Piri Piri Chicken on the menu!

It was a surprise, however, when although they ordered a glass of wine each, a full bottle arrived on their table with the meal.

"How are we going to manage to drink a whole bottle," Dawn queried. "We don't have much time left because it took us so long to find this place."

Just at that moment, they saw Brian walk by and they called over to him,

"Come and join us in our celebration."

Smiling, he did so and sat down at a small table opposite. When he gestured to the waitress, she brought over an extra wine goblet, and with much clinking of glasses they managed to empty the bottle before he strolled off again to complete his shopping.

* * * * *

Everyone, apart from Amy, was back at the bus by 2.30 pm and Brian took the opportunity to ask Anne about her meeting with Naomi.

"It was so wonderful to see her again," said Anne, "and we're going to keep in touch in future. It's just a pity that we received the news that her son has died. Thank you so much for arranging everything though. How did you do it?"

"I just contacted an old friend who used to live nearby when my home was in Johannesburg. He's a private investigator and he owed me a favour," Brian explained.

As the minutes ticked by Brian started to look agitated.

"Where was Amy?"

The reason Amy had scurried off so quickly when she left the bus was in order to find a quiet place from where she could speak to Ted on her mobile phone. Not taking any notice of the direction in which she went, she had finally found the ideal spot – a café where she could sit in a booth at the back and not be seen by any passers-by.

It was opportune that when his phone rang, Ted had just pulled into a service station to fill up with petrol. He immediately recognised the number displayed and greeted Amy warmly.

Then a long conversation had taken place as he detailed the plans he had made for where they would stay and when he would meet her.

Ted had left his rented accommodation near the Kruger National Park very early that morning and had also travelled to Jo'burg, but only because that was where he would find the junction for the N1 motorway that would take him to Cape Town. It was going to be a long drive, however; it was over 1,052 miles (1,693 km) from the Kruger to Cape Town. He was estimating that it would take him approximately 19 hours and, therefore, he was planning to find a place to stay overnight and complete the journey the next day.

Amy was excited when she left the café, and suddenly noticing the time, she had proceeded hurriedly in the direction from which she thought she had come. Unfortunately, she had soon found that she was absolutely lost. Luckily, however, she remembered she still had Brian's number programmed into her phone, and just when he was about to give Dan directions to take the others to the airport and leave him behind to search for Amy, Brian's phone rang.

"It's Amy," he said with relief in his voice, before asking her to describe exactly where she was. Then he went off to find her.

While they were waiting, Peter suddenly remembered:

"I've got your strap here Jerry," he said, "I'm so sorry. I nearly forgot to return it. We managed to find straps for our new suitcases in the shopping mall. Thank you so much for lending it to us."

When Brian and Amy returned, Dawn did a quick presentation to both Brian and Dan, thanking them for providing such a wonderful tour of South Africa and for looking after them so well. Then it was off to the airport.

* * * * *

Dawn had purchased a copy of The Zululand Observer at the shopping mall, and on the short onward journey to the airport she amused her fellow travellers by reading out extracts from the 'Vacancies' section:

"Qualified Seamstresses wanted for clothing factory in Alton. Good all rounder. No chancers please."

"Client Liaison Officer … must be an energetic people's person and be able to work under pressure."

"Bongiwe seeks full-time, sleep in work. Eng, kids, cook."

It was left to Jerry, however, to read out a more serious article from the Zulu Herald Tribune entitled 'Body found in Kruger National Park'.

> "A body identified as that of Robert Goodnuf Xulu, the well-known leader of the M & P Branch of the ANC Youth League, was discovered yesterday. It was found after Rangers noticed vultures circling an area in the Kruger Park known to be the territory of a large pride of lions. Unusually, the body had only been partly devoured making identification possible, but forensic experts have not yet determined the method of his demise, or how the body came to be in such a location.
>
> Throughout K Z N, Robert Goodnuf Xulu was actively engaged as a political leader known to have aspirations to become a member of the

163

next generation of Ministers in the South African Government. Educated at UNISA, Robert Goodnuf Xulu went on to gain a degree in politics at Oxford University in England and then returned to South Africa as a highly visible presence in the ANC Youth League. His death will be a great loss to this organisation.

Investigations are continuing."

* * * * *

By this time Ted, having filled up with petrol, was sitting in a café within the service station area where he was having a snack before continuing his long drive to Cape Town. Although he was going in the same direction as the tour party, the drive was going to take much longer than their flight, which was why he had started off so early that morning.

His car was loaded up with his personal possessions, and having just finished that long conversation on his mobile phone with Amy, he was reading the same article that Jerry had read out to the tour party.

Having already put a name to the person he had recognised pushing his way into the lift when he had been on his way to visit Joseph, Ted was finding the newspaper report very interesting.

"Could not have happened to a more deserving person." He then laughed to himself as he added, "and even the lions could not stomach him. That must tell people something."

Ted certainly did not believe that the death of Robert Goodnuf Xulu would represent a great loss to the ANC Youth League; in fact, he felt that it might prove advantageous as a new leader could help the future development of South Africa in a more positive way.

He then continued his journey in a much happier frame of mind whilst thinking,

"It's true – what goes around, comes around."

* * * * *

After listening to the article, however, Amy was now not so happy. She was worrying about Ted again.

"Has he made the right decision to get involved in investigating the poaching?" she was asking herself.

She didn't want him risking his life, and a dead body discovered in a safari park was not something she wanted to know about.

At this point, they passed a shanty town, and Amy, who was trying to change the subject, said,

"It's terrible that people still have to live in conditions like that."

To which Brian replied,

"I'm going to hold the microphone near Dan now. He lives in Soweto, and I'm sure he'd like to explain.

"That's right," Dan said. "I live in Soweto and it's a nice place to live. Everyone is friendly, and now we have brick-built houses and good roads. Electricity, water and sewerage services are all there, and because of Nelson Mandela the area has improved tremendously. It is the same with all the established shanty towns – they have all been supplied with electricity, water and sewerage arrangements, not like it was before Mandela."

"However, you have to remember that a lot of the people who live in these shanty towns are migrant workers; they only live there because it is close to where they can find work. They might move on to find work elsewhere, and most of them send their earnings back to their families living in the homelands. That is where they will retire to in their old age, so it could be that they are having nice houses built there."

"Also, inside these corrugated iron huts you might be surprised to find that they have nice furniture, even big televisions and the latest computer equipment. Yes, some people are still poor, but there are now many who are much better off than they were before Mandela."

Then he continued,

"There is a story (probably true) that when the Government supplied bricks to some families - and that is what Mandela's Government did for many communities so that they could improve their homes by putting up brick structures - the people sold the bricks. They probably did not understand what they should do with them, but they knew that by selling the bricks they could raise money to spend on other things. So they did so, and just reinforced their corrugated iron huts so that they could continue to live as they had always done, but they were better off in their own eyes."

When they reached the airport everybody alighted from the bus, collected their luggage and said sad goodbyes to Brian and Dan. Then the tour party, pushing trolleys laden with luggage entered the Departure Hall where more goodbyes took place with hugs and kisses this time, as it felt as though the small group had been together for a lifetime, not just for eight days.

Meryl and Peter were catching a flight to Victoria Falls where they were going to spend a further seven days, and Anne and Cathy would be returning to London, so the four of them made their way to International Departures. That only left Amy to travel to Cape Town with Dawn and Jerry.

Meryl, Peter, Anne and Cathy stayed together as they checked in their luggage (albeit at adjacent desks) and went through security control into the International Departure Lounge. There they found that their gates were at different ends of the room, and so regrettably they also had to split up.

Luckily, Anne and Cathy moved off without a backward glance otherwise they might have been worried when an Immigration Officer approached Meryl and Peter, and asked them to accompany him.

Meryl and Peter looked at each other in surprise, but did as they were told; surely it was not another problem with their suitcases!

They were shown into a small office and there, to their surprise, Lt Col Pieter Du Plessis greeted them with,

"I couldn't allow you to leave the country without letting you know the full story, after all you have been involved."

"Oh, thank you so much," Meryl and Peter said as they enthusiastically shook him by the hand.

"Perhaps we might be able to help you when we return to the UK," Peter suggested, not realising he had sowed a seed of an idea as far as Du Plessis was concerned.

They all then took seats around a desk while Du Plessis explained,

"When we last met, you asked how I knew that the money was going to be used for political purposes. Now I am in a position to tell you. As you know, Bearer Bonds are unregistered investment securities. No records are kept of transactions, or ownership, which is useful for those who wish to remain anonymous, and the person who actually has the bond in his hand is the rightful owner. Therefore, there is no recourse in the event of loss, theft or destruction."

"That's why they were so anxious to get hold of those in our suitcase," Peter could not stop himself from interrupting.

"Yes, that's true," Du Plessis went on, "but I don't think those ordered to undertake the theft knew exactly what they were handling. And those who sent the goods to South Africa made a big mistake."

"What was that?" Peter asked.

"They were so worried that the Bearer Bonds would not reach the person they were destined for, they put some special instructions on the envelope. These stated that the package could only be opened by none other than Robert Goodnuf Xulu."

"Who's that?" Meryl had now found her voice.

"Robert Goodnuf Xulu was a political hopeful who we have been keeping an eye on for sometime. He's been encouraging young Black South Africans to break away from the mainstream ANC Youth League and join him. His radical views could have lead to the destruction of South Africa as we know it."

"He's the one whose body was found in the Kruger National Park," Peter added, suddenly remembering the article that Jerry had read out from his newspaper.

"That's right. We don't know how his body got there, or how he died. We may never find out, but it has brought this matter to a satisfactory conclusion. We were hoping to capture him with his followers, but he got away. The breakaway groups of the ANC Youth League are in complete disarray. Many of their leaders are either in hiding, are dead, or are in prison. Therefore, it is going to be difficult for them to continue their political, and possibly criminal activities. Also, we have seized a lot of their funds, which will go to those in need, not to help individuals gain power that they don't deserve."

"So a fitting ending," Peter concluded, and everyone agreed.

Peter and Meryl then left Jo'burg in a happy frame of mind, ready for their next adventure.

*****

Jerry, Dawn and Amy did not have such a pleasant encounter at the airport.

As they were all travelling to Cape Town, Dan had put all three suitcases on the same trolley that Jerry was pushing along, with Amy and Dawn trailing behind.

When he stopped at the notice board to read the flight information, and announced, "Our flight's not on the board so we can't check in yet," he was overheard by a young man in uniform who informed him,

"Of course you can, Sir. Just follow me."

The young man took over pushing the trolley and now there were three people hurrying behind it as the young man was progressing at speed. He soon stopped, however, near a bank of automatic check-in machines, and instructed Jerry to put in his passport.

As Jerry was quite slow, the man took the passport from him and inserted it, whilst at the same asking the women for their passports.

Even though Dawn was concerned that their passports might disappear, she did as she was told and Amy followed suit. Jerry kept close to the young man, however, and observed what was happening, even becoming involved in choosing their seat numbers.

Afterwards he made sure that all the passports were returned to them, together with the printed out boarding passes, as by this time there were three young men in uniform surrounding them.

"Now we'll deposit your suitcases for you over there," said the older one who had now taken charge, and grabbing the trolley he wheeled it across to a check-in desk. Again, Jerry, Dawn and Amy quickly followed.

The check-in girl did not seem surprised to see the young men helping put the luggage on the conveyor belt, but Jerry was getting annoyed.

"Leave them," he said angrily. "I'll sort the luggage. We're not all together."

At that point some security guards arrived and the young men were asked to leave. Perhaps the check-in girl had signalled to them, or they had just happened to turn up at that point; the tourists were not able to tell. However, they were very pleased to be left alone.

After checking in their luggage, they made their way towards the Departure Lounge, but before they could reach the entrance, the three young men appeared again.

"That will be 150 Rand, Sir," the one in charge stated. "Fifty Rand for assistance with each suitcase."

"I'll deal with this," Jerry stated. "You girls go on ahead through security."

Dawn and Amy did as they were told, but Dawn looked back, worrying about Jerry. She saw that he was following them, whilst at the same time slowly getting out his wallet, and just before he reached the gate, he handed over some money.

"That's 50 Rand," he said. "That's sufficient payment for your help."

And at that point he slipped into the queue behind the two women, and the young men were so shocked that they couldn't stop him.

All they could do was look at each other and move away quickly before the security guards found them again.

"Well, 50 Rand is better than nothing," said Beni.

* * * * *

In the Departure Lounge, the three travellers found some seats and Jerry stayed with their hand luggage while Dawn and Amy went off in different directions to explore the shops.

Dawn returned quite quickly having found some finger puppets and socks both of which depicted lions, monkeys and giraffes.

"They'll be suitable for Isabelle," Dawn laughed and Jerry agreed as he played with the finger puppets.

It was some time afterwards that Amy returned with a glass of wine in her hand, and a carrier bag obviously containing bottles of alcohol.

"I've bought some presents for . . ." Amy hesitated and then continued, "for my husband."

Then their flight, SA367 to Cape Town, was announced, and they made their way to the Departure Gate.

"Amy's drunk again," Jerry whispered to Dawn. "Thank goodness I managed to book her into a seat that's well away from us."

So it was that they had a very peaceful, short flight to Cape Town, and the next time Dawn saw Amy was after they had landed.

Dawn was waiting in the queue for the 'Ladies' when Amy came out of a cubicle.

On seeing Dawn, she shouted loudly, "Hi, did you have a good flight?"

At which point she dropped the carrier bag full of alcohol. There was a crash as glass bottles shattered and liquid started to spread across the tiled floor.

"What shall I do?" Amy wailed.

"Quickly pick up the carrier bag and keep as much inside it as possible. Put it in the sink," Dawn instructed.

Amy did as she was told and then announced, "I'll find someone to clean the floor," before she rushed out of the room.

The next Dawn and Jerry saw of her was by the conveyor belt. The broken bottles were not mentioned, although Dawn had told Jerry about the incident.

However, it was obvious that Amy was not sober, and she was pleased when Jerry offered to get her suitcase off the conveyor belt and put it on the trolley with theirs as she was probably not capable of doing so herself.

* * * * *

CHAPTER 15
'Cape Town'

When Amy, Dawn and Jerry walked into the Arrivals Hall at Cape Town International Airport, their new guide, Ed, greeted them and then escorted them to a Magic Bus parked in an underground car park. He explained that there would only be two other people joining the group, and as it was such a small tour party, he would be their driver as well as their guide.

Then he left them in the bus while he went to collect their new fellow passengers. A short time later he returned with Marie and David who introduced themselves, and everybody settled down ready for the drive into the centre of Cape Town. As they travelled along, the tourists chatted together.

The journey from the airport proved to be only a short one, along nice new motorways and then through crowded side streets, before they turned off into the square containing their hotel, aptly named The Inn on the Square.

When Dawn and Jerry walked into their room, they were delighted to see that it was lovely, modern, bright and clean. They freshened up by having a shower in an enormous shower cubicle and then went down to dine in the hotel restaurant.

But a problem was awaiting them when they reached the hotel lobby. Amy was already in the bar and seeing them get out of the lift, she called them over,

"Join me for a drink before dinner."

Dawn and Jerry could hardly refuse.

While Jerry went over to the bar and ordered two Vodka and Cokes, Dawn sat down with Amy on a soft, low sofa in front of which there was a coffee table where a large glass of gin and tonic resided.

"Just a small pick-me-up before dinner," Amy confided.

Conversation was difficult as it was obvious that Amy had been there for some time, and having already consumed a large quantity of alcohol, she was garrulous. She even joked with the barman at times as though he was an old friend. As usual, Dawn and Jerry hardly managed to get a word in edgeways.

When they had finished their drinks, Jerry announced that they were going into dinner, and Amy quickly asked,

"Mind if I join you."

Dawn mumbled "okay", but Jerry could not even manage to reply. He just gave Dawn a look which said it all; they had fallen into the trap again.

After the waitress had seated them at a table by the window overlooking the Square, and supplied them with menus, Amy said,

"I'll pay for the wine this evening."

Again, Jerry did not say anything, but he was thinking,

"That will be a first."

Dawn and Jerry had already decided that they could not eat much after the plane journey, and told Amy that they were just going to have a main course. Amy, still talking continually, studied both the wine and the meal menus for some time, and when the waitress arrived asked,

"Could I have two starters served together, at the same time as their main course?"

"Of course," the waitress looked surprised, but she took down the order.

Then Amy ordered a bottle of wine.

As requested, Amy's two starters arrived at the same time as her companions' main courses, but they were on separate plates. She tutted at the waitress, and proceeded to scrape the food from one plate onto the other.

Then, as the first bottle of wine was practically empty, she ordered another one.

Dawn and Jerry looked on in surprise. They still had wine in their glasses from the first bottle, and it was unlikely that they would need more.

Amy tucked into her food, still talking all the time and knocking back one glass of wine after another until the second bottle was empty as well.

"Shall I order another?" she asked.

"We don't want any more," Jerry replied. "In fact, we've finished our meal, and I think it's time to get the bill."

Amy had to agree, and loudly called to the waitress, asking for the bill.

Dawn and Jerry could not hide their embarrassment, but Amy did not notice.

When the bill arrived, containing the charge for two bottles of wine, she announced,

"Shall we just split it three ways?"

At which point Jerry could no longer keep calm. This was getting too much. He picked up the bill that had been placed in front of Amy, and quite firmly said,

"No, we'll pay for our meals and wine, and you pay for yours. We had a glass of wine each so we'll say that's half a bottle. I had the trio of venison (warthog, kudu and springbok shank) and Dawn had the rack of lamb ribs. Therefore, our wine plus our main courses, amounts to 450 Rand. I'll put in 500 Rand and that will cover the tip as well."

Jerry then did exactly as he stated and put a 500 Rand note inside the bill folder and handed it back to Amy.

"You pay the balance."

Amy looked stunned, but managed to say,

"Are you sure that's right?"

before expressing her surprise at the total amount.

Jerry was not going to be swayed, and Amy sensed this before digging into her large purple handbag where she found her clear plastic bag full of banknotes. She made a great show of counting these out on the table in full view of everyone, and Dawn and Jerry could only look away in disgust.

Then they happily left the restaurant, but not before Jerry had to help Amy to her feet. Then she held onto his arm as they walked out.

Following along behind, Dawn managed to whisper,

"Thank you," to the waitress and then added, "Will you please pass on our compliments to the chef? That meal was superb."

Amy did suggest going to the bar afterwards, but Jerry managed to persuade her that that was not an option as he guided her into the lift. As their room was on a different floor, they got out of the lift before her, but not until after Jerry had pressed the button for her floor number.

"Do you think she'll be okay finding her room?" Dawn asked.

"She's always managed before," Jerry replied. "It's not our problem."

* * * * *

Amy, being Amy, found her room easily enough and flopped down on the bed. However, despite all the alcohol she had consumed, she found it impossible to sleep that night.

She had been worrying ever since the incident at O R Tambo Airport that might have drawn attention to her. What if the police had stopped her at the airport? She had suddenly thought that it was now over a week since she had left England, and they could be searching for her. With her name being easy to find on the passenger list, an airport would be the ideal place for them to arrest her. It would be a good idea to change her name as soon as possible.

Then she started thinking about the arrangements she had made to meet Ted. There was nothing to stop her leaving the hotel earlier than planned. She had her mobile if he needed to contact her, but he'd already told her where they were going to stay.

Therefore, she got herself ready to leave, and waited anxiously until she thought it was a reasonable hour to telephone Reception to ask for her bill to be prepared.

Appearing in Reception very early that morning, dragging her suitcase behind her and carrying her many bags, she explained that she'd received a telephone call from home and had to get to the airport urgently in order to fly back to England.

The Receptionist arranged a taxi for her and she set off without seeing anyone else.

When she reached the airport it was too early for the shops to be open, but she did find a café where she ordered a breakfast that she hardly ate. She just drank several cups of coffee as she sat there.

Then as soon as the shops opened, she bought the items she needed: hair dye, some old-fashioned, suitably dowdy clothes that included a suit that she could wear for a wedding and a large scarf, together with a very large, cheap, canvas suitcase on wheels which was her first purchase.

When she deposited her colourful suitcase inside the cheap, canvas one, the sales assistant looked on in surprise. Seeing this, Amy explained,

"Suitcases get damaged on flights, I'm protecting my best one, and anyway I might need the extra space because I'm going shopping in London."

Hearing this, the male shop assistant thought that sounded quite reasonable, after all women were always shopping.

When she had everything she needed, she went into the 'Ladies' and changed into the dowdy suit. She wrapped the large scarf around her head African-style, thereby hiding her blonde hair, and put her colourful, travelling clothes into the suitcase planning to get rid of them later; she definitely did not want clothes that could be recognised to be found at the airport.

Then she walked out of the terminal, dragging her new suitcase into which she had managed to fit everything apart from her handbag, and found a taxi rank outside the Arrivals Hall.

"Can you take me to the Smithland Self-Catering Apartments, 29 Hans Strydom Street, Parow," she instructed the driver trying to disguise her English accent by sounding slightly Afrikaans, before she sat in the back seat, and allowed him to put her luggage in the boot.

When she reached the apartments situated near the N1 motorway, she checked in stating that she was Ted's wife. Luckily, no one asked her to produce any documents to prove her identity; she was just directed to the rooms that Ted had reserved.

Once there, she got busy changing her appearance quite dramatically. Then she made herself comfortable and waited for Ted to arrive, knowing that it might be some time before he did so.

* * * * *

On going down to breakfast the next day, Jerry and Dawn found that they had to join a queue stretching a long way away from the entrance to the restaurant.

This was a shock, but there was an even greater shock awaiting them when they finally entered the breakfast room; it was crowded with people, mainly native Africans, the majority of whom were dressed in what appeared to be a uniform (white trousers and shirts with blue jackets for the men, red skirts and berets with white blouses and red cravats for the women). The tables were crammed full of both people and food, and there were still crowds swarming around the buffet, everyone piling up their plates with food as they conversed loudly. This was such a contrast to the breakfasts they had experienced previously on this trip that Dawn and Jerry could only watch in amazement.

Eventually they were shown to an empty table, but when they went down to visit the buffet, there was very little left. Dawn found some oranges and pineapple, and followed this with scrambled eggs, preferring not to eat the potato chips (fries), tomatoes, baked beans, stir fry vegetables, or help herself from a tureen of steaming, hot porridge.

However, a waitress did bring a small basket of fresh croissants to their table, which stopped them from making an assessment later that this was the worst breakfast on the trip.

When they returned to their room, they had to decide what to do that morning as originally they had been told their tickets would be for the 9.00 am sailing to Robben Island that day. Regardless of this, on collecting them from Reception, the tickets had turned out to be for the boat departing at 1500 hours. Therefore, there was plenty of time before they needed to get down to the Waterfront.

First of all, they decided to take a swim in the hotel pool on the roof. After this, they went for a stroll in the square where stalls had been set up specifically to sell souvenirs to tourists.

Jerry needed to exchange some travellers' cheques and, therefore, went to the Bureau De Change in one of the roads leading off the square. However, as they had experienced previously in South Africa, changing travellers' cheques was very time-consuming and involved a large amount of unnecessary bureaucracy. To calm him down afterwards, Dawn suggested that they sit outside one of the pavement cafes where they ordered coffee and muffins, and watched the world go by. Then it was back to their room to get ready for their Robben Island Adventure.

* * * * *

Amy was so happy when Ted arrived at the apartment just before noon.

It had been a surprise for Ted when the Receptionist told him that his wife was waiting in their room, but he managed to handle it well. He had not expected Amy to be there as the arrangement was that he would meet her at the Inn on the Square that evening, after she had enjoyed a tour of Cape Town and visited Table Mountain.

The second surprise for Ted was that Amy now had dark brown hair; she had dyed it while she had been waiting for him to arrive.

However, he was so pleased to see her that he just hugged her, and initially he did not even ask why she had changed her plans.

* * * * *

The transport that arrived at the Inn on the Square just before 1.00 pm took Dawn and Jerry down to the Waterfront where they were to board the ferry to Robben Island. By following the directions they had been given, that Mandela Gateway was near the Clock Tower, they found a building named 'Mandela Gateway', which was not exactly what they were expecting.

"Well, that wasn't there the last time we came to Cape Town," Dawn exclaimed. "I was just expecting to see a jetty where the boats would be moored."

The Mandela Gateway was, in fact, a very modern building, with large glass windows through which it was easy to see that it was absolutely packed, mostly with native Africans dressed in a similar way to those they had met at breakfast. They were queueing on the slopes and stairs in the building that led down to the jetty and singing gospel songs enthusiastically whilst swaying in time to the music.

When Jerry made an enquiry of a waiter who was standing outside watching them, he was told that it was a special day for members of the Pentecostal Church and that when a Bishop had appeared on the boat that had just left the jetty, his followers had all cheered loudly.

As there was still over an hour to go before their three o'clock sailing, Jerry and Dawn decided to take a look round the shops on the Waterfront in the hope that the previous ferry would have departed by the time they returned, and the Mandela Gateway would be less crowded.

However, although it was not quite so crowded when they went back to the building, there were still several queues. There was some confusion as to which queue they should join, but finally they joined the right one; apparently the other queues were for people waiting for a special boat because the one they had been booked on the previous day had been cancelled due to bad weather.

Eventually, Dawn and Jerry boarded a catamaran, found some seats with a good view, and enjoyed the trip across to Robben Island on a calm sea. When they reached Murray Quay, they were directed to get on a coach and it was explained that their guide would be an ex-prisoner on the island.

He actually proved to be a very amusing tour guide, and in addition to imparting a lot of information about the political prisoners, together with how Nelson Mandela and others had eventually 'Walked to Freedom', he had jokes for every nationality on the coach.

For example, when speaking to the Indians, he asked,

"Why can't Indians play football?"

"Because when they get a corner, they open a shop."

For the British, it was,

"The English have watches, the Africans have time."

To the Americans, he said

"Hilary Clinton came to visit, but Bill stayed in the White House."

Then it was a joke for the Dutch,

"In Holland you have to have cheese with every course."

And of course, he could not leave out the Australians,

"Eucalyptus trees are a problem here because they drink water like the Australians drink beer."

Their first stop was at a compound containing a building where Walter Sisulu had been solitarily imprisoned; he had not been allowed to talk to anybody for four years.

The next stop was to look at the gravestones of those who had died from leprosy; originally the island had served as a leper colony.

At the third stop, the guide explained the problems created by the importation of eucalyptus trees, cats and rabbits. Then they passed churches, houses where staff lived, a crypt where Indonesians had worshipped, the Governor's House (now a guest house) before eventually stopping at the beach where Nelson Mandela had collected seaweed.

Next it was on to the Limestone Quarry where prisoners had had to work for at least six hours a day, sometimes in blinding sunshine; as a result of the reflection/glare of the sun on the limestone some inmates had been blinded.

When they stopped by a cannon, it was time for the guide to produce another joke about the Africans having time as he explained that the defence weapons on the island had not been completed until 1947, ie after the Second World War had ended, and then he added,

"When Hilary visited, we asked her to take back a message to George Bush that we don't have any weapons of mass destruction."

During the tour, their guide also explained his role in the movement whose goal was to rid the country of apartheid, and the fact that he had travelled round the world promoting the cause.

Finally, it was on to the prison itself, where another ex-prisoner escorted Dawn, Jerry and their fellow coach passengers. He first pointed out the football pitch and then took them into a room where 60 prisoners had slept; they had access to just three showers and water was only available on three days a week. Then he explained that the prisoners were segregated into Blacks, Coloureds or Asians, and how rations and clothes were allocated. Asian and African political prisons were treated differently - short sleeve shirts and short trousers for Africans and long trousers and long sleeve shirts for the others. There would have been no glass in the barred windows at that time, each prisoner would just have had a mat on the floor and one blanket, and in the winter, it was extremely cold on the island.

When they toured the remainder of the building, Nelson Mandela's cell was pointed out. It was a small room measuring approximately 6 foot square, ie 3.25 square metres. Next they were taken out into the exercise yard where Nelson Mandela had hidden a copy of his book, and prisoners exchanged messages by tossing balls of paper over the walls.

Then Dawn and Jerry walked back to the harbour where they caught the last boat back to the Waterfront.

After another quick walk round the Waterfront where previously they had seen entertainers, they found a minibus style of taxi driven by a man who introduced himself as Saki and provided them with his card. On the drive back to the hotel, he explained how his son had recently been to the UK on a sports tour that had included a visit to Ipswich Town Football Club.

* * * * *

On going down to dinner that evening, Dawn and Jerry met Marie and David in the lobby.

"Have you heard about Amy," Marie exclaimed.

"No, whatever's happened?" Dawn asked thinking that some calamity must have occurred.

"She's disappeared," Marie replied theatrically.

"That's not quite true," David explained. "When we were all supposed to meet this morning for the trip to Table Mountain, she did not appear so Ed asked Reception to telephone her room. He was then given a note from Amy that said she had received a telephone call and because of problems at home, she was catching the earliest flight she could in order to get back to the UK."

"So, she didn't just disappear then," Jerry confirmed.

"No, but it's very peculiar," Marie just had to add. "Yesterday, she was saying that Table Mountain was going to be the highlight of the trip."

"Yes," Dawn had to agree. "When we were discussing with Brian that we wanted to go to Robben Island instead of Table Mountain, she was adamant she did not want to miss going up Table Mountain. In fact, every time it came up in conversation, she repeated herself until we had to say that any changes we made were our personal requirements and they would not affect her."

"Would you like to join us for dinner," David suggested. "Then we can have a chat about all our experiences today."

Everyone agreed that this was a good idea, and they went into the Dining Room together.

They had a very enjoyable meal sharing two bottles of wine and a lot of personal tales.

Marie, without allowing David to interrupt her, told Dawn and Jerry about their day,

"We were so lucky that the weather was good. On Ed's advice, we went up in the cable car to the top of Table Mountain first, before too many tourists got there, and the view was fantastic. Then we visited Kirstenbosch Botanical Gardens on the eastern slopes. It was wonderful. Do you know, it was proclaimed a National Botanical Garden in 1913. Next we went to the Castle of Good Hope (the oldest surviving colonial building in South Africa) and the museums housed there were so interesting. Finally, we walked through the Company

Gardens: there was so much to see – the Houses of Parliament, another Museum, a planetarium, a cathedral, an aviary, a fishpond, a restaurant, a library and the National Gallery. There's even a Synagogue and the Holocaust Centre. But what we liked most of all were the beautiful flowerbeds. Everywhere we went, there were such colourful flowers – the rose garden was spectacular. Then the grande finale! Well, it was a good thing we only had a snack for lunch, because the afternoon tea at the Mount Nelson Hotel was superb. The cakes – Passion Fruit and White Chocolate Cake, Gingerbread and Gianduja Cake, Baked Cheesecake and a Lemon Chiffon that was out of this world."

Finally, Marie stopped as she started to savour the cakes again, each of which she had had a small taste.

"So you won't want much for dinner then," Jerry laughed.

"Oh, that tea was hours ago," Marie came down to earth with a smile. "What about your day?"

Jerry and Dawn then told of their visit to Robben Island.

When they left the restaurant, having shared the bill between them, a sight met them in Reception: two large African ladies were standing at the desk dressed in their night attire, complete with fluffy pink slippers and hair in rollers covered in hairnets.

They were all so startled to see the ladies that they didn't see Ed standing there, until he greeted them.

"I hope you had a nice dinner," he started the conversation, making it obvious that he was anxious to talk as he did not wait for them to reply before continuing.

"I've just had to deal with the problems of Amy's sudden departure. Apparently, she left a lot of clothes behind, and although Reception said she booked a taxi to take her to the airport early this morning, I've checked with the airlines and I can't find out which plane she managed to get on. I'm now wondering if I should be worried about her. I've reported her disappearance to Head Office. Do you know anything about her going home?" he asked Jerry and Dawn.

"We don't know anything at all, but I wouldn't worry," Jerry advised. "I'm sure she can look after herself. The only problem we had was that she regularly got drunk, and there were a lot of occasions when her stories did not quite ring true."

"Oh, well," Ed continued dejectedly. "It's all part of the job. I'll deal with it."

Then he said good night, and walked towards the exit.

"Poor man," said David. "He does sound as if he needs cheering up. Hopefully, he'll be feeling better tomorrow."

At that point the lift arrived, and the four friends made their way up to their rooms, ready for a good night's sleep.

* * * * *

On entering their hotel room, Dawn and Jerry started to discuss Amy.

"Why had she had to return to the UK so quickly?"

"Could it be that her husband was ill?"

Taking into account the lies she had told previously, Dawn was even beginning to wonder if she had really returned to England, or perhaps something else had happened to her.

Jerry, however, was just pleased that she had gone.

* * * * *

CHAPTER 16
'The Cape Peninsula'

Lt Col Pieter Du Plessis was also feeling pleased that evening.

When he had entered his office first thing in the morning, he had found his second-in-command, Major Munro, waiting for him with some good news.

"A call was received last night on that telephone number you gave to the Rangers at the Kruger Park," he had been told.

"It wasn't about the identity of those killed in the helicopter crash, but it was a tip off about the transportation of a consignment of rhino horns. We now know the registration number of the vehicle, the route it's going to take and when."

"That's an interesting development," Du Plessis had replied. "We need to profit by this. It could lead us to those involved in exporting the horns and enable us to stop their activities. We need to plan carefully. When are the horns being transported?"

"Tonight," Major Munro had then stated.

"We'll have to act fast. Set up vehicle checking on that road, but not so that they are forewarned. We also need to make it appear as though they successfully pass the check, but put a tracker device in with the horns so that they can be followed."

"How are we going to do that?" the Major had asked, surprised at how quickly Du Plessis had come up with a plan.

"Send in that female Constable," had been Du Plessis' immediate reply. "The one I reprimanded the other day for using a personal mobile phone while on duty and for having red nail varnish on when in uniform."

Even though the Major could not begin to understand why the female Constable needed to be involved, he had done exactly as requested.

Constable Cila Shaka had walked into Lt Col Du Plessis' office in a state of consternation; was she about to receive another reprimand?

She was surprised, therefore, when Du Plessis had greeted her warmly and asked her to take a seat.

"I have a special assignment for you," he had told her. "It might be a way for you to atone for your previous behaviour."

Then he had explained what he wanted her to do during what would appear to be a routine vehicle check.

When she'd left the Lt Col's office, Major Munro reappeared to ask,

"Why have you chosen her?"

"She's just right," Du Plessis had replied. "She looks and acts like a complete scatterbrain. Nobody would think her capable of doing what I've asked her to do, but I'm hoping she'll prove me wrong."

He had then outlined his plan to his second-in-command, who arranged for a routine vehicle check to be set up on the main Pongola road. It was to be sited just after the road crossed the Mpeti River where the police vehicles would be hidden from view by anyone approaching until they actually reached that spot.

It was a place where vehicle checks had occurred previously so there would be nothing unusual for one to be there that evening, and he made sure that Constable Cila Shaka fully understood her role.

What was unusual though was that on that particular evening Lt Col Du Plessis and Major Munro were going to be present during a routine vehicle check, but they would be hidden from view in an unmarked car parked at the side of the road from where they could watch the proceedings.

Several cars, vans and lorries had been pulled in and checked before the one they were waiting for arrived. When it did it was Constable Cila Shaka who approached the driver asking for documentation, an explanation of where he was travelling to and what he was carrying (all routine questions).

She then asked the driver to open the back of the vehicle so that she could inspect the goods (again a routine request), but the driver had seemed nervous.

He got out, opened the back and had explained that the lid of the crate was nailed down. The Constable had taken a look and then removed a lever from her belt before starting to prise the crate open.

The driver had looked on, unable to say a word, when just at that moment the Constable's mobile phone had rung. She handed the lever to the driver.

"You open it," she had said to him. "I've got to take this call."

The driver had done as he was told, but had made little progress by the time she finished her call, only having made it possible for one corner of the crate to be lifted slightly.

The Constable had looked at him and the crate in a bored way. She tried lifting the corner, and had then said,

"I can't be bothered with any more of this. It's going to ruin my nails. Seal it up again and be on your way."

The driver had looked delighted. Suddenly, he managed to find a hammer and some nails that he used to fix the crate, and he rushed back to sit in the driving seat.

He then just about managed to say "Thank you" to the Constable before driving off.

Du Plessis and Munro had watched him disappear into the distance prior to getting out of the car to have a word with the Constable.

"Did you manage to put in the tracking device?" Du Plessis had asked.

"Yes, Sir," Constable Cila Shaka had replied proudly. "Job completed as planned."

* * * * *

The next day (Day 11 as far as Dawn and Jerry were concerned) proved to be gloriously sunny and warm when they joined Marie and David in Reception after yet another 'bun fight' of a breakfast, or as they learnt later, what David now called 'the assault on the breakfast buffet'.

When Ed arrived, he found them all eager to enjoy a tour of the Cape Peninsula. No mention was made of Amy when they set off towards Simon's Town in their Magic Bus, because they did not want to remind Ed of the problems he had had to deal with the previous day.

As he drove off at 8.30 am, Ed gave them a quick breakdown of their schedule for the day,

"First of all we will explore the Cape Flats, drive around the coast so that you can see various beaches before we reach Simon's Town where you can enjoy a harbour cruise. Then on to Boulders Beach to see the penguins, lunch at the Cape of Good Hope Nature Reserve and then back to Cape Town via Hout Bay."

"Sounds good," said Jerry and the others agreed.

As they travelled out of the Cape Town, they passed some very smart residential districts; Bishops Court and Sand Lake where Ed explained how towns had been laid out during the apartheid period.

"The CBD (Commercial Business District) would be in the centre. This would be surrounded by a 'Whites Only' housing area. Then around this would be the homes of Coloureds and Asians, and on the outer circle, there would be the settlements for Blacks and Chinese."

They soon reached False Bay, and while they stopped to admire the view, Ed told them

"This was named False Bay because many sailors tried to land here incorrectly thinking that it was Cape Bay or Table Bay. The water here is extremely cold, but it is a good place for surfers, seals and sharks. You will see shark watch stations along this coast. If they are displaying a green flag that indicates that it is safe to bathe, black is a sign of poor visibility, red that sharks have been spotted off shore, and white with a black image of a shark means 'get out of the water'. It is whale season here from July to December."

Then it was on via Culpe or Cork Bay to Fish Hoek where Ed explained,

"Property prices here are extremely high. For a 250 square metre, 3-bed home, prices are from 860,000 Rand upwards."

Then somebody shouted 'Whale' and Ed stopped the bus.

At first, they all thought it was a rock, but then it moved giving the tourists the satisfaction of being able to say they had spotted it.

Soon they arrived in Simon's Tour where Ed outlined its history.

"The harbour was built in 1686. Prior to that there was no safe anchorage and ships were not able to obtain insurance from Lloyds. Three hundred Allied War Ships called in here for repairs during World War II, and it is now the headquarters of the South African Navy."

Then they were invited to board a rigid-hull inflatable dinghy whose skipper gave them a guided tour of the harbour where two German War Ships were currently moored.

From the sea, he pointed out places of interest ashore:

- the training base originally built in 1743 as store houses, which was later used as a hospital and accommodation;
- the Methodist Chapel built in 1828;
- the monument on the hill in memory of sailors who lost their lives in WWII;
- Admiralty Estate visited twice by Queen Elizabeth, as well as by Rudyard Kipling and David Livingstone.

Then as they circled the Naval Dockyard with its anti-pirate gun,

- the Roman Rock Lighthouse built in 1861 (the only one built on a rock in South Africa) that was now solar powered and used as a helicopter landing pad,
- Ark Rock, known as Noah's Ark to the locals.

The tourists spotted snorkelers in the water, white-breasted cormorants and many other birds resting on a pipeline being used as a breakwater. A multitude of starfish and mussels resided on the jetty walls, seals regularly surfaced to observe the tourists and amusingly-named yachts were moored in the marina: Daydream, Compromise, Tenacity 2 and No Longer A Dream.

In the Naval Dockyard itself, they could see well-armed naval vessels, and they passed an old submarine S99 now a Museum and a South African Frigate & Cable Restorer now used for accommodation, visited by schoolchildren and maintained by the Museum.

Back ashore, Ed walked with them to Jubilee Square passing such establishments as 'The Salty Sea Dog (for fish and chips)' and Bertha's Restaurant. In the square, he explained,

"Jubilee Square was built in 1935 and the statue is of a Great Dane who lived in the town. The story is that the dog used to travel with the sailors into Cape Town and ensure that when they were drunk they managed to catch the last train back to Simon's Town."

"By the way, the railway line is over 100 years old and was built by Cecil Rhodes."

"The railroad wanted to ban the dog from travelling on the train free of charge so a request was sent to the British Admiralty for him to be enlisted in the Royal Navy. When permission was granted, the Recruiting Officer was supplied with the dog's name 'Nuisance', but he asked for a first name. The reply was 'Just Nuisance' and henceforth he was officially named 'Just Nuisance'. The dog was given a full military funeral when he died after being knocked down by a car."

Then it was on to the South African Naval Museum where they learnt about the expulsion of the Blacks from Simon's Town in 1965.

Their next stop was a complete contrast; Boulders Beach had been turned into a Nature Reserve especially for the preservation of African penguins (now an endangered species with only approximately 1,000 left in the world, mainly around the Cape coast) that nested in the sand dunes all around.

Then it was on to Cape Point, across rugged mountain scenery that was part of the Table Mountain National Park.

They were told that the peak above Cape Point was higher than that above the Cape of Good Hope. There were two lighthouses at Cape Point with the old lighthouse being the one at a higher level. Ed explained that the new lighthouse had been built lower down, closer to sea level, so that ships could see it clearly because foggy conditions occurred at higher levels for more than 900 hours a year.

They had lunch in the Two Oceans Restaurant in the Cape of Good Hope National Park.

Afterwards, they all purchased tickets for a bus that took them further up the hill on a narrow track. Then they climbed a short flight of steps leading to a viewing platform on the top of the hill, at the base of the lighthouse, from where Dawn and Jerry saw two more whales.

When they got back on the Magic Bus, they were taken for a drive around the Cape of Good Hope Nature Reserve (an area of 7,750 hectares that has been a reserve since 1940) where they saw ostrich and eland roaming, and were told that a unique species of fynbos grew.

Next they went down to the Cape of Good Hope (originally named the Cape of Torment), the south-west tip of South Africa, along a coastal road close to the sea where there was a terrific swell that day.

The group, together with Ed, had their picture taken behind the 'Cape of Good Hope' sign just like normal tourists before they drove on to Scarborough – a conservation village.

Then they went past the Slangkop (Snake Head) Lighthouse and through the town of Kommetjie that Ed pointed out was regularly visited by baboons.

At this point, he told the legend of the Chacma Baboons,

"About 1,000 years ago there was a terrible drought in this area and the tribe who lived here (the Khoi) initiated rationing. Stores were put in one hut, which was guarded day and night. Unfortunately, one of the guards succumbed to temptation, but was caught by another guard and taken to the Witch Doctor. The Witch Doctor asked that the warrior's wives and family also be brought forward and then he threw stones on the ground. The warrior and his family were changed into baboons. And to this day, the baboons regularly steal food and water."

The next town they passed was Masiphemele where people were living in tin shacks. Then it was on to Noordhoek and up to Chapman's Peak on a toll road.

Ed explained that the twisting road was often subjected to rock falls, as the sandstone cliffs were susceptible to erosion. To confirm this there was a sign that stated,

'Danger – Use the road at own risk'.

Then on their left there was a beautiful stretch of beach (7 kms long), with Hout Bay at the far end, protected from the wind on three sides by mountain ranges, one of which was Sentinel Rock (on the seaward side).

Ed explained,

"Sentinel Rock recently sold for 10 Million Rand. The town of Hout Bay is a residential area for fishermen, and the statue you will see on the rock shortly, is in memory of the Cape Lion, which is now extinct. It had a very distinctive black mane."

Finally, it was back to Cape Town via famous passes built by Thomas Bain, and then past Sugar Bush Hill, Llandudno (Cape Town's only nudist beach), the Twelve Apostles Hotel & Spa (listed as one of the best hotels in the world), Camps Bay with beautiful homes and rough seas, Brighton Court, Victoria Road with its restaurants and pubs (an ideal place to sit and watch the sunset), Beach Road and Mouille Point Lighthouse (the oldest lighthouse in South Africa), for their last night's stay at the Inn on the Square.

For Dawn and Jerry, it was a quiet, romantic dinner for two that evening after an exhausting day.

* * * * *

Beni, Bongani and Eli carried on with their scam at O R Tambo Airport for three consecutive days before it became obvious that the security staff were getting annoyed with them, and they had to stop.

They had obtained quite a good sum of money by then, however, and they decided to visit Sabatha Ntombela on Tuesday evening after a leisurely drive from Johannesburg to Zululand. With Zululand being their homeland, they would be able to stay with relatives and return to Johannesburg the next day without arousing suspicion.

Sabatha was pleased to see them when they knocked on her door. She was still not receiving many visitors, but her grandmother was now staying with her. She was even more excited when they gave her the money they had collected, and she agreed to spend it on items for the twins that she was expecting.

* * * * *

CHAPTER 17
'The Garden Route'

For the four remaining members of the tour party, the next five days just flew past. Ed was a good guide, providing information and introducing them to excellent restaurants when the meals were not included in the itinerary thus enabling them to sample a wide range of South African cuisine. He was not so full of information as Brian had been, but perhaps that was a good thing. After all, Dawn and Jerry did not want to hear repeats of what they had heard already, and Ed also had to concentrate on driving the Magic Bus, which he did extremely well. However, when they reached places of specific interest, he did provide a good explanation of what they were viewing, and in the meantime, the tourists could sit back, relax and enjoy the surroundings which were so different to what Dawn and Jerry had encountered on the first half of their tour.

Field after field of cultivated land and small homesteads built in the Dutch Colonial style, and pretty, well-maintained towns and villages flew past the windows of the Magic Bus during their tour along the Garden Route.

There was also a lot of mountain scenery and areas that had been designated as national parks, all waiting to be explored.

On leaving Cape Town on Day 12 of their holiday, Dawn and Jerry together with their new companions, Marie and David, travelled with Ed, their guide, to their first stop in Oudtshoorn where they visited the CP Nel Museum in the former Oudtshoorn Boys' High School. There they viewed a special exhibition entitled 'The Ostrich throughout the Ages'. This provided an insight into natural history, together with the historical and cultural influences that had affected the ostrich industry in South Africa. Then it was on to an Ostrich Farm.

However, there was sadness as they passed empty fields and Ed explained,

"This area used to be home to the world's largest ostrich population with a number of specialized ostrich breeding and show farms. These fields around you would have been

filled with ostrich, but many were wiped out as a result of the avian flu virus."

"Not many people abroad would even have considered how the virus could have affected the ostrich," said Jerry, "but it has obviously devastated the ostrich farming industry in his area.

When they reached a show farm, they were introduced to "Suzy the Stripper" and "Jack the Ripper", ostriches who would remain partners for life. Then they were entertained by ostrich races, and given a guided tour of pens containing different breeds of birds in the ostrich family such as emus. That evening Ed took them to a BBQ on another Ostrich Farm where they were able to meet local people.

They stayed for two nights at the Oudtshoorn Inn where, from their bedroom window, they could look down on tortoise strolling around the swimming pool in the hotel garden.

* * * * *

Late in the afternoon of that particular Wednesday, Lt Col Du Plessis received some interesting information.

"Sabatha Ntombela has come into money," Major Munro told him. "She was in Pongola today buying quite a few items for babies, and they were not cheap."

"So somebody is looking after Sabatha," Du Plessis replied. "I wonder who that could be? Can you find about any recent visitors?

"I'll try," Munro confirmed.

* * * * *

The next day the tour group were treated to an entirely different experience. After ascending the Swartberg Pass, they left the Magic Bus for a short mountain walk to the historic 'Ou Tolhuis', which is the base of the H.O.P.E. (Helping Our People and Environment) Foundation. It was there that they learnt how the Foundation created learning opportunities, and were able to sample a freshly baked Melk Tart served hot, straight from the oven.

As he drove along and the tourists viewed the stunning mountain scenery, Ed stopped occasionally to point out spectacular views and to explain,

"The Swartberg Mountains, or Black Mountains in English, comprise the best exposed fold mountain chain in the world with their magnificent geological formations, and some parts are UNESCO World Heritage Sites. The rust colour in amongst the rocks indicates deposits of iron ore."

"The Swartberg Pass runs from Oudtshoorn in the south to Prince Albert in the north. Thomas Bain, who used convict labour, built it between 1881 and 1888. You can still see some of the small huts at the side of the road where the convicts were housed during that time. You can imagine the hard labour involved. The pass opened on 10 January 1888."

Then they went on to the Victorian Room Restaurant in Prince Albert where they enjoyed a traditional Karoo Platter with wine tasting whilst watching veteran cars drive past. Afterwards, the tourists went for a stroll down the main street of this delightful small town where the buildings had been constructed in a variety of styles. There they saw some unusual sculptures produced by Richard John Forbes and his apprentices who had carved the stumps of five 130-year-old Blue Gum Trees into monumental landmarks for the town; the sculptures had been give the name 'The Burghers of Prince Albert'.

When they got back to the Magic Bus, Ed was ready with a commentary,

"Prince Albert benefits from water from the Swartberg Mountains, which enables them to breed the Karoo lamb, grow olives, produce olive oil and a variety of cheeses, all of which are local delicacies. The building styles are Cape Dutch, Karoo and Victorian, and thirteen of the structures have been designated National Monuments."

In the afternoon, they visited the 60 metre high waterfall at Meiringspoort by walking up a steep path and climbing over rocks. When they got to the top there was an impressive view of the waterfall that had previously been hidden from sight in a deep ravine.

Once again, it was Ed who explained,

"All the roads and drifts (that's what we call the fords) around Meiringspoort had to be rebuilt after floods in November 1996. That's when the picnic spots and this visitor centre at the waterfall site were constructed. You may also be interested to learn that Geraniums

(Pelargonium Zonale) originated from this area. You will see them growing wild all around."

Then, on their way back to their hotel, they visited the quaint South African town of De Rust that Ed informed them had received the award 'Best Town in South Africa'.

When they reached the Oudtshoorn Inn in the centre of the town of Oudtshoorn in the region of Little Karoo, Ed explained where they could find a good restaurant before he left the four of them to dine out that evening on another superb repast that included ostrich steak.

The four travellers then benefited from a quiet, relaxing evening where they ate good food and enjoyed interesting conversation.

* * * * *

Unfortunately, it cannot be said that the same circumstances were destined for Ed.

When he got back to his room late that afternoon, there was a message waiting for him; a request to ring his boss.

He did so immediately, and was surprised to learn that the tour company had received a telephone call from the British Police asking for information about Amy's whereabouts. As a result, his boss had repeated Ed's check on passengers departing on flights from Cape Town Airport since Amy had left the hotel, and confirmed that she had not been aboard any of them. So where had she gone after her rapid departure from the Inn on the Square in Cape Town?

Ed was even more confused, and promised to speak to his group to ask whether or not they had received any news of Amy's whereabouts.

"Please do, and let me have any information you obtain," said his boss. "At present, the South African Police are not involved. I want to avoid having them questioning our customers by keeping the British Police happy myself. It might spoil the holiday of the group travelling with you at present if we have to introduce them to the police, and also the reputation of the company is at stake. It does not look good if we have to admit that we have lost one of our guests."

Did this mean that the net was tightening on Amy?

* * * * *

The next morning, when he met his guests in the hotel lobby, Ed tried to keep the conversation light by first of all asking if they had enjoyed their meal the previous evening.

Then, he added in an offhand way,

"Anyone heard from Amy?"

"No," Jerry replied on behalf of them all. "Why should we? We didn't exchange contact details, and she's gone back to England."

After checking out of the Oudtshoorn Inn at 8.30 am, and passing the Backpackers' Paradise, the Bo Peep Nursery and the Cyber Ostrich Internet Café, the tour party left the town of Oudtshoorn on their way to George over the Outeniqua Mountains, with the Swartsberg Mountain Range behind them.

"This is known as the Four Passes Route," Ed informed them. *"Soon you will be able to see the Indian Ocean ahead. The Outeniqua Pass is 800 metres above sea level, and the road has recently been closed for three months because of a rock fall."*

As they drove along, the tourists could see the old dirt track road running parallel to the railway line above them, and the mountains all around looked as though they were covered in green velvet. Ed then added that this area was known as the Land of a Thousand Hills.

On their way to Knysna for an overnight stay at the Protea Hotel on the Knysna Quays, and a sunset boat trip across the Knysna Lagoon, they stopped to visit the Cango Caves in the Klein Karoo, at the head of the picturesque Cango Valley. They were shown around some spectacular underground dripstone caverns where the towering formations had been lit up to show off their splendour.

Before continuing on their journey, the tourists were told that not all the caverns were open to the public as that would involve entering via narrow holes, but some adventure trails had been installed.

The tourists also stopped to take pictures of the Indian Ocean when they reached Wilderness Beach where the

Kaaimans River flows into the sea. They saw the train known locally as the Oteniqua Chu Chu, as it crossed the river on the railway bridge, and then they took photographs of Dassies (Rock Hyrax) the size of large, plump rabbits, dozing in the shade on the concrete joists under the main road.

Eventually, they arrived in the town of Knysna, situated between lush forests and on the shore of a peaceful estuary, where Ed explained,

"Originally Knysna was the centre of a big game hunting area until the game was wiped out. There was also a whaling industry and forestry, but there are no trees any more. When timber used to be transported by boat from Knysna Lagoon to Cape Town, John Benn was a ship's pilot. On your cruise this evening you will see the dangers ships have to face to get into the lagoon; it is incredibly difficult because of all the rocks at the entrance, and at times, the sea can be extremely rough. But John Benn was an expert and he never lost a ship."

"Now Knysna is a tourist and a leisure centre. South Africans come here for holidays, or have weekend homes as it's not far from Cape Town."

* * * * *

Lt Col Du Plessis received some more good news that day when Major Munro reported that he had obtained the names of some young men who had visited their homelands recently. The homelands concerned were in the vicinity of Sabatha Ntombela's village, and these young men normally worked in Johannesburg. In fact, they were already known to the police.

Could these young men have given Sabatha's money?

Lt Col made arrangements for them to be watched very closely when they returned to Johannesburg.

* * * * *

At lunchtime the same day, Dawn and Jerry went for a stroll through a shopping arcade on one of the many piers built out into the lagoon, on their way to find a restaurant for a light meal. It was lined on both sides with establishments selling tourist memorabilia, jewellery and designer clothes.

Just as Jerry was saying,

"This place is a cross between Key West in Florida with its white clapboard buildings and Port Grimaud in France where there are smart houses built next to the waterways so that people can moor their boats,"

Dawn stopped suddenly and turned round to look back the way they had just come.

"I'm sure I just saw Amy," she said as she pointed. "Look that woman down there."

"That woman's a brunette," Jerry replied. "Amy was blond."

"Women, in fact anyone can dye their hair," Dawn continued, still utterly convinced.

But Jerry had turned away and started to walk on saying,

"You're wrong. That can't be Amy. She went back to the UK."

Dawn was still certain that she had seen Amy, however. Was it women's intuition, or was it something more? The woman she had seen walked in the same way as Amy, she carried a bag in the same way as Amy had done and she was the same shape as Amy. After spending eight days in Amy's company, Dawn knew that she was right, and that she would recognise Amy anywhere.

Then it flashed into her mind; the woven, multi-coloured plastic bag that Amy had purchased at the craft market. The woman, who had disappeared by now, had been carrying exactly the same bag.

As she could not now go chasing after her and prove that she was right, Dawn didn't say anything more to Jerry, and because of Jerry's scepticism, she did not even mention the sighting to their fellow travellers.

She just followed Jerry into the restaurant on Falcon Quay, but questions about Amy were on her mind.

The restaurant Jerry had chosen was a delightful open-air establishment positioned on one of the jetties jutting out into the lake. They sat down at a table right on the edge from where they could observe the water traffic as it passed to and fro. Then they ordered a light salad for lunch, as they knew that they would be eating dinner that evening. Jerry had a salmon and avocado salad, while Dawn ate chicken liver, avocado and bacon salad, both of which were extremely good. A gull catching a crayfish entertained them while they enjoyed their meal, and relaxed in the sunshine.

That evening Ed decided he would join them at the restaurant he had recommended, the Dry Dock Food Company. So it was that there were five of them dining together, but unfortunately, Ed had chosen a speciality fish restaurant not knowing that Dawn was allergic to fish, even the smell of it could upset her stomach.

However, they overcame that problem by once again choosing a table close to the water's edge so that there was plenty of fresh air to waft away the smell of the fish being enjoyed by all those in the restaurant, with the exception of Dawn and Jerry who both managed to find something on the menu that was not fish; Jerry had a lamb curry and Dawn had smoked pork ribs.

Then Ed pointed them in the direction of the quay from which they would board the pleasure boat 'John Benn' for a sunset cruise on the lake.

As they sat around a table on board with Marie and David for company, Jerry was saying,

"Cape Town, the Garden Route and the Cape Winelands, in fact the whole of this part of South Africa is just like being in Europe. With cultivated fields, good roads, smart towns and organised tourist attractions, you would never know you were in South Africa. It's so different from where we were last week. Now that was the real South Africa, with bushveld and open countryside stretching for miles and not a soul in sight,"

when the Captain made an announcement which shattered Jerry's illusions.

"By law, I have to go through the safety arrangements on this vessel, but I can only say that we have sufficient life jackets for the crew. And they know where they are," he joked.

Everyone laughed. They were definitely in South Africa.

Then conversations continued as they sailed across the lake, the shores of which were lit by bright white and multi-coloured lights reflected in the water. They watched the sun go down in a spectacular fashion before returning to the quayside.

* * * * *

All in all it had been a very enjoyable evening, but what would have made Dawn even happier if only she had known. Known what? That Amy was looking down on the pleasure boat 'John Benn' as it sailed around the lake that evening. Dawn had been right. Amy was in Knysna.

However, Amy had not seen Dawn in the shopping arcade as her mind had been on other things. Furthermore, Amy had not even remembered that Dawn and Jerry would be visiting Knysna, or that the itinerary for her and her previous travelling companions had included a cruise on the lagoon. In fact, Amy had not thought about them for some time. She was enjoying her new life too much to have occasion to remember the past.

Amy was smiling at Ted now while they sat drinking wine on the balcony of Ted's small bungalow overlooking the Knysna Lagoon.

"What's the plan?" she asked. "When are you starting your undercover work at the safari park in Mphekwa?"

"I don't know exactly when I start, but I have planned that we leave here early tomorrow, and take a slow drive north. We should arrive at Mphekwa on Monday morning. Accommodation has been arranged for us to live near the park while I'm working there. Although I believe that Robert Goodnuf Xulu was the organiser of a network of rhino poaching activities, and the poachers now have no one controlling them, we still need to find those who were working with him so that they don't get the chance to start up operations again."

"I'm looking forward to going back to Zululand," said Amy happily.

"And to getting married, I hope," added Ted.

"Oh, yes," Amy replied. "Today, I bought something special to wear on that occasion."

* * * * *

The tourists were also leaving Knysna the next day, but they were travelling via Mossel Bay to Franschhoek where they would spend two nights at another Protea Hotel.

Before they actually left Knysna, Ed took them on the Magic Bus up to the Heads and parked quite close to where Ted's bungalow was situated, but Ted and Amy had already left by then as they had a long car journey ahead of them.

From the Heads the tourists looked down onto the Lagoon with its nature reserve on the opposite bank and its dangerous outlet to the ocean where waves sent spray high into the air as they came into contact with rocks.

On the journey to Franschhoek, they made several more stops and gathered a lot more information about this region of South Africa.

As they went into Mossel Bay, they passed a large industrial estate and railway yard where some old steam engines were displayed, and Ed explained that Mossel Bay was a busy port as well as being a tourist spot. Then they saw the Cachalot Fish Market, blocks of apartments, signs for holiday lets, and roughly thatched holiday cottages facing the shore. Ed parked in the centre of town, and the tourists explored on foot, or took the opportunity to visit the Bartholomew Diaz Museum.

Then they continued on the Garden Route stopping at Riversdale for lunch and Cape Agulhas, which Ed explained, was the southern-most point of the African Continent.

Then it was through the mountain range that separated them from Franschhoek via the Franschhoek Pass (previously named Elephants' Pass).

When they reached Franschhoek, Ed stopped the Magic Bus alongside the Huguenot monument standing proudly at the end of the main street and provided a brief commentary:

"This area was settled more than 300 years ago by the Huguenots who brought with them their age-old culture of French wine and excellent food. Many of those who fled France in 1685 were given land in this valley by the Dutch Government. Then, because of the large herds of elephants that roamed the area, it was called Oliphantshoek (Elephants' Corner). However, the settlement soon became known as Franschhoek (French Corner)."

"In this village you will find plenty to explore: craft shops, art galleries, antique shops in the main street, plus many coffee shops and restaurants. I will take you to a special restaurant this evening, and then tomorrow evening and the following morning, there will be plenty of time for you to experience the unique atmosphere of this place on your own."

"Franschhoek has been chosen for your final two nights in South Africa because from here it is easy to travel to other parts of the Cape Winelands. Tomorrow we will go to Stellenbosch and the Manor House on the Boschendal Estate, together with visiting some vineyards for wine tasting. Also, it is only a short drive from here to Cape Town Airport.

* * * * *

When Ted and Amy left Knysna that morning they also took a scenic route travelling to Oudtshoorn and then on through Prince Albert before they joined the N1 motorway heading north.

As they drove along, Ted surprised Amy with the plans he had made for their wedding.

"We're going to get married this afternoon," he announced.

Amy gasped.

"How ever did you manage to arrange it all so quickly?" she asked, "and in secret too."

"I stopped off at a friend's on the way to meet you in Cape Town," Ted explained.

"He's an old friend. We joined the Ranger Service at the same time when we were young, and we've kept in touch ever since. He went off and set up his own private safari park with a small guesthouse that he runs with his wife. It's just outside Beaufort West, only about four and a half hours away from Knysna so we'll be there by lunchtime."

Then he added,

"The local clergyman is a bit doddery, but my friend has arranged for him to perform the wedding ceremony in the grounds of the guesthouse. It's a breath taking setting out on the Karoo Plains with the Nuweveld Mountains in the background – you'll love it."

"Don't you need to fulfil any legal requirements to get married there?" Amy asked.

"In South Africa marriages can take place in public buildings, hospitals, or private residences providing the doors are open, as well as in churches and other religious places. In fact, anywhere that is open to the public. The only legal document required is a Certificate of Non-Impediment, and I've obtained one of those."

"How did you do that?" Amy was full of questions.

"Don't ask," Ted replied.

"What time is the wedding?" said Amy with yet another question.

"Four o'clock this afternoon," Ted confirmed. "You'll have time to get to know my friends over lunch, and then get ready."

"How wonderful," Amy sat back dreamily, and concentrated on the beautiful scenery flashing by.

She was thinking to herself how lucky she had been to find Ted. He was so thoughtful. When he learnt that she had missed the visit to Table Mountain that she had dreamt of for so long, he had taken her there, and they had also visited many other sights in the Cape Town area during their short stay there. Now she was about to experience a wonderful wedding to the man she loved.

They turned off the N1 at the sign for Beaufort West, and as they drove through town, Amy saw market stalls all around.

"Stop, stop," she shouted at Ted. "It's market day. I need to buy some flowers for the wedding."

Ted parked as soon as he found space available, and Amy jumped out of the car saying,

"You stay here. I can manage to say 'I'll have those' and 'How much' in Afrikaans."

When she returned, her arms were full of yellow and white blooms.

"These will be suitable for buttonholes, and my bouquet," she explained as Ted drove off happily.

Leaving Beaufort West, they followed the signs for Matjiesfontein in the heart of the mountains. Then it was along a gravel track to the Great Karoo Safari Park.

As they drove up to the front of the main building, Ted's friends came out to greet them. They were immediately invited in, and then shown out onto the terrace where a beautiful lunch, including many specialities of the Karoo Region, was spread out before them.

As they ate and conversed together, Amy soon felt at home, and Ted's friends, Bruce and Maureen, quickly took to her as they were so pleased that at long last Ted had found someone nice to spend the rest of his life with.

Then it was time to get ready for the ceremony.

Maureen helped Amy with the flowers, sorting them out into buttonholes for the men, a beautiful bouquet for Amy, and a small posy for herself. There were even some flowers left to decorate Amy's dark brown hair. Amy chose the yellow ones, which matched the very expensive, bright yellow blouse she had treated herself to when shopping on the Knysna Quay. This smartened up the dull suit she had purchased at Cape Town Airport, and by 4.00 pm everybody was ready.

Ted felt so proud as he watched Amy walking across the grass towards him on Bruce's arm. He could not stop asking himself what he had done to deserve such a beautiful bride as he smiled at her, and the ceremony began.

It was quickly over, and then there was champagne and even more food as celebrations went on into the evening. The couple sat happily in the garden watching the sunset over the mountains, and then spent the first night of their married life in one of the chalets in the grounds.

Maureen and Bruce had thoughtfully decorated the small bedroom with even more flowers, petals on the bed and softly glowing candles all around.

Amy could not have been happier as she went to sleep that night.

* * * * *

CHAPTER 18
The Cape Winelands'

That same evening, Ed introduced the small tour group to another new culinary experience. He had booked a table for the whole group, including himself, at a restaurant in the main street.

As they walked along, he pointed out places of interest, and said,

"There's an extremely good restaurant over there – the best one in Franschhoek."

"That's where we'll go tomorrow night," Jerry whispered to Dawn. "Our last meal in South Africa needs to be something special."

When they reached the restaurant that Ed had chosen they found that it was certainly different. Instead of the normal dining tables and chairs, there were sofas placed around coffee tables, and the menu comprised of unusual delicacies not divided into separate courses.

Ed suggested that everyone choose at least two dishes initially as the portions were very small. Then by all of them deciding on something different, it would be possible to sample everything on the menu and then opt for the dish, or dishes, they preferred if they wanted to order more.

This they did and were intrigued when the small dishes of food arrived. It was all delicious and although the arrangement resembled 'tapas', the food included dishes that none of the group had ever tasted before.

With the food being accompanied by good quality, local wine, the whole group were relaxed as conversations ebbed and flowed.

This was just what Ed wanted as he tried to direct the discussions towards Amy. However, Marie and David explained that they had only spoken to her briefly on the drive from the airport, and Jerry, his attitude relaxed as a result of the alcohol, could only say how he was whole-heartedly glad that she was no longer with the group as he had been worried that eventually she would have ruined their holiday. It was only Dawn who said nothing. Should she tell Ed that she thought she had seen Amy in Knysna? Eventually she decided that she would speak to him when she could do so without anyone else around; Jerry would only argue that she was wrong and she did not want to spoil the evening.

So it was that Ed had nothing more to report to his boss when he telephoned him that evening. He had tried, he said, but it was obvious that if Amy had any future plans, she had not informed her fellow travellers about them.

* * * * *

The next day Ted and Amy left the Great Karoo Safari Park after an early breakfast with Bruce and Maureen. The safari park owners now treated Amy like a treasured friend, and sadly Amy waved goodbye to them as she and Ted, the newly-weds, drove off together.

Amy soon cheered up, however, as she thought about the fact that they would soon be back in Zululand undertaking important work.

They had to travel through Beaufort West in order to reach the N1, and then it was a long, boring journey along the motorway before they stopped at a motel for their second night of wedded bliss.

* * * * *

Keeping his promise, Ed took his guests on a journey through the Cape Winelands that day.

As they drove along, he explained,

"The Cape Winelands is the largest wine producing area in South Africa. It is divided into six main regions: Constantia, Stellenbosch, Franschhoek, Paarl, Robertson and Wellington."

"Our first stop will be at Fairview for a wine and cheese tasting."

When they arrived there at 9.05 am, they found everything very well organised with wines and cheeses laid out in separate areas, and members of staff encouraging them to indulge in sips of wine while sampling the many cheeses on offer.

"If Amy was here, she would be knocking back all the wine, and be rolling drunk before ten o'clock," Jerry whispered in such a way that only Dawn heard him.

Next they travelled to Stellensbosch. Once there, Ed pointed out that it was the only town with a University where Afrikaans was the main language.

After a tour of the town, they visited the Village Museum with four houses depicting different eras in the history of South Africa, and then it was time for a coffee in the Java Coffee where the directions to the toilets were quite amusing:

'In the basket at the end of the bar, there is a 3" pure bristle paintbrush at the end of which is attached a Yale key. Open the sliding door at the rear of the café. Follow the blue lights in the ceiling to get to the end of them. Turn right, go up the stairs and unlock the door to the toilet.'

After a quick walk round smart shopping streets, the group met back at the bus, and Ed drove out into the countryside again. His objective was to provide another quite different experience of South African cuisine.

He certainly fulfilled that objective at the Restaurant de Volkskombuis Aan de Wagen (loosely translated as the Nation's Kitchen on the Wagon) where one of the dishes on offer was 'Bobotie', a traditional lamb curry.

Here, they were served with rustic, traditional Afrikaans or Cape fare in the open-air courtyard at the front of the restaurant by very friendly staff, before they travelled on to visit Boschendal Manor House by going over Hell's Heights.

The Manor House was another historic building with its rooms laid out in the style of its era and where the staff wore traditional costumes.

The tour party also strolled around the extensive grounds where they discovered their first mulberry tree.

Then it was on to Allée Bleue for another wine tasting. Situated at the end of an avenue of blue gum trees and surrounded by fields of cultivated vines, was a modern building. There they were shown into a room where they sat on bar stools at counters and were issued with score cards on which they commented on the wines that they were given to taste.

Finally, they were invited to undertake a guided tour of the wine cellar that included climbing up metal staircases to look down into the vats. Most were currently empty, but the guide did explain the processes used to produce both red and white wine.

This was the first opportunity Dawn found for speaking to Ed without the others overhearing. Pretending that they were discussing wines, she made sure everyone else had moved on ahead before she said,

"I think I saw Amy in Knysna."

"Are you sure?" Ed replied. "Why didn't you say something before?"

"I wasn't sure," Dawn continued. "Jerry didn't believe it was her, but the more I've thought about it the more certain I am. It was the shopping bag that convinced me."

"Whatever do you mean?" Ed questioned.

"Amy purchased an unusual woven plastic shopping bag in Swaziland," Dawn explained. "She was carrying that bag in Knysna, and even though she no longer has blonde hair (she's a brunette now) everything else about her appearance screamed at me that it was Amy."

"Well, I'll report your sighting, but I don't know whether anything will come of it," Ed concluded.

"I just had to tell you," Dawn said resignedly. "But I agree, I realise that I may never know if it really was Amy."

That evening Jerry was true to his word and arranged with Reception to book a table for two at the restaurant Ed had recommended for a last romantic meal in Franschhoek.

Ed was also busy that evening. He telephoned his boss again, explained what Dawn had told him and then was told about the arrangements for meeting his next tour group. With his thoughts heavily engaged with future work, he did not think about Amy again.

It was left to his boss to contact the British Police to supply an update, and then it was their job to decide whether to check it out, or not.

The question was, "Would they do so?"

* * * * *

Ted and Amy had only just arrived outside their bungalow on the outskirts of Mphekwa the next morning, and were in the process of bringing in everything from the car, when Lt Col Pieter Du Plessis paid them a surprise visit.

"Let me help you with that," he said as he took a case from Amy and carried it indoors.

Ted then introduced them to each other.

"This is my wife, Amelia," he said to Du Plessis and then to his wife who was now using her full name, he added, "This is Lt Col Pieter Du Plessis, Amelia."

Amy greeted Du Plessis politely in Afrikaans, and then asked if he would like a cup of bush tea, again speaking in Afrikaans.

Du Plessis accepted the kind offer, and he and Ted proceeded into the lounge where they sat down on easy chairs.

"Didn't know you were married, Ted," Du Plessis stated before Ted had a chance to speak. "Have you been together long."

"For a while," Ted replied vaguely before asking,

"How did you know we'd arrived?"

"Ah, the bush telegraph," Du Plessis laughed. "I have my spies everywhere."

Then he continued,

"I needed to speak to you urgently, Ted, because there are a lot of loose ends that I would appreciate your help with. Also, I've arranged for you to start work at the local safari park tomorrow."

"Goodness, I wasn't expecting to start so soon, but I'm sure Amelia won't mind," Ted replied confidently.

It was now time for Du Plessis to explain the progress he had made so far, but as it was also the moment when Amy entered with the bush tea, he hesitated for a moment to thank her before she went back to the kitchen.

Ted filled the silence by saying,

"Amelia has a lot of unpacking to do, so she won't be joining us."

This prompted Du Plessis to continue,

"First of all, there's the helicopter crash. The pilot was easy to identify, and we interviewed those working at his airfield where we obtained some information, but it was all very vague. I believe some of them knew more, and were only pretending to help the police in the hope that it would prove they weren't involved. However, we couldn't get much useful information out of them, and there is no evidence of their complicity."

"With regard to the two Chinese passengers listed on the flight plan, we reported their deaths to the Chinese Embassy in Pretoria and we understand their families have been informed. It would appear that they really were businessmen who ran a factory in Beijing making quilts so their appointment with agents supplying quilting equipment can be explained. However, what can't be explained is what they were doing in the vicinity of the Kruger National Park – that's another matter. I know that they had a further reason for visiting South Africa and that was to obtain rhino horns, but again I have no evidence."

"Now we come to the Joseph situation – how did he die in hospital?"

It was at this point that Ted could not stop himself from interrupting Du Plessis.

"Did Robert Goodnuf Xulu kill him?" Ted asked.

"So you recognised him as well," Du Plessis confirmed. "He was the person pushing his way into the lift that we got out of."

"However, again I have no proof. Just that we know that he was in the vicinity at the time is not enough. He didn't leave fingerprints, was probably wearing gloves, and nobody saw him in Joseph's room."

"That brings me to the death of Robert Goodnuf Xulu whose body suddenly turned up in the Kruger National Park after Joseph's death."

Again, Ted could not stop himself from interrupting.

"Are you considering that his death could have been an act of retribution according to Zulu custom?" Ted asked. "Was it a vengeance killing?"

"Possibly," the Lt Col replied. "The fact that the body was found in the Kruger is significant, but how did it get there. Someone with inside knowledge of the Kruger must have been involved. To transport a body into the park and then leave it where there is known to be a pride of lions, would have necessitated the assistance of someone who worked there."

"That's just one area where I need your help, Ted. Can you contact old colleagues and perhaps go out for a drink with them. Find out what you can. After all, you're not very far away, and you have a good cover now that you're running a training course here at Mphekwa."

Ted agreed, but just had to add that he had not decided to undertake his current role in order to find out who had killed Robert Goodnuf Xulu. In fact, if it was Xulu who had murdered Joseph, he was glad that he was dead.

Du Plessis said that he understood and could sympathise, but pointed out that all murders had to be investigated and efforts made to solve them otherwise the law could not be upheld.

Then he went on,

"Your main role is still going to be finding out if there are any Rangers who are involved with those undertaking poaching of endangered species. We need to find out where the inside intelligence has been coming from, and to put a stop to help being provided in the future. Someone, or some people somewhere are making money, or have made money, out of this activity, and the fact that they have done so should be apparent. Are you still happy to work on finding out who these people are?"

Ted agreed that he certainly was, and explained that his wife already had some ideas on how she could help as well.

This satisfied Du Plessis who continued,

"We've had just two quite significant breakthroughs recently that I can tell you about."

"Although nobody phoned on that number I left with the Rangers at the Kruger to report on missing persons, it did result in a tip off about a consignment of rhino horns. Now we're in the process of tracking that shipment; as it is being transported, we are following it every step of the way and arresting those involved. Hopefully, this will also lead us to apprehending the customers as well."

"Blocking at least one route out of the country could prove advantageous, and if we can make an example by charging, or even imprisoning, those who are prepared to pay large sums of money for rhino horns, that could deter others from doing so in future."

"The other news is that Sabatha Ntombela has come into money. We have considered that it could be payment from those who worked with Joseph, or it could just be well wishers, but it is a large sum. We have information on who's possibly involved and we're keeping an eye on that situation as well."

"I thought I might take Amelia to meet Sabatha," Ted added, "but I don't think it's right to interrogate her. She probably knows nothing about what's been going on, and she's suffered enough."

Du Plessis agreed, and then Ted asked an unexpected question.

"Have you identified the other two passengers in the helicopter?"

Du Plessis then realised that in order to ensure Ted remained motivated, he needed to make him aware that he was trusted, and so to Ted's surprise, he confessed:

"We did actually know all along who the other two passengers were, but we had to make others believe that we did not," he said.

"One of them was Thembinkosi Cebekhulu who had been working undercover for us for some time. He had been accepted as a member of a breakaway branch of the ANC Youth League, and was travelling on the helicopter with the leader of the group, Thomas Mthiyane, otherwise known as 'Rocky the Red'."

"It was Thembinkosi who supplied the tip off that an attempt to poach rhino horns was to take place on that evening, but the location he gave proved to be the wrong one; it must have been changed at the last minute."

"We lost a good man that night. Since then we have been carrying out surveillance of that particular branch and its members. Arrests are planned to take place shortly."

Ted was so absolutely amazed that he could not say anything, but he was thinking that this proved that Du Plessis knew what he was doing and Ted respected that.

As Du Plessis stood up to leave, he gave Ted a slip of paper saying,

"That's my personal contact number. You can ring me at any time to report developments. They'll be a contract awaiting you at the safari park regarding your training commitments over the next few months. Any problems, let me know."

Then he abruptly left the room, calling out 'thank you and goodbye' to Amy as he passed the kitchen.

Ted and Amy stood at the window watching him go, and then Ted told Amy everything that had passed between him and Du Plessis. He had decided that from now on they were not going to have any secrets from each other, and when he explained this, she readily agreed.

* * * * *

On that same Monday morning, Dawn and Jerry had to say goodbye to Marie and David immediately after breakfast, as they were booked on an early flight, but Dawn and Jerry were not leaving the hotel until late that afternoon,

Dawn and Jerry then took a stroll down the main street, going in and out of interesting shops before they found a Chocolatier where lunch was advertised.

Thinking this might be something different, they sat at a table inside this small café. However, the menu was not that extensive and they both ended up with a lasagne before completing their meal with a large slice of chocolate gateau each.

Luckily, they did not have to vacate their hotel room until 4.00 pm, so they could relax by the pool that afternoon before they made sure that their cases were suitably packed and met Ed in Reception at 4.30 pm.

When they arrived back at Cape Town airport on the Magic Bus forty-five minutes later, Dawn and Jerry thanked Ed for a truly wonderful 'Magical Mystery Tour' of the Cape Province. He and Jerry then shook hands, while Dawn gave him a kiss before they went through to Departures.

It was only when they were boarding flight no BA58 bound for Heathrow that Dawn thought of Amy.

"She should have been on this flight. Where was she now?"

* * * * *

Ted and Amy were back in the small bungalow on the outskirts of Mphekwa after having undertaken a small shopping trip insisted on by Amy who had listed what she needed to make the place more homely. It was quite a well-equipped bungalow, however, and somebody had even taken the trouble to stock the shelves in the kitchen with food, but Amy was determined to make improvements.

If Ted was starting work at the local safari park the next day, she would be glad to have plenty to do in the bungalow. She was also going to continue with her studies of the Afrikaans language, to try and ensure that she could speak perfectly.

She was picking it up quite quickly, probably because she had laid down the rule to Ted that they should only speak to each other in Afrikaans. She had studied German at school, which made it easier, and she had always had a good ear for foreign languages.

It now seemed to be 'many moons ago' when she had fled from the hotel in Cape Town.

She also planned to learn to speak Zulu and to arrange coffee mornings to raise money for the local school where she could get to know local people, especially wives of Rangers. She would have loved to contact Mary and exchange ideas on how she could help South African children, but she knew that it would never be possible. She had to forget about her previous life.

"There are eleven official languages in South Africa," Ted had joked with her (in Afrikaans, of course) when she told him she intended to learn to speak Zulu next. "Are you going to study them all?"

"Two new languages are sufficient for now," Amy had replied.

"I'm going to enjoy talking to local people in their own language."

Amy had discovered her forte.

* * * * *

EPILOGUE

It was three days after Dawn and Jerry had returned from South Africa and they had not yet come 'down to earth'. In fact, they were still getting up unnecessarily early, dressing quickly and had to stop themselves putting a suitcase outside their front door before breakfast, such were the automatic habits they had got into. They laughed about this as they discussed all the marvellous sights they had seen and the people they had met.

It was then that Dawn remembered,

"I wonder whatever happened to Amy?" she queried. "She had a Ticket to Zululand, but she did not return to the United Kingdom with us. Did she go back home? We will probably never find out."

In fact, they never did as neither the UK nor the South African Police bothered to contact them about Amy's disappearance.

However, as soon as they got home, Dawn found the article she had seen previously in a wildlife magazine. She and Jerry were reading it again as it was now so much more relevant.

"It says here that London is the main hub for the smuggling of endangered species," said Jerry, "I would never have thought that was the case."

"If only people would work together to stop the poaching of endangered species, perhaps the rhino and other wildlife on the brink of extinction, could be saved," Dawn continued.

"I think that statement must be considered as being your dream," Jerry replied. "And it should be one that as many individuals as possible support.

* * * * *

Unknown to Dawn and Jerry, on that very same day two completely unrelated articles (or were they unrelated?) appeared in local newspapers in parts of the world far, far away from each other.

* * * * *

In the North East London Gazette, an article with the outstanding headline 'Man Found Dead in his Own Home' was followed by a story explaining that a man had been found by neighbours after being dead for nearly two weeks, but the death had been declared as being 'from natural causes'. The only peculiar thing was that his wife had disappeared.

The local GP had explained that it was his belief that the wife, who he had told at the end of his last visit that her husband only had a few days left to live, had refused to accept this fact. She had been looking after her husband for over 30 years, most of their married life, and had always refused to discuss what would happen when he died. She had also refused to allow him to be taken into care, even though she had no relatives, or friends to help her look after him.

In the final paragraph of the article (which was not even on the front cover of the Gazette as this had been dominated by pictures of hoodlums carrying out looting after riots in the area), it stated that the police were making attempts to trace the wife, but as the death of her husband could be explained, they had no reason to charge her with foul play.

* * * * *

In the Zulu Herald Tribune on the same day, there was a report entitled 'Poachers arrested in Mphekwa'.

'Three men have been arrested in connection with the deaths of rhino killed by heavy calibre gunfire in the Mphekwa area last September."

"We are heavily involved in fighting this crime against endangered species," said Lt Col Du Plessis who then added,

"I can assure you that more arrests will be made shortly, and when sentenced, the names of the individuals concerned will be made known to all in the Zululand Roll of Dishonour".'

* * * * *

Dawn and Jerry would also have been surprised to learn that Amy and Ted were in Mphekwa on that day reading the above article that confirmed Ted's success in quickly finding a group involved in killing rhinos for their horns.

"You did really well, Ted," said Amy, "to find them so swiftly."

"I was just lucky," Ted replied. "I happened to overhear a conversation, and reported it to Du Plessis."

"There's still more work to do," he continued, "and I wouldn't be able to do it if I did not have you at my side to encourage me."

Was this one of the benefits of Amy's
'Ticket to Zululand'?

* * * * *

Anne had been true to her promise to Naomi and shortly after Anne and Cathy's return to the England, Naomi's daughter-in-law was offered a job at the UK Trade & Investment Offices in Johannesburg.

Also, eventually Naomi and her daughter-in-law learnt the truth about Thembinkosi.

* * * * *

Furthermore, when Peter returned to the London office of HM Customs & Excise after having had a wonderful time at Victoria Falls, a message from Lt Col Pieter Du Plessis was waiting for him:

"Assignment of rhino horns due to arrive at Heathrow on 15 October. Please intercept and apprehend the purchasers if possible."

* * * * *

Did this all mean that Dawn's dream was slowly coming true as more people were now working together to combat wildlife crime?

We can only hope so.

* * * * *

REFERENCES

Ladysmith Gazette (September 2011)
Lonely Planet published by the BBC
Zululand Observer (September 2011)

www.ask.com
www.bbc.co.uk
www.britishbattles.com
www.expedia.com
www.iucnredlist.org
www.sagr.co.za
www.sahistory.org.za
www.wikipedia.org
www.wwf.org.uk

Special Notes:

1. Extracts from newspaper articles have been inset and attributed where applicable.

2. Factual information quoted in dialogue has been displayed in italics.

Other books by the same author include:

A Ticket to Malta

Malta, a small island offering tourists the benefit of brilliant sunshine, blue skies and a clear, azure Mediterranean sea, has suffered more than its fair share of strife in the past. Now its friendly, welcoming people are having to cope with the problems brought about by a tide of illegal immigrants landing on their rocky shores.

For two particular families, life gets more complicated when the past comes back to haunt them: a past that some people would prefer to forget.

Innocent tourists become involved. But are they so innocent? What really happened in the past?

* * * * *

A Ticket to Cusco
'The Land of the Inca'

Was the Inca civilisation completely wiped off the face of the earth after the Spanish Conquistadors executed the last Inca Emperor Atahualpa on 16 November 1532, and brought diseases from Europe which decimated the population? Or did some Quechua speaking people survive, living deep within the high mountain ranges of the Andes, and carry on instilling the Inca traditions within future generations?

Although 'A Ticket to Cusco' is a fictional account of a tourist trip to Peru, it does raise some interesting hypotheses – could there really be those working in secret, following the ideology of the Inca in order to help the people of Peru solve some of their current problems? What is happening behind the scenes? There is obviously more going on than is apparent to tourists, but could they actually be meeting people who are direct descendants of the Inca? Are they experiencing events which far exceed reasonable explanation?

Due for Publication in 2013